The Jump Artist

AUSTIN RATNER

PENGUIN BOOKS

PENGUIN BOOKS

Published by the Penguin Group
Penguin Books Ltd, 80 Strand, London WC2R ORL, England
Penguin Group (USA) Inc., 375 Hudson Street, New York, New York 10014, USA
Penguin Group (Canada), 90 Eglinton Avenue East, Suite 700, Toronto, Ontario, Canada M4P 2Y3
(a division of Pearson Penguin Canada Inc.)
Penguin Ireland, 25 St Stephen's Green, Dublin 2, Ireland (a division of Penguin Books Ltd)
Penguin Group (Australia), 707 Collins Street, Melbourne, Victoria 3008, Australia
(a division of Pearson Australia Group Pty Ltd)
Penguin Books India Pvt Ltd, 11 Community Centre, Panchsheel Park, New Delhi – 110 017, India
Penguin Group (NZ), 67 Apollo Drive, Rosedale, Auckland 0632, New Zealand
(a division of Pearson New Zealand Ltd)
Penguin Books (South Africa) (Pty) Ltd, Block D, Rosebank Office Park, 181 Jan Smuts Avenue,
Parktown North, Gauteng 2193, South Africa

Penguin Books Ltd, Registered Offices: 80 Strand, London WC2R ORL, England

www.penguin.com

First published in the United States of America by Bellevue Literary Press 2009
First published in Great Britain by Viking 2012
Published in Penguin Books 2013
001

This book was published with the generous support of Bellevue Literary Press's
founding donor the Arnold Simon Family Trust, the Bernard & Irene Schwartz Foundation
and the Lucius N. Littauer Foundation

Typeset by Palimpsest Book Production Limited, Falkirk, Stirlingshire
Printed in Great Britain by Clays Ltd, St Ives plc

ISBN: 978–0–241–96139–1

www.greenpenguin.co.uk

Penguin Books is committed to a sustainable
future for our business, our readers and our planet.
This book is made from Forest Stewardship
Council™ certified paper.

ALWAYS LEARNING　　　　**PEARSON**

For Kristin, Virgil, and Gabriel

Author's Note

This novel is based on a true story, an early chapter of the Holocaust that is now mostly forgotten in the English-speaking world, and in telling it I've been inspired by André Gide's statement that 'fiction is history which *might* have taken place, and history is fiction which *has* taken place.' In keeping with this idea, I've tried to heed the known facts about Halsman's history and to confine the pure fiction to what might plausibly have been the case. I was guided by Halsman's letters to his girlfriend, published in 1930, by the newspaper articles in two well-respected Vienna newspapers of the time, by his defense attorney's account, and by many other primary sources. The goal was to use the techniques of fiction to imagine subjectively what Halsman suffered and overcame, while still honoring the truth of what happened and the truth of Halsman's character as it's revealed in the source material and in his work.

All that having been said, I did not know Philippe Halsman and I don't think anyone who actually knew him could read my book and say, 'That is Halsman.' What's inside these pages is instead a character inspired by Philippe Halsman, like him in some ways, undoubtedly unlike him in many others, and based on much guesswork and invention, not only because I've tried to re-create his inner life, but also because I've supposed the path he took from boy to man. My book is not a biography so much as an artistic tribute to Philippe Halsman – more like a portrait or a sculpture. It isn't the 'final word' on his life and doesn't pretend to be, any more than Rodin pretended his sculpture of Balzac *was* Balzac.

Acknowledgments

The writing of this novel depended on significant research and translation from German and French primary sources. I am indebted to many people for help: to Julia Goesser, Gabika Bockaj, Kenji Ouellet, Susanne Mair, Clark Mitchell, Liza Tripp, and Andrea Hacker for their excellent assistance with research and hard work in translation – without them this story could not have been told in English; to Ralph Horwitz, Martha Keil, Laurent Zimmern, and Brigitte Berg for help accessing archival material in Austria and France; to Peter Goller and Niko Hofinger, who shared and discussed their historical research; to Jonathan Leiken and David Sternbach for consultations on legal matters; to Philippe Halsman's daughter Irene Halsman, his son-in-law Steve Bello, and his grandson Oliver Halsman Rosenberg for their willingness to hear out my project despite trepidation, and for hosting me at the Halsman Archive; to Halsman's niece Liliane Emanuel; and to his grand-niece Nicole Emanuel for her ample assistance and friendship.

For help in preparing the manuscript for publication, I wish to thank Leslie Hodgkins and Anne Edelstein first and foremost, Andrea Chapin, Tish O'Dowd, Betsy Seifter, Chandra Speeth, and Erika Goldman; thanks also to James Ratner, Susan Ratner, Deborah Paris, Zack Paris, and Jonathan Kandell. For enabling me to jump the Atlantic, I thank Penguin's Will Hammond, Jenny Fry and Andrew Smith, Victoria Hobbs and Krista Ingebretson, and the Rohr family. Finally, more than thanks to Kristin Ratner, who proves by her toleration that Robert Frost was right when he had Warren say, 'Home is the place where, when you have to go there, / They have to take you in.' And he was righter still when he had Mary improve upon the point and say, 'I should have called it / Something you somehow haven't to deserve.'

PART I
Der Vatermörder

1. The Hunters

I think, however, that on a beautiful winter day,
immediately after a snowstorm, when millions of
coniferæ, bowed down beneath their crystal burdens,
render the mountains dazzling with silver-powdered
forests and pyramids of prisms, this journey offers one of
the most glorious sights I have ever looked upon . . . For
this old thoroughfare is a thread on which are strung the
souvenirs of two thousand years.

JOHN L. STODDARD, *Lectures: South Tyrol*

10 September 1928, the Zillertal, Austria

Eduard Severin Maria, one of the elder princes of Auersperg, led a hunt that day in the valley. His horse fell and was
later found beheaded in the grass.

But Eduard gave little thought to his horses. The Auers-
pergs took greater pride in their hunting dogs. They were
Weimaraners, direct descendants of the Chiens Gris de Saint
Louis, the unicorn hunters of medieval tapestry, and they
had for centuries guarded over the meadows and moraine of
western Austria and lower Germany. Their colorless eyes
reflected the mountain wastes like white amulets.

The prince had in fact personally overseen his dogs' breeding in order to meet the standards of the German Weimaraner
Club. Doing so wasn't hard with animals of such pure stock.

One had only to look out for the longhair trait, forbidden by the club's studbook. Eduard was convinced that careful breeders like himself would soon eradicate the flaw from the hounds of Bavaria and Austria.

Yet only that morning of the hunt, he'd discovered two drowsy dun-colored pups who, not needing the warmth of their brothers and sisters, lay apart on the rug in the drafty minstrel's hall. Longhairs among his own dogs! If word got out, the club could expel him, or sterilize his dogs. And worse, the source was almost certainly Mars: Freya had littered sixteen pups with short coats before mating with Mars, and Mars had never sired before. Prince von Auersperg would prefer not to shoot the animal; he was the best hunting dog the prince had ever had. He never failed to bring back the quarry, each time laying the marmot or grouse at the prince's feet and turning right around to watch the mountain again with those eyes still and pale as an old moon. But the dog's breeding was a problem that remained unsolved, and it worried the prince all that day.

The prince tested the air with a wave of his palm. A warm and dry *Föhn* had blown down from the mountaintops in the last days, bringing clear weather and turning the mountains cobalt blue, but the dust now hovering on the roads portended rain. Well, he was not yet too old to hunt the Zillertal in September, whatever the weather.

The hounds ran, and patches of morning mist rolled over the cracked limestone, so that the dogs' wild barking seemed at times to come up out of the ground itself. The horses sailed the riders over the mist with loud clopping on the stone and quick thuds on the turf like a pelting of gunfire. The rifles creaked against the leather saddles. The horns echoed from the *Kammë* and ravines loomed up so suddenly in the hazy morning light, one had to be very skilled on a horse to avoid a nasty fall. By the time the sun had burned away the mist, a fox was caught, but the prince's horse tumbled down the brook leading to the Zamserbach. The prince was unhurt. He ordered the horse shot through the brain, and it was done under a midday sun. The hunters headed off to the inn at Breitlahner for lunch.

When the prince had gone, carrying his fox by the neck, the steed was beheaded, washing the grass in blood.

2. The Zamserschinder

Tell me, have you ever dreamt you were flying?

Philipp Halsmann, letter to Ruth Römer,
Innsbruck Prison, 30 July 1929

In the beginning, on the path through the mountains that
was called the Zamserschinder, all he wanted was to get away
from his father.

'Philja! Wait!' his father commanded. Papa was not so tall
with strong short arms and legs and a big head. His hair was
short and white and slick like the coat of an otter. He ran his
thumb over the wet hair and then flung the water and sweat
onto the path. He started up the rocks as though he were not
in the least tired and kicked and climbed all the way up to the
tall iron cross standing in the sun. There was a boy in the
shade of the rusted cross with a goat on a leader, another
one of these boys selling garnets from a tin can.

'I thought you wanted to make the train,' Philipp shouted.

'I do,' Papa shouted back. Papa would not buy gems from
a tin can, but a whim had once again moved him.

Philipp sat on a rock to rest. A stitch had been burning in
his left side off and on since the Schwarzsee, where Papa had
challenged him to a swim across the lake. His mouth was dry.
His feet hurt and his skin was chafed with layers of dried-
sweat salt.

Where did these boys come from? Where did they get

their garnets? You could go a day without seeing another person up here in the lonely green hills, the sun shining down on the dumb goats and wildflowers, then you'd come upon a lone figure, like the boy under the cross, standing there as if on the spot where he'd been born, like a gnome or spirit of the hills.

The boy said nothing as he poured the stones out into the palm of his hand. Papa said nothing as he pointed at them. Even with the water falling everywhere over this green land in rills and rushing brooks, what prevailed up here was quiet. The great unpeopled silence of the hills dwarfed human voices and the glacial *Eiswelt* presided above the hills like a span of gods. You were somehow too small to speak before the vastness, as in a temple or a church.

'Do you know the distance to Mayrhofen?' Papa said loudly to the boy under the cross, who didn't answer. Papa held one of the garnets up to the sun, then placed it back in the boy's palm. The goat was nibbling the petals of a purple flower, and the boy jerked on the rope around its neck. Then he held out his hand again with the garnets in it.

Philipp got up and wearily climbed the pile of rocks. 'Let's go then!' he said. He touched his father's back and could feel the heat of his father's body through the cold, wet shirt.

'All right,' Papa said. He turned to the mute boy again, shrugged and laughed. 'What will I do with my heir, here? I think he would like to be rid of me.'

They trudged down the ridge to the path, Papa's feet falling loudly on the earth, buckles on his rucksack jingling like bells.

'You haven't soaked my pack have you?' Philipp said. 'My diary is inside.' Papa had been drinking from the stream below the footbridge.

'What? No,' Papa said. He then dragged Philipp's pack up

from the ground and fished his arms through the leather straps. He slapped the pack on his chest with both hands, puffing up a small cloud of dust from the dusty canvas, and heaved it up higher on his chest. He looked at his son then with sage amusement, gold crowns gleaming in his open mouth.

'I should get out the camera,' Philipp said. 'You look very striking there, with the footbridge in the background.'

'That's foolish.'

'Let me carry my pack the rest of the way at least,' Philipp said. 'Mama will be angry with me.'

'Listen to the doctor,' Papa said. 'You need the sun on your back.'

'I should listen?' Philipp said. 'What about you? You'll never listen to a doctor in your life!'

'Why are you standing around?' Papa said. And he strode ahead on the trail with both packs. Philipp felt so light by comparison, he thought he would float into the sky. 'Next year, when you pay your own bills, you can do as you like,' Papa called over his shoulder.

It had been this way since they got lost on Monte Generoso. There had been a woman atop the scree and Papa called to her and started up the sunny steep rocks three times in three different places, but each time he tilted backward off the scree and had to backpedal to the trail. Once, he got his foot stuck. But Philipp stretched himself for a foothold that was the obvious key to the operation, and he made it up with ease on the first try. At the top he spoke to the little woman having lunch on the rocks. She advised they double back. But when he got back down, his father was annoyed with him for wasting time and pretended he had never wanted to ask directions in the first place. He said he'd already figured out the right way. And he'd proceeded onward at a furious pace as if he meant to leave Philipp behind on the mountain. In the morning, when they set out again, he went charging on at the same furious pace and now, by Philipp's estimation, they were hiking thirty-five kilometers a day. They would scour the entire Alps with the Halsmann family eyeballs, personally testify to everything in the guidebook and a few more places besides, and then discard the guidebook like the rind of a squeezed lemon. They'd been up at 5:30 that very morning and vaulted up the Schönbichlerhorn into its frigid airless winds, had their retinas oxidized in the ether, and their hands seared on the snow and the flint rocks, hot as sunburned metal. They had broken themselves on the mountain and been baptized there above the timber line at the top of the world, where the river of air meets the river of fire. And Papa still insisted on making the evening train at Mayrhofen.

They pushed on over the trodden grass to the Zamserschinder, below which the Zamserbach roared through the leaning pine trees in a torrent of mud between sun-bronzed rocks. Philipp hurt his ankle and they argued again about the pace and the train. 'It's not healthy for you,' Philipp said.

'Senna leaves?' his father yelled above the roar of the water. 'Does a doctor treat a serious heart condition with senna leaves?'

'The doctor in Chamonix was a fool,' Philipp said.

Two young men came up over the hill on the trail. Philipp fell silent. The sound of rushing water closed over everything that had been said, as though it had not been said at all. His father shouted to them in his loud Yiddish-tinged German – 'Guten Tag! Do you know the distance to Mayrhofen?' – and his mouth hung open, showing the gold teeth. But the two boys didn't stop. One of them cupped his hand behind his ear as though he couldn't hear, and they walked on and laughed when they had passed.

9

'Did you hear what they said?'

'No,' Papa said, in a tone that warned, *Do not go any further with this irrelevancy*. He hurried on.

'They said, "It's the two Jews from the Berlinerhütte." Remember? We saw them up there.'

'They said nothing of the kind,' Papa said.

Papa could not be embarrassed. But just today at the Furtschagelhaus the Austrians, staring unashamed and blowing at their coffee mugs with red cheeks, had studied him and his father as though they were insects.

'Ach,' Papa said. 'Nature calls, I'm afraid. You go on ahead, Philja, and I'll catch up to you.' Papa took Philipp by the arm, raised the bare skin to his mouth, and kissed it.

'I'll wait for you,' Philipp said.

'You may be staying in Breitlahner tonight,' Papa said, 'but I have to get all the way to Jenbach.'

'What's so important in Jenbach?' Philipp said. He knew. Papa would teach the rocks of Monte Generoso a lesson and break these mountains like a horse.

Papa said nothing.

'What's so important in Jenbach?' Philipp said.

'Mama,' Papa said quietly. The only time his father's voice quieted was when he was cornered into a confession. It was like that time when the boat had capsized in the Aa – Papa was not good in the stern – and Papa had lost the watch that Mama had inscribed for him. When they'd righted themselves, Philipp kept trying to push off, and Papa kept saying, 'Wait,' and Philipp kept dipping his paddle, and Papa said, 'Wait,' and Philipp dipped the paddle, until Papa lowered his voice and said, 'I need a minute.'

'Okay, Papa,' Philipp said.

His father dropped the first rucksack to the ground and Philipp went over the stone footbridge and down the winding path between the alder bushes, where the mountain rose up steeply above the path and cast it in shadow.

He felt something almost like peace then. It had become a lovely day. Crisp pure air, newly minted by the wind gods of the *Eiswelt*, blew down over the trembling grass. The sound of the rushing water and the damp pine smell enveloped him. What would be truly lovely would be to have Ruth there beside him. Why was it that he loved her so much more when they were apart? *Love* – there was that word again. *Lugano. Love. Does it mean you're 'in love' if that's what comes to your mind? How many times should it come before you can say you're 'in love'?*

Who could say?

Philipp heard a sound of barking dogs and stopped. The sound was so faint, he couldn't be sure if it were real. But then a louder sound: a sharp cry from behind him on the trail. Just one cry and then nothing but the ceaseless roar of the Zamserbach. He thought it might have been a trick of the Zamser's waters on his ears, but when he turned it seemed that he saw through the leaves a flash of movement: his father, falling. It was pictorial and still, like an image on a photographic plate – his father tilting backward off the trail at an incredible angle, hands clutching the straps of his rucksack.

He rushed back toward the stone footbridge, and even before he got there, what he suddenly wanted to do was to rush back in time instead of space: to the deck of the Furtschagelhaus, where they'd together looked up at the glacier, the icy firn like massive shining stairs from the rocks of the grassy moraine up into the heavens; to go back before that, to the Schwarzsee, the Black Lake, with its shrunken trees and supralunary mirror that inverted the heavens. His father, who couldn't swim, had challenged him to a race across the lake. He clung to those memories, though they had not until now been good ones, like a child, suddenly homesick and clinging to the memory of home.

When he reached the footbridge, he saw his father lying below on his back, murmuring.

3. Dr Pessler

That is why I cite the saying backwards: *'Dum spero, spiro.'*
['While I hope, I breathe']

PHILIPP HALSMANN, letter to Ruth Römer,
Innsbruck Prison, 1929

February 1929, Innsbruck Prison

They'd been let out of their cages. It was the first time Philipp had breathed the open night air in months and it was so caustic, alpine, and pure it stabbed his lungs. But someone had started a fire in the cigarette bin, so Philipp stood shivering in a corner of the courtyard. He remembered the sound of a real fire, of hot wood coals ticking and popping like needle raindrops tapping on the roof, but dry – like a twinkling of snow crystals slowly packing into themselves.

Horst came back, big boots stomping through the snow puddles. *'Nein,'* he said. He dumped a bucket of water on the fire and herded them back in. *'Von jetzt an sind Zigaretten verboten.'*

Snow blanketed the Innsbruck Prison. The dungeon doors were locked one by one in a long and echoing recession of bolts clanking in rusted holsters. Horst was angry. But Philipp hadn't seen a fire since he had been free, in the Gasthaus Stern at Jenbach, with Mama and Papa.

He lay down on the paillasse, blowing on his frozen fingers.

He wouldn't sleep tonight as he hadn't the night before, because in the morning the new lawyer was coming. So he lay awake, thinking about fire. It was nice, in a way, to be near a fire. Papa used to light a fire on Friday nights in Riga, when the men played pinochle. That one night, the vodka bottle had sat in the snow by the firewood and left puddles among the cards, which stuck to the water, like bugs dragging along a table with wet wings. Mama had baked an apple pie, and Philipp had seen up Esya's dress. It was after the dog died.

Mama had been able to stand death then. If Papa were here, he would tell her to buy herself a new sweater, a whole new wardrobe. He would stuff the crumpled bills into her hand.

Through the high window in his cell, if he stood on the chair, clung to the ledge, and dragged himself up, Philipp could see the tops of three of the limestone peaks north of Innsbruck: the Brandjoch, the one they called 'Frau Hitt,' and the Sattelspitzen. From the ceiling, maybe he could have seen down to the green Inn River at the foot of the mountains, but there was no way to climb up so high. So he stared out at the mountains, which had killed his father. They were, he imagined, three people very much like the Innsbruck prisoners, malformed of conscience and immune to regret. But no person had killed his father, only rocks and thin air. His father had fought the mountains heroically and had lost only because of the moral flaw there among the mute rocks and snow and goats. Today clouds were boiling up like steam from the mountaintops into the empty blue stratosphere over Tyrol.

The new lawyer did not understand this. He believed that it was a murder, like these other fools of the Tyrol.

The pass-through on the door slid open. Horst poked through a heel of yellow bread, pinched between two chapped and hairy knuckles. '*Sie haben einen Besucher*,' the guard said. Philipp took the bread and put it on his stack of books. Friends again.

Then he pulled the chair away from the wall, switched on the light bulb, and placed the chair in what he imagined was a welcoming position. He couldn't help but take ownership now of the cell with its cracked, dingy white paint, piles of books, newspapers, and parcels, the stack of writing paper on the floor beside the metal bedpan, the paillasse and the little sewing kit on the blanket, the orange with its scarred rind. And he was determined, this time, to be calm so he would not have any more nightmares and so he would not have to discipline himself with push-ups or by skipping another meal. He turned over the picture of his father so it lay face down and pulled his sleeve down to cover the scar, then called out, '*Kommen Sie herein!*' At the last minute, he tried to pat down his hair. He was skinnier than ever now, and pale, with spectacles that seemed too big and an unkempt and bushy dark beard and coarse brown hair standing up tall on his head. He hated to see his face in the bathroom mirror most of all because he looked so weak.

The door opened, and in came Franz Pessler, short but fit and handsome. He didn't even look around, just dropped his attaché case on the concrete floor, lifted the chair, and slung it under himself, quite at home. 'Sit,' he said.

Philipp held out his hand, but Pessler pulled the attaché case up onto his knees and flipped it open immediately. The attorney had light sea-blue eyes, somewhat narrowly spaced and deeply recessed under a serious blond brow, and they were creased at the outside corners as if from many years gazing at the brightness of the ocean or the desert. The face was slightly round – not in a corpulent way, but substantial like the face of an Argentine race-car driver whose photograph Philipp had once seen. A faint scar slanted on the right cheek: a healthy Aryan face, accustomed to the weather of the mountain. Though his voice was high and staccato, like a sound made in the body of a bird, he was strong, at least in a rude Tyrol sense, not like the cross-eyed Vienna Jew who had screwed everything up already. But Pessler didn't understand what had happened and this had caused Philipp to fly into a rage.

Pessler looked up from his papers and stared quizzically for a moment. 'Sit,' he said again, and Philipp immediately lowered himself onto the paillasse, the prickly sack of straw on the concrete floor where he slept. He would obey at any cost to his dignity; the prison food had once again filled his bowel with air. He drew his thighs tightly together.

'Our new republic is a worrisome place, isn't it?' Pessler said. 'Let's hope there'll be no riots when the decision is reversed.' Pessler opened up a folder in his case and began reading: '"While the father struck me as a very open and agreeable fellow, the son immediately struck me as suspicious and cold."' He looked at Philipp inquisitively. Then he continued reading: '"The father was friendly, laughed loudly, liked to tell jokes. The son was unfriendly and sullen." Hans Bauer. "I immediately thought that there is something dangerous about him." Maria Rauch. "He seemed uncomfortable in the society of other people." Another witness.'

'I need no reproval,' Philipp said. 'I will be good.'

'Yes, those are quotations from the transcripts. Then there are the newspapers. "The accused makes a most unfavorable impression." "Philipp Halsmann is strange in appearance, with a truculent personality. His testimony is marked by aggressive outbursts." "*Vorsitzende* Larcher is only trying to help the grumpy little man, who comes across as disagreeable and un-likable." A Jew, even, who wrote that in *Die Wahrheit!* "The accused is argumentative and hostile."'

'A Jew, even? In *Die Wahrheit?* You mean a fellow member of the worldwide Jewish banking conspiracy has broken ranks? Ha! And I thought you were educated by Jesuits.'

Pessler did not respond with so much as a twitch of his blond mustache. 'This is Tyrol,' he said. 'The Jewish race is unfamiliar to the people here. Not like in Vienna. And, to be frank, your hair and lips do have a Negroid look.' Pessler swept his hand through the air as if the point were irrelevant. 'But let me ask you, are you disagreeable?'

'I would be less disagreeable if I were not in prison because of a bunch of Heimwehr goatherds who think due process of law means asking the opinion of the local innkeeper's dog,' Philipp said.

Pessler again was perfectly still. Everyone who came into the cell always looked up to the high windows as if they themselves were imprisoned, but Pessler was staring straight at him with his sea-bright eyes, examining him like a doctor. Philipp looked out the window at the clear patch of blue.

'How did he die?' Pessler said.

'My father had a heart condition,' Philipp said. By an act of supreme self-control, he did not raise his voice, though they were now back on that ground which had caused him to pound his fists against the wall and break the chair. 'He fell.'

Pessler shook his head. He cast his eyes around then, as if he might find some evidence to prove his point there in the room. He pointed to the picture frame turned face down on the bench. 'May I see?' Pessler said.

Philipp handed him the photograph. It showed Papa sitting in a meadow, looking out at a lake.

'Why face down?' Pessler said.

Philipp said nothing.

'When is the last time you remember seeing him alive?'

'When he fell.'

Pessler rested his head despondently in his hand.

Philipp said nothing. These were the coarse terms in which the Tyrolean mind worked – murder, blood libel, race, Jewish perfidy.

'You're disappointed with me,' Pessler said.

Philipp said nothing still. He would not yell, because if he yelled he would have to skip lunch and he was too hungry.

Pessler held up his hands in a calming gesture. 'Things were hidden from you. Listen to me if you want to get out of here.'

'You think I want to get out of here?' Philipp said hotly. 'I'll stay in prison a hundred years. No one killed my father but the mountain. All that stupid ice and rock you call your home. And I'll stay right here until it's proved!' He had gone ahead and shouted. He rubbed his empty belly.

'I didn't say *you* killed him,' Pessler said. 'I said he was murdered.'

'You didn't know my father. He was too strong for anyone to kill. I once saw him get into a fight with a horse and win. A mountain could kill him, but not a man.' Philipp breathed in the stale air of the cell for a while. It was cold in the cell. Pessler's hands were white on the attaché case, though he'd left his suit jacket unbuttoned and looked perfectly comfortable. He was steady, clean, blond, impervious to the cold because he was raised on glacier water and pure Alpine wind. And he was impervious to the filth of the cell because he was free and would take with him only what stuck to the soles of his shoes.

'Your story has to change,' Pessler said. 'And the beard makes you look like a criminal.'

18

'They don't allow me to shave here,' Philipp said.

'That can be remedied.'

Philipp pulled back his left sleeve and held up his wrist. On the underside, which was clear and thin and white, there were two small scar lines. 'You didn't read about it in the paper?' The warden said he would never see another pencil sharpener.

'I seldom read about trials in the newspapers,' Pessler said, still leaning back, unmoved as though he hadn't understood the meaning of the scars.

Horst pushed open the door.

'Well,' Pessler said, standing up, 'we have more to discuss.' He placed his foot on a rung of the chair, which Horst had screwed back together, and pushed it against the wall. 'Is there anything I can bring you when I come back?'

Philipp flipped his father's picture face down again and watched Pessler with the rage and humiliation still rising like a vapor from his ears. He pulled off his spectacles and washed away the sight of the attorney. He would now have to read *Corinne*, by Madame de Staël, instead of eat, or maybe he would do a hundred push-ups.

Pessler rapped ceremonially on the doorjamb and was already out in the hallway when Philipp blurted out, in a voice that was hoarse with sudden tears, 'Apple pie.'

4. Dr Meixner

His mother didn't understand why he'd attempted suicide. It
was because the guilty verdict had forever sealed for him *The
Fundamental Principles of the Metaphysic of Morals* by Immanuel
Kant. When the boys in school made fun of the old Russian's limp, he had not. He'd attuned his will to the angels as
on a pitch pipe, and calibrated his every action against a
rational principle of universal good. But what he'd learned in
the Alps was the supreme irrelevance of a 'good will' in this
world. Whatever harmonies resided in his soul, and in that
of his father, they resonated nowhere in the cold crevasses
and goat skulls of the mountain. Here, law was a ritual carried out in the hearts of goat men, and the lawyers were the
minions of the goat men and chased after them in order to
decorate their rituals in casuistries. The only rational moral
action, then, the only brave action, had been to absent himself from this irrational and untruthful world. But he had by
now revised this position somewhat, and he made sure no
one knew that he starved himself for punishment, especially
not his mother.

It took a long time for Pessler to return. But it may have been a short time. Ten minutes passed like an hour and an hour like an afternoon. You couldn't see to the end of a month. That was like a schoolchild in Russia trying to see across a Russian winter.

'Horst,' Philipp said. 'What does the sun look like today?'

'I don't know, Philja, I'm in prison here with you.'

'What does the river look like then?'

'Mud.'

He spent a few hours (minutes) thinking about Horst. *Horst needs gratitude, so he's probably lonely too, he probably lives alone, he probably drinks Obstler Schnapps by himself in a room with no telephone. He calls me Philja and I've never mentioned my childhood nickname, so he must read my letters. He probably reads other people's mail and peeks at ladies' underclothes in the Hofgarten.*

'*Sie haben einen Besucher*,' Horst said through the door.

When Pessler entered the cell, he did not say hello and he did not have any apple pie. All he said was, 'I'm going to have to show you the autopsy photos.'

His excursions, as Horst called them, were another vagary of Austrian justice. It was as though they were aping the Western courts of law without really getting the point or much wanting to. So the prosecution brought him back to the 'crime' scene and examined him there in the field, and the defense argued about it, and they all pointed to sticks and rocks and he was given his turn to argue too. It was like a science experiment performed without controls, wild, contaminated, a farce. Pessler said that Karl Meixner, the forensic pathologist who wore his hat indoors, would not permit him to take the autopsy photos. And so they would have to go to Meixner if they wanted to see them. 'But don't worry,' Pessler said. 'I won't let him torture you.'

From the Dürkopp, they walked up shady, cold Müller-strasse, where the windowsills were lined with empty flower boxes. No one seemed to be at home. At the end of the street, just beyond the quiet tombstones of the Friedhof, sat the Institute for Juridical Medicine, still and quiet as if it were another of the grave buildings in the cemetery. The sun lit the entire amphitheater of blue mountains above and shone individually on each of the polished gravestones, one of which, perhaps, belonged to his father.

Meixner was waiting for them inside, but nothing stirred behind the Institute's dark demilune window high above. They stopped there before the door.

'Now, you must address him as Herr Doktor,' Pessler said, steam pluming from his nose. Two bird shadows crossed the bright square sandstone pillars, entombed in their Egyptian silence, and disappeared. 'Never say "you." Say "Herr Doktor."'

'As Herr Doktor wishes.'

Pessler stared at him and tugged once at the lapels of his topcoat.

Then the gendarme – what they called in German a *Polizist* – pushed Philipp inside into a musty, unlit hallway, and on after that into a bright room of steel butcher tables that stunk of formaldehyde. There, lying naked to the air, was a corpse, bloated, wet, and white, horny yellow toes pointing at each wall, face compressed and corrugated on one side like a plucked chicken in an icebox. The *Polizist* pinched his nose shut, then dropped his arm again. Pessler strode past the body and the tables, which had drains in the center for the blood. Philipp strode after him and looked directly at the body and did not pinch his nose shut.

In the adjoining hall, the *Polizist* stopped by an open door-way and Pessler and Philipp went on into a room full of bell jars. There was no one there. At the base of the tall window facing the door was a row of skulls, a huge one in the middle with a cracked forehead. An enormous stuffed eagle, wings spread in flight, thrust its beak at Philipp from a wicker stand, and in a bell jar by a little writing desk sat a submerged human fetus, its large head bowed over a body thin and curled as if it had been cursed with some disease. In another jar was a bizarre animal, perhaps a mollusk, shelled and pluming with torn inner tissues. It was labeled HERMAPHRODITISMUS VERUS. Or maybe it was a jellyfish. A view camera on a tripod leaned against the wall, and above the camera hung several watercolors of mountain meadows, which were signed 'K. Meixner.'

'Herr Doktor?' Pessler called out.

No answer came, but beyond the doorway by the black marble laboratory bench someone pushed back a chair, and then Herr Dr Meixner emerged. He didn't acknowledge either Pessler or Philipp but simply opened a dossier on the bench and began sifting through photographs. Philipp wouldn't say a word, no matter what they showed him, he wouldn't move, and he certainly wouldn't cry. If he cried or acted nervous, he would fast for a hundred days.

Meixner wore a long white lab coat over a taupe suit and black tie. He had on his queer yellow-brown alpine hat, with its high and unpinched crown and its wide slanting brim, like that on a pith helmet. One of the doctor's dark brows was hitched up higher than the other, as he looked down at the dossier in silence, flicking his crocodile eyes around. His head appeared to be shaved up under the hat and his falling cheeks weighted his big bald head like a pineapple. He had long pendulous earlobes and, amazingly, he wore a wedding ring.

Philipp was debating whether the doctor or his wife were the more insane when Herr Dr Meixner said loudly, 'You are interested in *Hermaphroditismus verus*?' Meixner kept looking at the photographs, but pointed right at the bell jar with the jellyfish. 'Those are the genitalia of a juvenile human hermaphrodite,' he said.

'To whom is Herr Doktor speaking?' Philipp said.

Meixner snapped his head up and looked at Philipp fiercely. 'To you.' Then Meixner said, 'Look here,' and pointed to the dossier. 'Come, Herr Halsmann, and look! This boy was hit with a shovel.'

Philipp did as he was told so as to avoid future punishments on Madame de Staël's chopping block. The photograph was taken from directly above and it showed a boy of fourteen or fifteen lying on his back. No blood. The mouth hung open and the fly of his pants was undone.

'And here a son has killed his parents and stored the bodies together for three weeks,' Meixner said, looking at Philipp's face for the first time. It was a mask of perfect calm. Meixner flipped a photograph of an unhappy looking young man on a country road and pulled out another picture showing two corpses, one bloated, the other thin. Philipp kept his spine ramrod straight, and his face completely still. He didn't turn away. 'What is fascinating is that the obese mother is relatively preserved,' Herr Dr Meixner said. 'The eyeballs have been destroyed by maggots, as you can see, but the internal organs are completely preserved, with no maggots present inside the integument and subdermal fat apart from the *Schädelhöhle*, the cranial cavity, where many maggots were found in liquefied brain matter.' He pulled out another picture. 'The mother was shot just once through the heart. Now the skinny father was shot and stabbed multiple times. The flies laid their eggs not only in the natural openings of the face, but also in the many wounds, and, by contrast, all his body cavities were occupied with maggots with the internal organs thoroughly destroyed.' Meixner now stared at Philipp for a good long time.

'It's interesting work Herr Doktor performs here,' Pessler interjected. 'Can we see the Max Halsmann photos now, please?'

Meixner grunted and went through the doorway by the bench. Moments later he returned carrying a large glass bell jar like those that held the fetus and the hermaphrodite genitals. This one contained in the clear fluid a white organ the size of a pot roast, and many floaters, which swayed in unison in the tippy water.

Pessler grabbed Philipp by the shoulders and spun him around, so that he faced the stuffed eagle.

'Herr Halsmann shows no reaction,' Meixner said. 'Only a prison sentence can stir him from his apathy, it appears.'

'What is that?' Philipp said, with his eyes still fixed on the beak of the eagle. 'In the jar.'

'It's your father's head,' Meixner said loudly. His voice said he was a man who liked for people to hear the truth no matter how weak or ashamed they were before it. Because he was not weak. A good rude truth is like milk to a real Austrian man!

'Herr Doktor wishes to embarrass me, Philipp,' Pessler said. 'I have already informed him that the Institute's handling of the remains constitutes a criminal act.'

'No one has violated the little laws of this pygmy state, except *der Vatermörder*,' Meixner said. 'Anyway, the remains were released. We only require the head as a specimen.'

'I needed to show you the photos, Philipp,' Pessler said in his ear, 'to show you that your father was murdered.'

'A fact of which Herr Halsmann is no doubt aware,' Meixner said. 'This case has consumed enough of the faculty's time already, mein Herr, at great cost to its reputation. I believe

I've been overly gracious, as have many others, in acceding to the demands of Jews and Viennese mercenaries.' He added contemptuously, 'The demands of this sacrosanct... Halsmann family.'

Pessler was pushing him almost into the eagle's beak, but Philipp wouldn't turn his head. If the beak touched his face or cut his flesh, he would not cry out.

'Show us the photos,' Pessler said.

'No,' Meixner said. 'A proper demonstration should be made on the specimen itself.'

Philipp heard the lid of the jar come off with a *ping*, and a wet noise and then *plum, plum, plum, plum, plum* a heavy rain of formaldehyde into the steel basin. 'Let me turn it this way,' Meixner said, and there was a sound like someone tossing and catching a cabbage. 'As the examiners have said repeatedly in court, a fall is impossible. The wound you see here above the root of the nose is seven centimeters across and penetrates the forehead of the skull into the *Schädelhöhle*, the cranial cavity. See this in the wound? *Das ist Gehirn.* Brain.' Again came the sound of Meixner tossing the heavy wet head. 'Here, above the right ear, an egg-shaped cavity on the skull. The bone is *zersplittert* to a degree that indicates eight to ten repeated blows with a blunt object. The skin is macerated from repeated bludgeoning.' Meixner enumerated many other wounds all around the head, while Philipp stared into the beak of the eagle. 'Beaten, *ja*?'

'The photographs,' Pessler said.

There was a thump and a clank of metal. 'Okay, we are finished then. You can uncover your eyes, Herr Halsmann,' Meixner said.

But when Philipp turned around, there was the head in a puddle, eyes and mouth closed, like the head of John the Baptist on a platter. It did bear some resemblance to his father, but it had no hair and no eyeglasses and there was a deep hole in the forehead. The professor wiped his hands on a towel, and with a scissor forceps he lifted a stone from another tray. 'One more thing,' Meixner said. He held the stone to another wound over the right ear, where a piece of yellow fat was hanging on the white pinna. 'The stone is from the crime scene. Same exact size as the wound. Now look.' He held the rock under a magnifying glass on a stand. He turned it back and forth with the glinting pincers. 'You see? Skin. Blood. Hair. It matches Max Halsmann's hair. He was beaten to death with a stone.' Meixner then set the stone down and with the forceps pulled a flap of skin down from high on the bald pate of the head, covering its eyes. '*Der Knochen ist so klein zersplittert, dass sich die Splitter gar nicht mehr zusammensetzen.* Like Humpty Dumpty.' Philipp's German had begun to abandon him, as if he were still at the Tiedeböhl Gymnasium, but he held fast and scarcely blinked.

Meixner left the room, and Pessler stepped in front of the head. *Die Wunde.* The wound. The wound. *Um den Schädel fand man eine grosse, tiefe Wunde an der Stirn, oberhalb der Nasenwurzel, durch welche die Schädelhöhle eröffnet wurde.* There was no time to work it out.

Meixner came right back with the pictures and spread them on the marble. Another corpse.

'It's your father,' Pessler said.

'No,' Philipp said. 'This man has no hair.'

'The head was shaved,' Meixner said.

Philipp looked at the man in the first picture. There was something very gentle and docile about this body in the photograph lying peacefully on its back, eyes closed, lips just barely drawn together. The man was big and thick like his father, and the nose was like his father's. But the spectacles were missing.

'*Die Wunde*,' Meixner was saying again. There was talk of centimeters and angles again. Especially the deep wound on the forehead did look like the result of violence. But not by a stone – rather by something sharp – as if someone had hammered a piton down into the forehead.

In both the supine and prone photographs, the head of the man appeared to be resting on the edge of a wooden board. In the photo where the man lay on his front, the neck was extended, chin lifted like a Christmas goose, arms aligned obediently at his sides, palms up.

Philipp reached past his attorney to the head on the platter as if he would touch it. 'Could I see inside the mouth please?' he said loudly.

Herr Dr Meixner looked distantly at his skulls and bell jars.

'Just lift the upper lip there on the left side,' Philipp said. 'Herr Doktor.'

Meixner inserted his naked finger into the mouth and drew up the lip, revealing the teeth. There was a gold tooth there, wet and dull like a coin under cold seawater.

'If your curiosity is thoroughly satisfied,' Meixner said, pulling his finger away. The lip and cheek of the severed head fell back into repose; the head was a very compliant patient. A dog's mouth was slightly different in death. Muschka had died with her lips hanging open, revealing all her pointed teeth and black gums as she never would have in life, and it was impossible to put her hanging blue tongue back into her mouth.

'Go ahead, Philipp,' Pessler said.

Philipp went out to the hall, where the *Polizist* was standing with his gloves still pressed against his face, covering up his nose.

'The smell?' Philipp said. 'It doesn't bother me.'

Pessler backed through the door. 'If you play your games in the retrial,' he said into the room, 'I'll have you charged for defiling the dead.'

No reply came from the room, but the door closed quietly in Pessler's face.

'He didn't even fight,' Pessler said, helplessly. 'This Burschenschaft fascist, decrying foreigners in beer halls, and then when the war breaks out he keeps his feet dry with the chaplains and doesn't hear a single shot fired.'

Philipp watched coldly while the attorney wrung his hands. 'You fought, then?' Philipp said.

Pessler said nothing.

'Forget it. I don't care,' Philipp said.

'Yes, I fought,' Pessler said.

They walked in silence back down Müllerstrasse to the Dürkopp, which was parked under the naked limbs of a pear tree. The other *Polizist* was reading a newspaper in the front seat.

'And you believe Herr Dr Meixner?' Philipp said. 'It seems to me that he's deranged.' He didn't even feel like yelling.

'He may be,' Pessler said, screwing his hat down on his head. 'But the facts are what they are.'

As the Dürkopp bounced over the cobblestones, Philipp felt the scar at his wrist. He had no intention of harming himself, for he felt harmed enough to satisfy him, but when he got back to the cell, he found they had again taken his newspapers away, and he threw the chair at the window bars and splintered it into forty pieces. Horst would never repair it now. Its life as a chair was over. He collected all the broken wood into a pile and thought what he would tell Horst. That he had been standing on the chair when he slipped and accidentally slammed the chair against the steel bars in the window and, seeing that two pieces of wood were still attached to one another, he had accidentally slammed them into the bars a fourth time so that the chair was reduced irreversibly to firewood. Pessler had fought in a war; and Meixner knew what to do; but Philipp didn't know what to do. Meixner was right as far as that went. Philipp was a child, and he was afraid. And to punish himself for his childish loss of control with the chair, he picked up one of the loose screws and held it up over his wrist, but he merely traced his old wounds with it rather than stabbing himself.

5. Love

That which you found so good and right, and by that I
mean the *Angst vor dem Herzen* ['the fear of the heart'], I
find, forgive me, wrong. It is not fear but shame . . . When
I see you again . . . I will not be embarrassed, Gioconda,
to throw down all the fig leaves. And I will invite you to
do the same, to be as old-fashioned as Adam and Eve.

PHILIPP HALSMANN, letter to Ruth Römer,
Innsbruck Prison, 1929

So there had been the fall, but then, it seemed, someone had
driven a piton through Papa's forehead. Philipp considered
the fact (since there was no one to say it to) in the most direct
possible terms. He turned his mind's eye directly on the
mountain man who slaughtered pigs, hunted birds, built
roads. The idea of the goat man out there almost made him
want to open up Kant again, as though the damaged coils in
the machinery of justice might now realign themselves by a
reflex of universal reason. And they would all live happily
ever after. All he had to do was go find out what happened
and compel the murderer to come to jail and take his place.
However, there was the problem of the door.

'Horst!' he yelled through the door. 'I have to get out of here
for a few days, OK? Can you let me out? It might be a week, or
at the outer limit, three months. But possibly longer. Yes, I
think I just need to get out of here for ever, OK? It began so
auspiciously, but I'm afraid this arrangement just isn't working.'

The other guard came, the one with the red schnapps face and dimple in his chin. 'What are you saying, Halsmann? Is that Russian? Speak German only or the warden will put you in *der Keller.*' The black eyeballs of Schnapps Face went to and fro at the pass-through.

'Not me,' Philipp said in Russian. 'His prized possession? Incidentally, the warden's wife is a train-station whore. You're drunk and impotent. Go find the warden and marry him.'

'If you persist, you will be reported,' the voice said across the door.

What would Kant do? He would definitely desist from speaking Russian. Because it is a universal principle of reason that all men falsely accused of killing their fathers should not be allowed to speak Russian. '*Gut,*' Philipp said, and added in Russian, 'I think the warden suits you.'

Then he got out Ruth's picture. And he did go to Kant, but not to the *Metaphysic of Morals.* Instead he looked up beauty, which Kant said was the 'object of a universal delight.' And because he couldn't go anywhere, or do anything about the mountain man lurking among the frozen pine needles of Frau Hitt, and because he'd already asked his sister to hire a detective in Vienna, he turned his thoughts to beauty.

A prison was a funny place for love to flower, but he supposed it could happen, like a weed springing up in a crack between bricks. And it was a funny time to be in love, if it was in fact love, yet it seemed to him that perhaps he was in love. It took him days (hours) to get himself to print the words across the slightly curved page: I LOVE YOU.

Each of the envelopes had the same inkblots caught in the loops of the *p*'s of his first name, the same Berlin postmarks – two black and clear, one half-vestige in red. They arrived open, neatly slit down the side, and when he withdrew her letters, which were marked with stripes of black ink, he didn't read them for an hour or more. He often removed his eyeglasses so he could only see the letters' feminine shapes and not make sense of the words. He'd watched her write a précis in her little room in Berlin; her thumb bent and unbent around the pen like an inchworm inching across the page. And so from her pen strokes he could infer her living hand, and from her hand, he could infer her whole body, could almost imagine she were sitting there before him. He'd even sat in the chair himself and then got up and placed his hand there, imagining the warmth were hers. She was one of those unattainably beautiful girls, even his friends agreed, the kind who pretended you didn't exist. Her portrait ignored him still: widely spaced and huge light eyes not returning his gaze, and her dark hair in a pageboy, as it had been in Berlin, and an old-fashioned dress with shoulder frills.

There was just enough perfume left on the paper to detect it through the censor's ink, which embalmed the perfume smell with its smell of paint. Her perfume was a door in his memory that led to a bedroom. But before Lugano it had led to the Tiergarten. His friends and her friends. She would speak only to her friends. His friends didn't even try with her – they aimed lower, at the loud sisters who would talk to anyone. He'd seen Ruth before when the same girls came to listen to jazz, but he didn't know her name. Andreas was there – tall, sunburned, with a chin a foot long, never serious. He even laughed about the man eating his lunch alone in the garden, who had complained to them about the crumbs they left. Ruth had liked that about Andreas, she later confessed, that he was always light. He cheered her up. She said she envied her cat, who did not have problems, who did not have to think but only react in the moment.

He walked behind her through the garden, so she wouldn't

see him looking, and his friends made fun of him and said loudly that he was in love, so she would hear it. But he had to look because of her beauty, which was not only a beauty of the body but one of mind. It could be read in the ungarish gentleness of motion in her limbs; you could tell just from looking that she didn't fully understand her effect on males, or that she didn't care about this effect, and didn't flaunt it, because she knew she possessed even greater advantages in her mind. This picture of beauty pleased his eyes like Winged Victory, so much so that he couldn't look away if there was any choice between looking and not looking. When he'd seen Winged Victory on the Daru staircase at the Louvre, Papa and Mama and Liouba had had to leave him behind to go see the Persian friezes. He'd soaked up the pleasure of it in his eyes for more than an hour, and when he looked at his face in the mirror in the hotel, his eyes were wrecked with burst vessels.

There was shame in his uncontrollable need to look, but greater shame in hiding. And there was fear that she would think him a bore or too short compared to Andreas. But he would have to talk to her in order to see if this were really the girl about whom he'd dreamed, a mate worthy of his heroic future and ready to accompany him in his conquests, as his mother had accompanied his father (according to those old stories told on Friday nights). He was ready to set forth into that future now, his eyes begged to look upon its beauty that very day, and he was not about to forfeit his heroic future to some German with a big chin who excelled at drinking beer in the afternoon and whose destiny lay in the sales department of some Ruhr manufacturer. So he did speak to her, when Andreas had gone. He'd said she ought to move away from the truck in the Grosser Stern with the propane tanks on it, and, not wanting to be seen as a boring engineer who thought about propane tanks all day, he'd asked her about art. She was a dancer, she said. He told her about Winged Victory at the Louvre and invited her to Dresden to see the Museum Johanneum.

His heroic future had commenced. Because, even if she said no, the question had been a daring act, worthy of any knight of the Order of St Arbuthnot's Finger. She'd said she loved Dresden, and made frequent trips there, and in this had helped him to believe he'd stumbled upon his destiny — but still the invitation had been heroically brave.

She came in two weeks and met him in the medieval gallery. He was silent and so was she. She'd waited for him to speak. He didn't speak. He looked at the Chiens Gris de Saint Louis on the sage tapestry and at the triptychs and up at the electoral sword of Frederick the Warlike hanging over his head. The air was cool as marble and smelled like the slightly damp stone of a wine cellar. They walked on in silence until they stood before the regalia of the king of Poland and he said, 'Shouldn't it be in Poland?'

She laughed, but when they went out of the museum she said she had to go meet a friend.

He remained quiet while they walked down the street. Then he'd said, 'Did you know I used to be a dancer? Watch this. *Entrechat!*' And he jumped up and crashed into a garbage can.

'Hmm. That's not exactly *entrechat* as I learned it. But your height was very good,' she said.

'Yeah. Look, *grand jeté!*' He leapt right over the fallen garbage can, lifting his right arm like the neck of a swan, and as he landed he clipped his left foot on the garbage can, which caused him to fall onto the sidewalk. 'Ow. Do you want to see my *pas de poisson?*'

He took her to get some apple pie on the windy Altmarkt

instead of to her friend's, and they ate it together under an umbrella. She ate it with her fingers and got chunks of the greasy *Apfelkuchen* caught up under her fingernails. Afterwards, they went to his apartment and there she'd demonstrated for him a proper *demi-plié*, fending him off with an arm extended and perfectly still, face turned serenely to the radiator.

They hadn't kissed in Dresden, but in Berlin she'd stood next to him at the boathouse and their arms were touching, standing so close he knew it was deliberate, and he felt as if she were embracing him there in front of everyone, while the fireworks went up over the Linden and the Brandenburg Gate. In the infernally hot and tiny attic where she lived, he had finally kissed her. And then Lugano came, where he had taken every step toward knighthood, beauty, and experience that might be taken besides the loss of his virginity. He had vanquished his shame and had adventured in a land that never ceased to surrender up to him new vistas of beautiful sensation, a wilderness of clefts, folds, and caves, each enclosing some new and exquisite orchid. The land surrendered its hidden treasures easily, unprotesting, as though he were always meant to find them.

He thought about Lugano all the time and those secret places on Ruth's body she'd allowed him to visit. But she couldn't say the things she'd said to him anymore, and he couldn't say the things he'd said to her in Lugano, because of the censor who was reading all the letters.

In fact it lately gave him fits of shame when he thought about Lugano, because his heroic future had been taken from him. He would not live up to his father now and he was scared and Ruth was out there with Andreas, while he slowly transmogrified from a boyfriend into a sickly *cause célèbre*. He even began to wonder if Ruth looked down on him because he was a Jew, as his mother had once looked down on Ruth for being a gentile. Sometimes when he thought of Lugano, when it no longer seemed the act of a knight to do so, but of a craven and scared boy who fantasized too much and didn't know how to act, he then punished himself with fifty push-ups. Today he had written I LOVE YOU, but before today he had signed all his letters to Ruth, *Mit festem Händedruck* – 'with a firm handshake.' He didn't feel brave anymore. And after the visit to the Juridical Institute, he saw not fertile valleys but pitons in his mind, and he had an almost unstoppable urge to kill himself again.

6. Censorship

Palmstrom conceives the Alps to be a cube
And climbs it through his telescopic tube.

CHRISTIAN MORGENSTERN, from 'Alpinism II,'
Alle Galgenlieder (*Gallows Songs*)

Liouba said it was because he saw Papa in the Institute that he had sunk deeper into despair, but it seemed to him that was merely a coincidence. Several other things had happened at the same time to drive his soul downward. For one, Ruth wrote to him about Andreas. And in the next letter, she did not say 'I love you' – was it because he'd written, 'Your face repays familiarity a thousandfold, just like La Gioconda's'? She hadn't liked that. And then a new prisoner had joined them in the yard. The man was deathly thin with lank blond hair and a consumptive cough – a vision of prison death. To make the others laugh, he would wheel himself right into the brick wall and collapse on the ground, grinning as he clutched his knee and rocked on the ground, blinking away actual tears. And often when he fell he began to cough, a deep vibration of the bronchi and a squeak, and the man would not grin then but dribble long trembling ropes of saliva to the ground. Sometimes the coughing went on for ten minutes or more. But the other prisoners roared with laughter every time the man sank to his knees coughing like a drowning goose.

Home. Home. Home. His mind chanted this when he wanted

to think of anything besides home, anything besides his room, where he'd stayed up late with Liouba talking across a candle flame. *Home, home, home*, like a painful pulsing of blood in his swollen throat. Or sometimes the pulsing said *Lugano, Lugano, Lugano*, and he needed to tell Ruth how much he loved her perfectly symmetrical face, huge eyes, and full lips with their slight overbite. He needed to tell her immediately, but there was no way to tell her and there was no lust in it at all. It was a thoroughly chaste and fearful love of her beauty that transfixed him now, like love of a beautiful landscape, like love of the Blue Lakes at home. He needed to make sure that the nickname La Gioconda still pleased her, as it had when they were under the palm tree. He had said it was her *nom de guerre*.

Well done, Halsmann, you're really holding it together like a man, Papa would be proud.

He wrote to her. He wrote and wrote but he didn't say anything about the nickname. He wrote about *Gallows Songs*. He wrote, 'You should in no way feel beholden to me, Ruth, you are young and single and I may be here for my whole youth. We don't know. Let me be the first one to set you free.'

He was indeed sinking. The ghoul face of the coughing man stood before him all the time, with eyes starting from the skull and too many teeth showing from within the withered mouth so that the skeleton seemed to be showing itself unmercifully through the skin. And in the bathroom he couldn't resist seeing his own face as some skin attached tenuously to a skull with eyes like buds on lily stems growing temporarily in the inhospitable bones. Now he found a need to order the blank hours by actually writing out his schedule. *Obey the schedule. The schedule will save you. It is a map through time. It will carry you through, day by day, to the end.*

Six o'clock, wake up. Every morning he awoke before the priest arrived, and waited for the priest as if in a vacuum, as if his father had just been there seconds before. And then the sound of the priest approached him in the darkness, *shoop, shoop, shoop,* as the priest drew aside the pass-through doors one by one and incanted upon the darkness a prayer to Christ for His forgiveness.

Shower. Let them laugh when you hide your body from them. Don't listen to them. They have nothing to do with you. 'Shy as Susanna at her bath,' he'd written to Ruth. Udo would whistle at him every single day and call him 'Frau Halsmann,' and every day, no matter how prepared he was, he'd just say nothing and blush. He hated this the most, when he would see the other men in the dank latrine with the gummy greenish drains. It smelled in there like a place no one would ever want to be, like a natatorium, like body smells, like . . . not home. A man had punched him in there once and the next day disappeared. First into *der Keller,* Horst said, and then out of Innsbruck prison altogether, because the warden didn't want a story in the newspapers, Horst said. No one ever touched him again, but they stared at him as though they wished to, and sometimes whispered '*Vatermörder*' and told him what they would do to him if Mother were not looking after him. It often seemed to him in the latrine that his failure to fit into prison life was an indictment of him instead of an indictment of the criminals, because if nothing else they were men and knew how to be men.

Return to cell and dress. His clothes were snaked by now with stitches, and the orange which he used as a thimble was wounded over its whole rind like a scarred-up moon. He could never clean the soles of his feet before putting on his socks, and the socks were always damp with yesterday's sweat because he would not wear the prison socks. *Going strong and almost to the end of the first hour. One down and just fif-teen more to go.*

Eat. Thank God for Udo's threats – they let Philipp eat alone in his cell. *Take bread, porridge* (even the words '*Geriebene Ger-stel*' gave him abdominal cramps), *and cup of water from the pass-through. Pour half of water into Gerstel. Chew gummy porridge and bread for more than half an hour to spite captors with continued existence.* His alimentary system had no interest in food.

Walk. Between 8 and 9 A.M., they goose-stepped in a circle in the empty courtyard, sucking in the painful Nordic air, Udo scratching at his empty eye socket and not saying 'Frau Halsmann' but broadcasting it into Philipp's brain. There had been a little tree out there, but the warden cut it down after the fire and now there was nothing.

Read entire newspaper (one to two hours).

Eat again. At lunch there was thin soup with leaves float-ing in it, strudel, wet and colorless boiled pork with horseradish (they called it *Krenfleisch* – how could a people name their food 'flesh,' like birds of carrion?), there were canned apples that Herr Glaser had sent, and, if it was a good day, there might be a boiled egg. If it was a very bad day, *Knödel*, Tyrolean dumplings of minced ham.

Read books. Now it was *Gallows Songs* by Morgenstern. Gide. Dumas – *un jour viendra.*

Analyze dreams or write poems. He dreamed of flying a lot. Sometimes he flew and no one noticed. He couldn't con-vince the others he could fly. But once, Ruth saw him in his dream.

Supper. Instead of an egg, a square of dry shortbread with apricot paste.

Read mail and write letters. He tried to save the letters till the end. This was almost a nice time. Now the sunrays softened and faded on the ceiling and he switched on the electric light.

He was almost through. The cold of night was descending on the mountains outside and at that time, the obliviousness of nature to humankind seemed peaceful and orderly and wondrous because it swept away Udo and prison and every custom of men.

Wrap Ruth's symmetrical, perfect face back up in wax paper to protect from the filth that dropped from the rotting pipes.

Lights out. Then it was dark as an inkblot until the eyes adjusted and the subtlest hint of light crept into the black ceiling, the weak far reaches of the last lights of Innsbruck. Then he would think of the huge mountains lying there, though they couldn't be seen, invisible as whales.

Sleep. Dream. Forget.

On *Fastnacht*, Philipp hauled himself up onto the window ledge and looked out through the bars. He could hear the people in the Hofgarten far below, singing to the winter spirits, but all he could see was Frau Hitt, purple and shining at the top in a sky with no clouds. One of the guides on the Schönbichlerhorn said Frau Hitt was a greedy woman who'd turned to stone. She'd given a starving peasant a stone to eat and reaped her just reward.

The guards came in at two in the afternoon and left him another tray of food for dinner. Then they went to join the festivities in the Hofgarten. The halls were empty and quiet except for someone yodeling at the end and another crying out occasionally to the other to shut his mouth. Schnapps Face said they would not return till very late. The schedule was all ruined. He thought he would cry.

The day passed as an eon, but it did pass. The singing in the city below never relented until the sun fell behind the mountains. He knew the guards did return as promised, because he was awakened by them banging on *Bettnässer*'s door in the middle of the night. They had written that in chalk on the boy's door for all to see – 'Bed Wetter' – and they clanked the bucket on his door at night and then Philipp would hear the boy groaning and watering the tin with his urine – a tall and thin eighteen-year-old who in the daytime would lean against the courtyard wall with his eyes mostly closed as if wilting under the judgment of the human gaze. Philipp was falling back to sleep when the banging came to his door and Schnapps Face came in with his *Schlagstock* out. The guard flipped on the lights. His face was redder than usual. Drunk.

'*Der Keller, zum Keller, sofort!*' The guard began tossing Philipp's bundles of newspapers out into the hall. Then he took the letters and the box of pens and the picture of Ruth and the picture of Papa looking onto the meadow and the picture of the family, when Mama had been well and happy, and tossed it all into the hallway with a crash.

He pushed Philipp out, too. A slight draft was moving through the hall. Then Schnapps Face took him down to the lightless *Keller* without a chance to put on any shoes. At the bottom of the stairs, he hopped on the gravel in his bare feet. Schnapps Face pushed him into the cell there and locked him up in the total blindness of the inner earth, where not even the vigil lamps of Innsbruck reached.

He thought about the broken pictures in the dark. Mama's chin upraised and squinting into the sunlight with a naïve happiness, her mind unimprinted with the tragedy. She was sitting in the chair on the patio, with Liouba sitting on the armrest in a white short-sleeve dress and long necklace, himself perched on the other armrest, sleeves rolled up, hand half-shoved in his pocket, thinking himself very worldly, an arm around his mother, and Papa was standing, leaning into the frame behind them in a three-piece suit, fist on his hip, and on his round head hair close-cropped and shining, avid for the silver of the photographer's glass.

When they'd been photographed in Switzerland, Papa had told a joke to the man in gray puttees.

A French soldier told me this in Berlin. He'd been arguing in the trenches with two other soldiers, an American and an Englishman, about the meaning of 'savoir faire'. The American claimed to know. He said, 'When you find your wife in bed with another man, and you say, "Pardon me," turn around, and walk out. That's savoir faire.' But the Englishman says, 'No, no, not at all. When you find your wife in bed with another man and you say, "Please continue." That's savoir faire!' And the Frenchman says, 'Non. You are in bed with another man's wife. He walks in and says, "Please continue." If, then, you can continue, that's savoir faire.'

It wasn't the last photograph of him taken, as it turned out.

Not abhorred in my imagination, not quite, though they filled your head with holes and cut it off. Not abhorred, still loved, even if it were a skull in the grave, stinking from its rotted seams. I love your bones, Papa. I love your head. Your hair so neatly and carefully combed when you came back inside with the bottle dripping snow on your new and slippery shoes. The tie around your neck loosened but not removed, a brown tie just purchased in Berlin. You told me to be a doctor. I can't hear you anymore. I can't see you. The tie around your neck, hanging just below that spot where the vein always bulged when you laughed. That was where Herr Doktor placed his razor.

Papa in a boat, drifting past the Daugava's mirrored white birches and old forest ruins. Two herons quietly flapping across. Papa drifting away on the quiet yellow and orange mirror of the autumn Daugava, away under the gleaming arcade of birches, white as time. Not rowing, but drifting past leaves and rocks in the smoothly sweeping glass. Smaller and smaller. Still just barely visible by the bend in the river. Gone.

The lazy autumn light of the Blue Lakes, slipping, sliding down through tree limbs, fading. Evening. Cool air. *He hasn't dressed properly, will be cold.* Serene cool air troubled by turbulent water – the whirlpool of the Blue Lakes where men drown.

No, he couldn't remember a thing about the tenth of last September anymore, when his father died – just that odd picture of him tilting backward. The Zamserbach had been roaring, so it was all a kind of silent movie, not real. Dr Rainer standing so close he could see the pores on his nose. *It looks like rain, you can tell by the wind, better hurry to Breitlahner.* Dr Rainer led Philipp on the path that he and his father should have walked together. *Walking in front of or behind the father?* That had been a headline in *Arbeiter Zeitung* last December, during the first trial. Before they'd left on their trip, his shaving mirror had broken. He remembered that now. Wasn't it an ill omen? And there had been a carpenter ant in his bedroom, and in the morning he found another huge black ant on the doorjamb, this one with ornamental wings like the flightless wings of a devil, a symbol of death.

Liouba said she would call on all the good and just people of Europe to save him if it came to that. Albert Einstein, it was said, was a man of infinite kindness. Among the things thrown into the hall was a photograph of the great physicist: hair going white in the front, as if under the abstractive influence of the Solomonic brain underneath it. A newspaper snapshot. He could make a better photograph himself. He'd started making photographs with Papa's view camera when he was fifteen. There was some miracle in that machine called a camera, the miracle of perception: Liouba had appeared on the glass plate from out of a cloud like the Lady of the Lake.

The dark in *der Keller* was cool and rather airless, like a place nobody went into very often, a place crowded with junk and rags and machines. He could hear a machine rumbling somewhere nearby – the boiler, probably. Was that a centipede crawling there? They were common enough in the cell, probably more insects down here, but he couldn't see. He thought he could feel the light, prickly feeling of an insect's legs on his skin, but when he swept his hand across the spot he felt nothing.

Sometimes, when he was small, he saw a sea dragon circling in the dark. And in the extreme quiet of night, he would half hallucinate the sound of migrating geese, a sound of tuneless horns that wouldn't stop, as if a thousand skeins had filled the sky. Now he heard instead dogs barking, barking, barking, almost imperceptible, as if muffled by the rushing waters of the Zamserbach. The dogs were running, circling in the fog, their barks jostling one another, interrupting and barking over one another, then fading as the dogs ran on ahead. The Prince von Auersperg's horse remained behind, fallen, slumped down the hill toward the Zamserschinder, kneeling alone in the wet grass.

PART II
Der Fall

1. The Root of All Evil

Let's hope that the Aryan population has now finally learned
what they can expect from the Jews and what it means to
grant to the Jews in our country rights which they never
deserved – rights they use to undermine the state and to
corrupt the morals of the *Volk* . . .
The son of Israel, the murderer of his father, Halsmann
was this time the cause for Jewish mockery of the Aryan
Volk. Aryan, take note!

'HALSMANN, The Son of Israel,'
Deutsche Arbeiter Presse, 26 October 1929

Long before the afternoon of Monday, 14 March 1938, when
Hitler's motorcade came rolling into Vienna with swastikas
unfurled along the Heldenplatz and church bells swinging in
the belfries, pilgrims from across Tyrol journeyed to Kirche
Judenstein.

They went to the church in the little town of Rinn, five
miles or so to the east of Innsbruck, to honor a martyr
named Anderl von Rinn. It was said that in 1462 three rich
Jews returning from a fair had stopped at a farm near the
town. A young child, two or three years old, was playing there
in the grass and the three Jews admired him very much
indeed. They inquired at the farmhouse: could they buy the
child? The father, a poor Christian farmer, was shocked by
the question. The Jews, however, produced such a sum of

money as he had never imagined. With so much money his troubles would be ended, and, thinking the Jews might give his son a better life, he agreed.

But the three Jews did not have a better life in mind for young Anderl. Instead, they brought him into the forest without delay. They carried the child screaming in terror to a great flat stone – the *Judenstein* – then pinned him down there and cut his throat. While he squealed, they collected his blood in a silver bowl and drained his young and innocent flesh completely white, because they required the pure blood of a Christian child for their Passover matzah; they sacrificed Christian children to commemorate their sacrifice of Christ. The wailing mother found the child's silent dead body hanging from a birch tree.

Anton Koberger had visited Kirche Judenstein in 1929 and in every other year in memory, and he recounted all these details to his nephew. The story had been passed down through the ages in many versions by many tellers, yes, but its basic features did not vary. A painting at Kirche Judenstein showed the three Jews cutting the throat of Anderl von Rinn with the inscription: SIE SCHNEIDEN DEM MAR-TERER, DIE GURGL AB UND NEMEN ALLES BLUT VON IHM. *They cut the martyr's throat and drained all his blood.* And Pope Benedict XIV had granted Anderl *beatificatio aequipollens* on Christmas day, 1752. Miracles at the tomb of the child attested to the martyrdom, and the story was told in writing by the Brothers Grimm. They said that when the deed was done, the money that the Jews had paid to the farmer turned to leaves.

That is not a miracle, his nephew said, that is a fairy tale. It was clear to Anton that the boy had lost his religion under the decadent influence of Vienna. When he returned home from school, he now refused to go to Judenstein and ridiculed the martyrology. Ah, said Uncle Anton, but was there not a kernel of truth to all fairy tales? Anton could even accept that most Jews no longer sacrificed Christian children, but, he said, perhaps they did at one time. Perhaps? Could anyone answer that question definitively? His nephew would not hear of it. During the last argument, he had so baited his uncle that Anton had spat on him in a fit of rage. Anton had apologized to his sister, but he wouldn't trade away the interests of his homeland to a cabal of foreign Jews simply because it was 'offensive' to speak out.

Anton knew better than to accept uncritically the 'objective' views of a student under the sway of Jewish professors and the Jewish newspapers. Let the Jews cry 'anti-Semite!' but the fact was that they ran the newspapers, had infiltrated the Viennese universities, and they were experts at propaganda. Even a Jew would admit to that. But the *Volk* were catching on now. Anton read *Der Eiserne Besen* and *Deutsche Arbeiter Presse* and *Der Stürmer*, he had heard the cries of the Nazi party on behalf of the neglected German *Volk*, and so his knowledge was insulated from the insidious propaganda of the Jewish press. The Aryan papers had unmasked, for example, the Jewish papers' campaign to promote the Jew Einstein's theory of relativity, now discredited, and their suppression of the rival *Welteislehre* theory, now gaining acceptance – the brilliant work of a poor and simple Austrian, Hans Hörbiger.

And the Aryan papers had told him of the Jewish press's smear campaign against the Austrian courts after the Halsmann verdict. They showed how Jewish influences had sought to overturn the verdict against the father murderer, Philipp Halsmann. But Anton was at the Serviten Church when the Pastor, Anselm Wimmer, spoke the truth about Halsmann: he was a Jew and so lacked a conscience. Anton was there on the courthouse steps as the second trial began. He was among all those swastika placards prodding the gray air and the signs proclaiming HINRICHTUNG, *'Execution,'* in dark Gothic print, and he shouted at the nervous fools with their pitiful signs saying UNSCHULDIG! – *'Innocent!'* He laughed at the silly women forcing their way up the steps of the courthouse to get a look at Halsmann inside, shrieking, pulling hair. The fat one cleared a path through the others with a rug beater – what a sight! And when he saw Franz Pessler fight his way inside behind two gendarmes, he shouted *'Tod dem Verräter!'* – *'Death to the traitor.'*

2. Court

Who can see into the minds of these men?

said of the Halsmann jury, *Die Wahrheit*,
Vienna, 20 September 1929

An ant was crawling across the flat gravestone where his father lay, and Philipp crushed the insect under the slick new sole of his right shoe. The guards were watching him from under the yew tree. Pessler was standing by the low iron fence, staring down at the grass. The sun burned on the polished headstones and on the rough old ones, melted in a century of rain. *Friedhof.* It meant 'cemetery', of course, but it was made out of other words. *Friede*, peace. *Hof*, yard.

Though he hadn't been outside the prison more than a couple of times for his 'excursions,' Philipp couldn't look anywhere but up above the pines on the mountains and beyond the barren peaks at the sky, as the pale air seemed the only neutral aspect of Innsbruck, clouds drifting on to Switzerland. The clouds were different from those he knew. Those visible from the cell, frozen high over the Sattelspitzen, wouldn't move for a day or more, and during recesses in the courtyard he was too exhausted to lift his head, and looked mostly down at his own feet, swinging over the dirt in a goose-step that hurt his right hip. But he noticed now, gazing directly up at a cloud for the first time in many months, that every part of a cloud was in fact in motion. The cloud was not still, but rather slowly advancing, a frontier of white all convoluted within itself by rolling spirals and eddies, thin tendrils evanescing in midair, new galaxies of vapor stirred into being.

He dropped his gaze back down to the earth. MORDUCH HALSMANN, the gravestone read, in the same Gothic lettering used in the Austrian newspapers.

Pessler came to him. 'It's time,' he said.

Philipp looked the attorney up and down with all the contempt he had for all the little martinets of Germany and Austria, but Pessler stood his ground and looked calmly at him out of the small sea eyes, glowing in their caves. He touched Philipp's back and shepherded him with a gentle hand toward the gate.

There was no canned fruit anymore and the eggs had stopped coming in, too. Perhaps because times were hard in Austria, the lights were kept off for most of the day in the courthouse. The high windows above the gallery glowed weakly, but the room was blindingly dim, washed in undersea gloom like the cabin of a submerged wreck. The gray walls were stained with water and there was even a dampness in the air. A brass chain hung low across the break in the half-wall between the bench area, where Philipp sat, and the gallery – the scarred-up old pews where Uncle Moritz, Mama, Liouba, and the others sat, the gawkers and gossipers, maybe 100 people, many with stenographer's pads. It was like his bar mitzvah, all they needed was a spread up there on the bench with some inedible whitefish salad, and his grandmother's friend Minda going around with her kreplach and asking the *Polizist* his salary. Just like that, except that Mama was alone and looked terrible, like an old nag with the ribs showing, and he felt a wish to poke his own flesh with nails.

More and more people were pressing themselves inside the courtroom, and as each person did, the *Polizist* pointed over the half-wall with his *Schlagstock* and commanded loudly that they bare their heads. He was big, an arm breaker like Schnapps Face, with two narrow rows of unreflective copper buttons down the chest of his green uniform and black hair curling out of his too-short shirtsleeves, and his blue eyes were arresting as searchlights, like those of a father who has just told his son he's reached his limit.

The *Polizist* shouted, '*Ruhe!*' and the judge entered. He was an old man with half-closed eyelids and hair the color of champagne, parted as if with a razor blade. '*Der Vorsitzende* Josef Ziegler,' the *Polizist* said, '*das Landesgericht* of Innsbruck, Austria, trial of accused Philipp Halsmann commencing 11 September 1929.' Then the jury came in, the men in white shirts, a grocer, Pessler had said, a carpenter, some merchants, some landowners. More people, more hearts, warming up the chilly damp air of the court.

The judge knocked his gavel. Philipp was alone at the table they called *der Zeugenstand* in a row of empty wooden chairs. Pessler was at a different table and at another sat the prosecutor, Herr Dr Siegfried Hohenleitner, with cheekbones that glowed like polished apples. Hohenleitner got up, greeted the judge and the jurors calmly, politely. *Guten Tag, Geschworenen.* Very civilized.

'What happened?' Hohenleitner said, looking directly at Philipp and waiting as though he might answer. He would not speak, however. Pessler had given him strict instructions not to speak, and he would not speak, not if they brought out his father's head. 'It's a proven fact that Max Morduch Halsmann was brutally murdered by bludgeoning to the head between two-fifteen and three o'clock P.M. on 10 September 1928 on a path along the face of the Olperer Massivs. All agree that only four people besides Max Halsmann and his son' – the prosecutor pointed at Philipp – 'are known to have been on the path from the Dominikushütte to the Breitlahner Inn between two-fifteen and three P.M. that day. These four have already testified in the first trial against Philipp Halsmann, the trial in which Philipp Halsmann was convicted of murdering his father Max Halsmann. We know the character of the other travelers. The defense won't even attempt to cast suspicion upon these travelers from Leipzig, Murzzuschlag, Zell, and Ginzling.

'What do we know about Philipp Halsmann from Latvia? First and foremost, we know that young Halsmann was the only person present at his father's death and second, we know that he lied about what occurred. Third, we know that young Halsmann did not get along with his father. Fourth, the medical faculty at the University of Innsbruck has examined the accused and the body of the victim and found it forensically certain – *zum Rand der Gewissheit* – that the accused is guilty. A leading expert in criminology, Herr Dr Karl Meixner, will tell you so himself. On this basis, Philipp Halsmann was already convicted of murder. But some foreign peoples who don't have faith in us here in Tyrol have prevailed upon sympathetic ears to obtain a special dispensation. Some people in Vienna are not certain of our court's ability to decide a case in Tyrol all by ourselves, so they ask us to do it once more, and slowly, in order to calm their nerves. After all, in such times as these, what better way to spend our hard-earned schillings?'

Ziegler sat there stoic as a mountainside below the portrait of Franz Josef, peering down from dark hooded eyes. Franz Josef I, emperor of an empire that no longer existed: a slender man with the zealous red muttonchops of a lynx, hair incongruously short like that of the unwigged transvestite in the Jūrmala bathhouse. A red-and-white sash over a double-breasted waistcoat, medals, red trousers embroidered with gold braid, and a decorative sword with a red tassel hanging from the pommel.

Pessler uncrossed his ankles, got up, and took Hohenleitner's place in the center of the courtroom floor. 'Certainty,' he said. 'A confusing subject, and one of the most important in the law. To help clear away confusion, I too have only a few points for you to remember. No evidence. No motive. And no lie. Now. We are here today not because of the demands of foreigners, but because of the demands of Herr Generalanwalt Pietsch of *der Obersten Gerichtshof* – the Aryan judge of the supreme court of Austria. Herr Dr Theodor Rittler – professor of criminal justice here at the University of Innsbruck, an Aryan, and also Herr Dr Hohenleitner's mentor – is among the many prominent Aryan legal minds from all over Austria, Germany, and Switzerland who closely followed the first proceedings, found Philipp Halsmann innocent, and stated so in writing. They did more than that, actually. They stated that the first trial was a disgrace to the courts. But certainty and truth are not about which authority says what. The truth of what happened rests upon a method of investigation. And it's a method that any person with common sense can apply, and when it's applied correctly, all investigators will reach the same conclusions.' Pessler explained about induction and deduction and burden of proof, but in simpler words for the benefit of the hill people. Then he picked up from the table the *Strafprozessordnung*, a huge volume bound in gilt leather, and thumbed through its crinkling tissue pages. He read aloud the legal definition of certainty in a criminal case, a list of criteria that mirrored the points he'd asked them to remember: physical evidence, motive, witnesses, false alibi, etc. *Well done, Pessler. Bravo.*

'One of the sheep in the flock has died,' Pessler said. 'Should we slaughter the flock because of rumors of mange? Or should we look for signs of mange and look for signs of a wolf before we take the drastic step of slaughtering the sheep? If a wolf has driven the sheep over a ridge to a fatal fall, then it is the wolf who must be slaughtered, not the sheep. We must know for certain. We can't decide in haste and ignorance. We must inquire. And if we find evidence of a wolf, we must not ignore it. We must find and kill the wolf.'

Judge Ziegler slammed his gavel down, unmoved by the speeches as the mountains themselves. Pessler stopped at Philipp's table and said into his ear, 'You just be a lamb. I've done this a hundred times.' But the speech did not alleviate the rainy dimness of the courtroom. They didn't have the wolf, or the goat man. They had him.

How strong that goat man must have been to kill a man as strong as Papa. And how big the mountain that broke Papa's heart. Philipp sat and thought of ugly things. He thought of Stein, the big prison near Vienna. The inmates always talked about Stein. Some of them had been there in the windowless labyrinth, making buttons or boxes for a year or more. It was where you went to die of tuberculosis. He would die there. The prisoner with the terrible cough had come from Stein and now he was gone, no one knew where. Philipp would die young, but unlike his father, who died like a man, fighting the mountain and fighting the goat man, too strong even to hate the goat men. Unlike Papa, he would die a prisoner, having achieved exactly nothing. It was easy to think of ugly things.

3. Mama

At night, an old man by the sea with pebbles in his mouth yelled and yelled at him. *The Tyrol trekkers: 'Where did they get those funny trail shoes!' Papa smiling, sun blazing in the astral blue air and glinting on his gold teeth, not getting it, saying to the trekkers, 'Where did you get your sunglasses? I need some like those. My eyes are burning.' 'Oh, they are not, Papa.' Then the other trekkers: 'Look, here come the two Jews from the Berlinerhütte.' Right, O illiterate wonders of the mesosphere – two Jews! Aren't we fascinating? My horns are very useful in these mountain climes. And someone in the Furtschagelhaus had said, 'Look at the glasses on the younger one.' He couldn't stand another second in that Viking mead hall, no matter what Mama had said.*

He tried to replace the ugly things in his memory with the beautiful things from Ruth's letters. All the things, the ugly and the beautiful mixed together in his mind:
*my brother came with us to Zittau
the landlord hasn't yet fixed the heat up here
the little attic where they kissed, it had been so hot
my new roommate a Mexican tenor of mixed race*

Angora cat, Luchl, she had a litter of five kittens

legless Russians returned from the War

I think I will sell them, there are five

her head tilted to the left, straight brown hair spilling across her brow, and that undimpled ass

Maybe they will let me touch your hand this time

Kommissar Kasperer, on the Zamserschinder, where your father has died

the sound of the water coursing through the dirty pipes in the shadows above – Palmstrom wraps himself in the noise of water pipes – Demosthenes, the Philippics, ha. Ha ha.

landlord comes wheezing up the front steps

When the sun had already risen on the mountains, casting a single beam onto the cement floor, Philipp woke from a nightmare.

He dressed, and sat on the table to wait for his mother. Once, he went to the wall, leapt up on the window ledge, and tried to see his reflection in the window in order to fix his hair, but all he could see was the mountains.

Horst knocked on the door.

When it swung open, his mother stood there shyly smiling and crying, as people do at funerals. The buttons on her sweater dangled like loose teeth. Her hair was coming unpinned and falling down about her neck. What would Papa do for her now? What would Papa want him to say?

'Mama,' he said, 'you're dressed like a crazy person.'

His mother entered the room, frowning. She lifted his blanket from the paillasse and turned around. 'Mein Herr, I requested a new blanket for my son when I was here last.'

Horst remained in the hallway and shrugged.

'May I close the door?' she said.

'No,' Horst said with a chuckle as if she had made a joke.

'Do you get beef, Philja?' she said. She bowed down awkwardly and straightened the thin blanket. 'Do you get beef?'

'Yes, Mama,' he said. 'Get a new sweater, Mama. You're not taking care of yourself. You look like a crazy person.' He repeated it several times more, as if it too were a casual joke, something Papa might have said on a Friday night: 'Look at you, you look like a crazy person!'

4. Kasperer

At the front [of the courtroom] there is a famous map of
the scene of the accident where different parts of the
path are marked with numbers. The location of the
accident is indicated by a swastika.

Die Wahrheit, Vienna, 20 September 1929

They'd probably write about his thumb in the newspapers. It
twitched and twitched again like a peristaltic worm.

'Old Halsmann was not the victim of an accident as the
accused has maintained,' Karl Meixner said. In the first trial
the inspector, Kasperer, had framed for the jury a simple
choice: did Max Halsmann fall to his death or did his son kill
him? Meixner clearly could not understand why anyone
would bother asking the question again when the answer was
so obvious, but he loved to discuss head injuries and so he
carried on with enthusiasm. 'The first blow stunned the victim, because he never used his hands to defend himself,' he
said. 'The hands are pristine, uninjured. May I demonstrate?'

Pessler interrupted him: 'The defense stipulates that Max
Halsmann was murdered.'

Meixner fell silent and scratched his massive bald gleaming head. Then all the voices Philipp couldn't understand
rose up in the courtroom. He thought the sound was like a
sound of one being: rumor was a monster of many eyes and
ears and tongues, as Virgil said.

It was, in a sense, a good morning and a good beginning to things, because it went off according to plan. Pessler was looking good, like the race-car driver. Meixner was dispatched out of the courtroom without the opportunity to speak another word of his beloved smashed craniums and spraying blood. And Hohenleitner was so upset, he started tossing papers around and yelled out, 'The defense cannot stipulate to a photograph!' and the judge had actually to open up his eyes for this excitatory exchange and had silenced the prosecutor with a bang of the gavel. There was nothing this judge liked so much, Pessler had said, as a harmonious stipulation between prosecution and defense.

Hohenleitner called his next witness, and a young man in his mid-thirties came out of the gallery and sat in one of the chairs beside Philipp. The sides of the young man's head were shaved completely after the style of the Red Baron, a dark shock of hair hanging down toward his right eyebrow.

'Will Herr Doktor please identify himself for the jury?' said Dr Hohenleitner.

The man was gazing off distractedly in the direction of the dark gaslight on the wall. He said: 'Wilhelm Kasperer.'

'Do you recognize the man sitting to your right?' Hohenleitner said.

'Yes, I do,' Kasperer said, still looking at the gaslight. He wouldn't look at Philipp at all, ignored him as if he were an opium addict.

'How do you know him?'

'As the *Kriminalkommissar* in the investigation of the murder of Max Halsmann, I interviewed Philipp Halsmann in the Breitlahner Inn on 11 September 1928 and again in Innsbruck some time later.'

'The defense now agrees that Max Halsmann was murdered,' Hohenleitner said. 'Philipp Halsmann has consistently denied this for the last year, but perhaps he has changed his mind now that a second verdict looms.'

'Objection,' Pessler said.

'Sustained,' said the judge. The volley of rulings around the gloomy court recalled tennis or chess or some other game in which every move is recorded and officiated.

'In your opinion as the chief detective,' Hohenleitner asked, 'did Philipp Halsmann murder his father?'

'I believe he did,' Kasperer said. This caused a quick reflex in the rumor monster, which siphoned air across its many gills and filled the courtroom again with whispering.

Philipp would not wipe off his eyeglasses or mop up the sweat creeping out from under his hair. He would not speak, he would not speak; he actually bit his teeth together in fear that some unholy words would escape from his mouth.

Do you just throw a person away, Halsmann? A human being should be given the honor of a decent burial, should he not? Did you care nothing for your father?

'What makes you conclude that he murdered his father?'

'The suspect lied.'

No, it's Jewish custom, you see. To desecrate the dead? No, to bury the body immediately. I see. Well, that has its uses, doesn't it? Herr Kommissar, how can I prove to you that I loved my father? Photographs and letters can be provided; I have only to ask my mother. 'That won't be necessary.'

'He lied?' Hohenleitner said.

'The accused maintained in the first interview and in subsequent interviews that he saw his father fall. The autopsy showed that the victim was bludgeoned to death.' Kasperer was now looking at the courthouse doors as if he couldn't wait to escape.

'Is that all he lied about?'

'No.'

Kasperer rose and crossed the room. He unfolded an easel in the corner and set upon it a white placard with a hand-drawn and numbered map of the Zamserschinder on it.

'Herr Dr Mahnert has drawn us this useful diagram,' Kasperer said, seeming to cheer up a bit. 'The Zamserschinder is a path approximately eight meters above the stream called the Zamserbach. The slope, which is indicated here, is covered with bushes and grass, and there are bushes up on the path as well. As Herr Dr Meixner mentioned, we found the blood sprayed up to eighty centimeters on the grass and bushes,' he said. 'It rained heavily that afternoon, but even so we saw the blood. This is point five, the spot where Philipp Halsmann claimed his father fell off the trail. We examined the trail on the afternoon of 11 September 1928. There was a drag mark at point five, but no blood. The *Blutspuren*, the blood sprays, started here at point eight and led to point fifteen, here, where the drag marks go over the side of the trail and down to point two. The blood stains and *Schleifspuren*, drag marks, clearly suggest the victim was attacked at point eight and pushed or dragged over the retaining wall, down the slope that leads to the Zamserbach. Point nine on the trail, here, is where the murder weapon, the bloody stone, was found.'

Can I trust you? Rain falling over everything, bouncing all the leaves in the gray weak light, water drops swallowed silently into the roar of the river. Yes, of course. You don't suspect me? I only want to know what happened. I'm not sure I can remember. Try very hard because it's very important. He cannot have been killed. Of course not.

'So Philipp Halsmann lied about seeing a fall, and he lied about where it took place. From the copious outpouring of blood at point eight, you conclude that the assault took place there. Did Philipp Halsmann have a recollection of point eight?'

'Yes, he did.' Kasperer, standing with hands in his pockets, pinched the bridge of his nose with a look of pain and embarrassment, as if it were he on trial, as if all the misunderstandings and lies had fallen on his head and not Philipp's and as if it were he and not Philipp who'd been imprisoned for the last year of his life.

'And what was his recollection?'

'The accused and I walked together along the Zamserschinder on the afternoon of 11 September 1928. I asked him to show me where he was standing when he saw his father fall. He stopped right here.' Kasperer held his forefinger against the chart. 'Point eight.'

The audience now broke out howling again, as if something very significant had been revealed. The court filled with a screen of white noise against which little else could be heard, a sound vaguely like the rushing of water in the Zamserbach, a sound that pressed right up to the ears. One could hear only near sounds against it, or something very loud, such as a cry of pain.

'So when asked to show where he was at the time of the murder, Philipp Halsmann indicated the very spot of ground where the murder occurred. Point eight. In other words, by his own admission he was present at the murder. Correct?'

'Objection,' Pessler said.

The judge sat still as a lizard on a wall.

'The accused was a very difficult interview subject,' Kasperer said, as if in his own defense. 'He insisted that I read back to him all my notes, then made numerous amendments to his statements. What I wrote had to be in perfect agreement with him down to the last letter. My secretary was surprised by my patience with him, actually. All I can say is, Herr Halsmann indicated he saw the fall from point eight and that is where the trail of blood began.'

'In other words, he was there at the time and place of killing, but claimed that he saw an accident,' Hohenleitner said.

'Argument,' Pessler said.

The judge issued no comment. Hohenleitner returned to his seat and began lining up his fountain pens. Kasperer plucked his coat from the chair and put it on again. It seemed that the proceedings were greatly injuring his neck, which he rubbed with much evident sympathy for himself.

In all their discussions in the little cell, Philipp detected in Pessler a contempt for Kasperer, Meixner, and Eder, the three morons, but Pessler said little to disparage them and he never let it show in the courtroom at all. When he stood before Kasperer, he asked his questions very calmly and neutrally, as though he were merely curious and the answers were trivial to him.

'How many criminal investigations had you overseen before the Max Halsmann murder?'

'One.'

'I see. And how many did you oversee after the Max Halsmann murder?'

'None.'

'I see. You resigned afterward?'

'Correct. But I never planned to stay with the police a long time. It so happened that a job at the Justice Ministry was offered to me as the Halsmann investigation got underway.'

Kasperer wriggled and squirmed. Did you examine the footprints? No, it rained. Did you look for signs of a robbery? The *Polizeikommissariat* was satisfied with my investigation. Did you, for instance, look inside the victim's wallet? No. Did you find blood on Philipp Halsmann? On his hair, clothes, skin, or belongings? No, but he could easily have washed it off in the stream. Did you consider other suspects? No.

'No? It was never possible that another person killed Max Halsmann?'

'I interviewed everyone in the vicinity. I worked until quite late at night, in fact.'

'You said "the vicinity." It's my humble impression that murderers often flee the vicinity.'

'There were no leads that suggested a fugitive.'

'Let me be more specific. Did you look for anyone known to have been carrying a pickax?'

'Why would I do that?'

'Did you ask any questions of the men working above the trail on the Friesenbergeralpe? The men building the road there.'

'I could have questioned everyone on earth, I suppose,' Kasperer said.

'I didn't ask if you questioned everyone on earth,' Pessler said. 'Just the men on the Friesenbergeralpe, who, unlike Philipp, carried pickaxes.'

The courtroom was growing dimmer and shadow had engulfed the dandified mien of the former emperor. The man from the Friesenbergeralpe road, the goat man, was still out there and no one was even looking for him except for the private detective, one lonely man all by himself looking for another solitary man in the vastness of the mountains. In fact, it wasn't the machinery of justice that frightened Philipp most anymore, but the machinery of time, winding events among its cold coils, cogs, and spindles, winding many things into being all at once and all at once taking them back again, into the interstices of the machine, where everything vanished, never to be seen again or ever to be understood.

5. Apple Pie

Des Herzens Woge schäumte nicht so schön empor und würde Geist,
Wenn nicht der alte stumme Fels – das Schicksal – ihr entgegenstände.

The heart's surging wave would not foam up so beauti-
fully and become spirit, did not the ancient cliff of Fate
stand silently opposing it.

Friedrich Hölderlin, *Hyperion*;
inscribed in Halsmann's copy of *Vie de Beethoven*

'Quiet down,' Horst said, and banged the cell door with his
Schlagstock.

'I've never heard you laugh before,' Philipp said.

'That's because you're not a very good comedian.' Pessler
set the empty dish on the bench.

'Where do you live?' Philipp said suddenly.

Pessler's face was wood again. 'By the University. On
Anichstrasse.'

'Will you have me over to dinner when I'm free?'

'We'll celebrate, surely,' Pessler said.

'I'd like to meet your wife.'

Pessler said nothing.

'Do you have family here?'

'Linz.'

'And your children. Do you have children?'

'We might have,' Pessler said, 'if not for the War.' Then he
added, 'We could. I mean, there's no physical reason why not.'

'The war's been over for a dozen years,' Philipp said.

Pessler watched him and said nothing.

'Look at me,' Philipp said. 'I'm conducting a great romance in prison. Like Don Giovanni. Never a dull moment.' He picked up the orange on the table and tossed it in the air.

Pessler sat quietly for a while, thinking. 'You are very lucky to be supplied with oranges,' he said. 'I wouldn't know where to find one in Innsbruck.'

'If I were you, with the freedom to go wherever I choose,' Philipp said, 'I would impregnate all the ladies in the free world.'

Horst walked past the cell door, boots clicking on the cement. 'Five minutes!'

'Will we find him?' Philipp said.

'Who?'

'The goat man. I'd like to return his pickax to him.'

'The detective has made some progress.'

Philipp scooped up the last bite of pie and set his plate down on top of Pessler's on the bench.

'What have you done to your wrist there?' Pessler said.

'Nothing,' Philipp said, and crossed his arms. 'I hurt it on the window ledge. I jump up there sometimes to look at the mountains.'

Pessler's eyes went up to the window ledge. He again sat quietly, thinking. Then he said, 'I knew an inspector from Styria who'd been a sapper in the war. He had to leave the police force afterwards.'

'Like Kasperer.'

'Kasperer was a paymaster in the war. Quite safe. But this man had come under heavy mortar fire at least once, probably many more times, and after the war he suffered what some people call "nervous exhaustion." The *Polizeikommissariat* dismissed him because he opened three separate murder investigations, and it seems in each case the victims were cows.'

Philipp affected a laugh. He was trying to cultivate in himself a Tyrolean sense of humor, and he guessed this was supposed to be funny.

'It's not a joke. I knew him before and he was a very ordinary sort of man who liked to trek and hunt and belonged to the usual clubs. I don't know what happened to him in the war except for one thing that happened in the Ardennes. I know he was in a meadow with a cow that was nursing her calf and the cow was hit by a mortar shell.' Pessler's eyes, already distant in their recesses, had unlocked and withdrawn their light from him.

These days the sun was persevering a little longer against the mountains, so there was a half-light in the little cell that rendered the bulb useless but also obscured the cracks in the paint and the crazy joints of the water pipe that shot right and left across the gloomy ceiling. 'What about him?' Philipp said.

'Death can play tricks in the mind,' Pessler said.

'And you think I'm crazy.'

'No.' He began another story then, this one about his friend who died in the war in 1917, and there was something confessional in his voice, the kind of factual courage one uses, for instance, to describe an embarrassing malady to a physician. His friend Volker Koppelin's legs were severed by a landmine, he said; he'd taken Pessler's place on the Monte Grappa road in the rain, probing the gravel for mines with his bayonet because he'd lost at cards. The explosion had flung Volker off the road and into the mud. He'd lost one leg at the knee, the other at the pelvis, and lost his helmet, too; and he'd bled so much that he died with his mouth open, and he leaned forward and slowly lowered his wide-open mouth and nose deep into a pool of mud. Buttocks half-naked and

71

stuck up in the air. 'It's the most surprising thing about the dead,' Pessler said, 'their profanity.' They didn't button their pants or close their mouths or cover their genitals anymore, he said. Their wounds farted gangrenous gas. They were careless about everything they should most have cared about – all of them, as though they'd all joined the same cult, like they were all citizens now of some different and very fucked up place. The uncivil polity of the dead. And by the most devious means, he said, they tried to make us join them, to make us barbarian too because we were their keepers, and we'd neglected them. We were already barbarian like them, and the punishment was to be dead like them too, or to live in fear of death. 'I think I saw Volker's cards,' Pessler said. 'He was drunk. I can't remember anymore.'

In one of Philipp's more Kantian moods, he'd interviewed the old Russians who sat on the veranda at Jūrmala, peering at the Baltic with sad blue eyes and medals across their chests. They never spoke of artillery, hardtack biscuits, trenches, or bivouacs. All they spoke about was death and the dead.

'You have a nice glow for a corpse,' Philipp said.

'It's too late for me,' Pessler said. 'But not for you.'

Horst came in and led the attorney out. 'Just remember what's true when tomorrow comes,' Pessler said as he went into the hallway carrying the bundle of dirty dishes. 'They're going to tell the story the way the dead would have it.' The door clanked shut with a hollow, dismal ring. Horst slammed the bolt home and looked in the pass-through with a wink.

When the lights were out, Philipp's trial nerves crept back, but different from before, instead of shapeless fear, a little more fight in him, and he was able to fall asleep as the yodeler way down the hall sang out into the darkness. Perhaps it was the changing of the guard; there seemed to be no one around to stop him.

6. The Murder

A half an hour before we reached the Dominikushütte,
I called upon him to stop and rest. I am convinced
the accident would not have happened if he would have
taken a rest.

PHILIPP HALSMANN,
as recorded in the 1928 psychiatric report

The grass was trampled, and it looked as if
somebody was dragging a bleeding pig over it.

JOSEF EDER, innkeeper and owner of the
Dominikushütte, testifying during the second
Halsmann trial, Innsbruck, 1929

In the afternoon, when the light was dimmest, the witnesses came, all those people from the Zillertal. They came back the following morning too, when hail was falling noisily on the shingles of the courthouse roof and all the spectators looked up and listened. Hohenleitner shuttled the witnesses back and forth as if he were majordomo of the Landesgericht, with many excessive bows and nods. Pessler made a formal request to turn on the artificial lights, but the proceedings continued in the half-light of a closed restaurant.

Johann Geissler first, the Alpenrose innkeeper, tanned, black beard trimmed, cleaned up, no longer a mountain man.

'They wanted separate rooms. I thought it was strange. And I thought they must have a lot of money.'

Then Josefine Gewolf of München, twenty-nine years old, pretty, straight blond hair, asymmetrical eyes, the left slightly higher than the right; Philipp would have photographed her in a three-quarter view. Next to her, Josef Schmied of Nürnburg, older, thirties, big head, direct, unafraid of questions. All together once again, just as though they were again at dinner in the Alpenrose with the odor of boiled Brussel sprouts in the air – or had the plumbing been backed up? Philipp could never quite tell with Austrian cuisine, and with Austrian toilets. Neither were very good.

'*Guten Tag,*' Philipp said. They said nothing.

'What disturbed you about your meeting with the Halsmanns that night at dinner in the Alpenrose?' Hohenleitner asked.

Gewolf said, 'I was sitting next to the Halsmann father and the son. The son said he wanted to climb a 3,000-meter mountain.'

Schmied said, 'They made an uncongenial impression.'

Gewolf said, 'I told them even for the Schwarzenstein, they must take a guide. The son opened a little red Baedeker and said it wasn't necessary.'

Schmied said, 'I told them a guide for the Schönbichlerhorn could be obtained at a cost of twenty schillings. Old Halsmann said it was too much.'

Gewolf said, 'I told them the Schwarzensteintour is dangerous. So old Halsmann said, if it was dangerous, he would indeed have to hire a guide because his son had already for some time been waiting to inherit his estate.'

Pessler asked if Philipp had laughed at the remark.

Schmied said, 'No.'

'Fräulein Gewolf,' Pessler said, 'you testified in the first trial that Philipp laughed at this remark.'

Gewolf said, 'I don't remember anymore. I only remember that the son looked unhappy and depressed.'

Next, Hans Bauer, a man with a little triangle mustache pointing up into the middle of his nose. Two of the mountain guides as well, Steindl and Pfister. Bauer lived in Mayrhofen, met them on a hike at the summit of the Schwarzenstein. 'No, the father didn't seem especially winded or tired.' The guides agreed. 'Old Halsmann was in high spirits. He told a dirty joke.' Philipp remembered it. The punchline was '*Jungfrau besteigen*' – 'screwing the virgin.' It had embarrassed him. 'I noticed they were not well equipped for mountain climbing,' Bauer said, 'but old Halsmann was confident. He said he'd hiked all over Switzerland already in the same boots. I warned of a possible fall. He said he wouldn't give his son the pleasure. His son wanted him to fall to his death in order to collect an inheritance, old Halsmann said. The son said to one of the girls, "See how little my father thinks of me."'

'Did the elder Halsmann give any indication of being afraid of what might happen on the mountain?' Hohenleitner said.

'Old Halsmann said he'd had a guide write him a confirmation that he'd taken the Schwarzensteintour.'

'Wasn't Max Halsmann boastful about his many tours in the Alps?' Pessler said.

'Yes, he was something of a braggart.'

'Philipp said in the first trial that his father collected such confirmations in order to boast of his accomplishments later. He liked conquests more than the outdoors. He wanted the confirmation in order to brag, did he not?'

'The witness cannot speculate,' Hohenleitner said.

'And did you take the inheritance comment seriously, Herr Bauer?' Pessler said.

'I do now.'

75

'In the previous trial,' Pessler said, 'you said it sounded like a joke.'

'I thought it was a joke at the time, but in light of later events, it appeared more sinister.'

'You mean, in light of the first verdict – which has now been annulled,' Pessler said. 'And did you merely ask about the hiking gear, or did you laugh at it?'

'I was trying to be helpful. They were not prepared for a tour in the mountains.'

'What about the others on the summit?' Pessler said. 'Johann Krumbauer, and the two sisters Marianne and Priska Oberforchen, from your home town. Did they laugh?'

'I don't remember.'

'Wasn't it true that the Halsmanns' hiking gear was the subject of much amusement among the others there at the summit? Do you remember that the sisters laughed at the Halsmanns' boots, which had been purchased in Riga?'

'I don't remember.'

Bauer seemed himself faintly amused, smiling there with his little tweed cap sitting on the table between his thumbs.

'Fräulein Gewolf,' Hohenleitner said. 'What happened at the Schwarzsee? The Black Lake.'

'Halsmann and his son were bathing in the lake. The father challenged the son to a race across. The son was annoyed and told us his father didn't even know how to swim.'

The Schwarzsee. Water pure and cold and reflecting the sky. Vision untrammeled over vast volumes of air. Enormous mountains. The clouds and bottomless blue sky parting and rippling as he waded into the water as though wading into the sky. At night one could have bathed in the stars, in space. He wished they would all go away and leave him alone with the sky. Mud between his toes. Couldn't get his feet dry or clean before going back in the socks. Cold air on his nipples. The blond girl with the high voice, Josefine, watching him. Was he too thin? He

76

thought he had grown a bit stronger of late. His father talking inces-
santly. Don't you see they're laughing at you, you fool? He could have
been off kissing Ruth by the palm trees in Lugano instead of dragging
around on this unending trip.

More witnesses. Elise Dehn, a doctor's wife from Heidel-
berg, nervous, with hysterical shaky fingers that pointed all
around the room.

'When did you meet them?'

'We met them on a climb up Monte Generoso and again
on a steamer in Lago Maggiore,' Frau Dehn said.

'What were your impressions?'

'The father seemed talkative and friendly. The son was
withdrawn. He rolled his eyes several times when his father
spoke to us.' She coughed a few unnecessary coughs.

She had seemed like an enemy even then, Frau Dehn, on the boat in
Lago Maggiore. A man playing an accordion and another playing a
violin as they passed the green Islands of Brissago in the slate-blue
water. Scarcely a wave. Champagne punch in a bowl with sliced peaches.
Liouba danced with a man twice her age when the music started. Papa
didn't like that, carried his drink outside onto the deck.

Herr Dr Wilhelm Geilenkirchen from Bonn, tall with a
round gut, bald head with wrinkles like a Shar Pei. 'The old
man smells of money,' Hohenleitner said, flipping pages.
'This was your thought when you met the victim, Max
Halsmann?'

'Yes.'

'Where did you meet them?'

'In the wind gap under the Schönbichlerhorn. We were
taking shelter from a freezing wind. We noticed them right
away because of their foreign appearance. I remember dis-
tinctly: the father was big and carried a walking stick, the son
smaller and wearing knee breeches.'

Dr Geilenkirchen had been friendly. Philipp had seen

beauty that day: the whole valley empty of people and gray, the air at the bottom heavy, a chore to breathe, the damp empty picnic tables outside the Furtschagelhaus, the white brook behind it pouring over the moss-green hill, a long white lock of witch's hair hanging wet over the green rocks, not a person or animal in sight. And at the top of the Schönbichlerhorn, rocks like the spines of dead dinosaurs embedded in blinding snow, baptismally cold air, no trees, and a high towering cross made of iron, anchored to the rock with two slanting cables like a ship's mast. Philipp told the man how in the summit book he'd advised the prompt installation of central heating. They had all laughed at the joke. Geilenkirchen had invited them to accompany him.

'At what time did you hear Max Halsmann call his son his "heir"?' Hohenleitner said.

'I don't remember him using that word,' Geilenkirchen said.

'Thank you,' Hohenleitner said.

'Did you notice any strain or conflict between father and son?' Pessler said.

'No,' Geilenkirchen said. 'I could easily see traveling with the old one. He would have been an entertaining tour partner.'

'You work in Bonn,' Pessler said. 'You're a lawyer. As a lawyer, as an Aryan, do you think it likely that this young man you met on the Schönbichlerhorn is capable of murdering his father?'

'No.'

Out in the Blue Lakes, some of the Riga children had gone to catch butterflies with a teenager named Herman Getzel. Philipp was five years old. It was before he had gone to school, while Mama was still teaching him at home. Summer of 1911, it must have been. Before the *Titanic* sunk, before the Great War had begun. *Chasing the white butterfly into the shadows of the*

birches with his little net. The butterfly embroidering the grass with its
white wings, then through the shady trees and gone. The others gone too.
Couldn't even hear them anymore. Wandering at the edge of the trees at
sunset in the long shining grass where the gnats tumbled in the orange
light. He sat down on a hard tree root to cry. Lost. One could cry for a
long time at that age. One hour, two hours, perhaps more.

Then crunching in the weeds and the rough red shirt with ox-horn
buttons and the gold-trimmed spectacles. Papa limping out of the grass.
Bits of bark and dirt clinging to his sleeves; sweat and blood on his
neck. Papa saying, I climbed over a woodpile. I went into the cage of the
barking dogs behind the cottage – laughing, yes, right, Philja – I
climbed a fence. I passed through a field of pricking nettles. I crossed the
lake in a boat with one oar to find you.

Hohenleitner began congratulating the witnesses for their
love of country, and apologizing abjectly for the inconven-
ience of testifying yet again, and he directed them off of the
Zeugenstand.

When the people from the Zamserschinder came up, Judge
Ziegler at last consented to turn on the electric lights. Karl
Nettermann, a stoker. His travel partner, Max Schneider, a
bookshop assistant. Marianne Hofer, who was picking berries at the Wesendlealpe. Her brother, Alois Riederer, a
goatherd. All of them young, roughly Philipp's age, all sitting
in a row at the *Zeugenstand* beside him, separated from him by
one empty chair. Only Marianne Hofer looked at him as she
took her seat, a horrible excess of makeup on her face and
hair braided back in two tight rows so that he hardly recognized her as the girl from the Wesendlealpe. She watched
him with sad brown eyes. Karl Nettermann sat nearest, tall,
solid from many months of heaving dampers and wheeling
coal on the railroads.

'Ms Hofer,' Hohenleitner said. 'You are a milkmaid?'

'Yes.'

'And where do you live?'

'We live in the meadow between the Dominikushütte and the Breitlahner Inn. Some people call it the Wesendlealpe.'

'What kind of a place is that? Busy? Crowded with people?'

'No. There's no one ever there but me,' she said. 'Just grass and wind and the cow.'

'How did you first learn of the murder?'

'I was picking berries when a young man appeared on the mountain slope above.'

'And what did he say?'

'He stopped and called out from far up the slope: "My father has fallen." Then he stood there, not moving, looking very odd, looking up to the sky with both hands pressed flat against his temples, like this.'

'You say you climbed up the hill, and still he only stood there, frozen,' Hohenleitner said.

'Yes,' Frau Hofer said.

'Was he dressed normally?'

'No. He had no shirt.'

'What happened next?' Hohenleitner said.

'I said, "Where is your father?" He said, "Back there." I said, "Where do you mean?" He said, "I don't know." I said, "Is he far away?" He said, "I don't know anymore." I said, "Is he still alive?" He said, "I don't know." Then he beat his chest with his fists and screamed, "My heart! My heart!"'

'And then?' Hohenleitner said.

'I got my brother and sent him with Herr Halsmann to try to rescue his father. I ran down the hill to Breitlahner for a doctor.'

'And did you ever see the victim, Max Halsmann?'

'By the time I got there, a man had taken charge, Herr

Eder, the landlord at the Dominikushütte. He told me a woman had no part in such matters and I should go home.'

'Herr Riederer,' Hohenleitner said. 'Your sister says she summoned you to help.'

'Yes,' Riederer said. 'I went with the son.'

'What did the son tell you?'

'He told me his father had fallen into the water and had an entire head full of holes. He said his father was too heavy to move out of the water but he'd pulled his father's face out to let him breathe.'

'Did he say his father was alive or dead?'

'He said his father was still alive, because when he left, his father was flapping his head and hands around.'

'When you arrived, was the scene as Halsmann described it?'

'No. The dead body was lying still with the face in the water up to the ears and the body in the water until the knees, and the water was full of blood. His rucksack was still on his back. He was dead.'

'How did Halsmann act when you got there?'

'The son came up the path after me and he yelled: "Is he okay?" When I said, "He is finished," he slapped his hands together and began to scream. What he was screaming I don't know. They were not German words.'

Hohenleitner read from his pages. 'You said before, "I immediately thought the son did a bad job pulling him out." Yes?'

'Yes. That's what I thought, right away. He was lying face down in the bloody water,' Riederer said.

'Did you try to pull the body out yourself?' Pessler asked.

'Yes, but it was too heavy.'

Philipp could no longer pay attention; he had to translate into Russian instead of simply hearing the meanings. He saw

Uncle Moritz. Mama sat beside him, staring down at her shoes. He thought he saw a white flower in her hair, but then saw it was just an empty glove in the hand of the woman sitting behind her.

What was your friend Schneider doing in the meantime?

And what did Eder do?

you'll be disinherited, Papa said

Did you notice the young Halsmann immediately after you came there?

I saw him, but I don't think he had heard me, because I had to call him a couple of times before he raised his head.

the victim's glasses were never found – lost in the great flow of rain on the Zamserbach. Haggling over a walking stick at the Alpenrose. Three schillings handed to Franz, Franz angry over the price. Look at this, Philja. I'll hang it over the divan in the library. Put my head over the divan, will you, Negroid Lips? Well, save my teeth, at least.

Halsmann spoke broken German –

Did you observe him working around the dead body?

No, he was just sitting there.

walking stick two meters above the body

the accused walked behind his father without a shirt

Nettermann and Schneider looked at each other. When we arrived at the scene of the accident, we found the young Halsmann sitting with his chin in his hands, mumbling to himself, 'How terrible, how terrible!'

anguish can teach even a Jew to pray, Dr Mahler said

Schneider. Halsmann was wailing that we should pull his father up the hill, so that he does not stay lying down there.

Nettermann. I thought maybe one ought not to touch the dead body. The police should examine it first. But because Halsmann was insisting again and again, I told him that I couldn't do it, because the body is too heavy. Despite the fact that it would be easy to pull it up with a rope.

The blood covering the rucksack was already dry.

Little bit further his rucksack was lying and on top of it a stick

my heir

Old Halsmann was lying under the slope with his head in water and was already dead. With great difficulty we persuaded the son to tell us what happened.

Halsmann said, 'It happened here. I immediately looked at the spot, but I could not explain to myself how it is possible that here, somebody could fall to his death.'

Some pieces of documents showed out of the wallet.

Philja, I have to step aside for a moment. You can just keep walking. We have no time to lose! Walking in front of or behind the father?

Nettermann and Schneider spoke at once.

We wanted to go on, but the son was adamant that he should be the one to inform the mother.

He convinced us to remain behind with the body while he went on alone to Breitlahner.

I noticed Eder's dog was going crazy

blood spattered to a height of

'Let us look around, maybe we will find a revolver,' Eder said to me. He began now to poke around in the grass with his ice pick, and suddenly he came upon a stone that was covered with blood and hair. 'Well, what is this!' He was shouting and showing me the stone. I could see clearly that on the stone there was blood and a tuft of hair.

There were also white traces which I assumed are from the brain or bones

Could you remember which parts of the dragging trace on the path showed the most blood?

Philja, I have to

Pessler knocked on the table in front of him and woke him from reverie. He pushed a folded piece of paper across the table. Calmly, rationally, inscrutably, he asked just two questions of Herr Riederer. 'What was the position of Max Halsmann's body when you came upon him?' he said.

'Parallel to the riverbank.'

'And in what position were the feet of the dead body?'

'The legs were drifting outward with the flow of the river. The water was swinging the feet back and forth.'

Philipp opened the note. It said, 'Don't listen to the dead.'

7. Herr Eder

[T]he traveller in the Alpine valleys will find a race healthy to the core, firmly rooted in the soil, solid, and virile. Here the loneliness of the mountains has created some of the finest personalities and characters ever produced by the German stock.

PROFESSOR DR NORBERT KREBS,
'A Geographical Sketch of Tyrol,'
Baedeker's Austria, 1929

Hohenleitner's eyes were pleased half-moons over the rose spots on his cheeks. 'Josef Eder,' he told the jury, 'is the owner of the Dominikushütte. He was the first to discover the evidence of foul play.' The man came limping forward from the gallery, a stocky and powerful man with a creased, red Tyrol face, chewing an unlit pipe. He wore a suit that was much too small and carried in both hands a red alpine hat with a shock of gray chamois wool on the brim.

'How did you learn of the accident?' Hohenleitner asked.

'The Riederer boy told me,' Eder said. His voice was very deep, as if it had been sawed from his lungs by mountain wind. He laid his pipe on the table.

'What did he say?'

'He asked if I had a stretcher, because on the path a man has fallen to his death.'

'Did he tell you where?' Hohenleitner said.

'It was a place I knew well because I repaired the retaining wall there in May. I asked him, "For God's sake, what happened? Did he have a stroke?" He told me, "I don't know. I only know that his head is completely smashed."'

'And what did you think of that?'

'I thought, something is wrong. I better go to see for myself what happened. I felt responsible, because I have repaired this passage. I tried to get there right away, but I wasn't able to walk so fast because I have broken my feet recently and could only walk with a limp. My wife sent my waitress after me to make sure that nothing happens to me. I bring my dog, also.'

'And what did you find when you arrived?' Hohenleitner said.

'There I met two men, Nettermann and Schneider. Nettermann asked me, "What is your dog looking for?" I wanted to chase the dog away, but as I was bending down, I have noticed some traces of blood.'

'Traces?' Hohenleitner said. 'How much blood?'

'The grass was trampled, and it looked as if somebody was dragging a bleeding pig over it,' Eder said.

'But the body was below in the water?' Hohenleitner asked.

'Yes.'

'And why was there blood on the path, do you think?'

'Well, from the dead body, I expect,' Eder replied.

'What I mean is, Herr Halsmann has said that his father had a stroke or heart attack and fell from the path, from the top of the retaining wall. If so, why was there blood on the path?'

'The witness is not an expert,' Pessler said.

Judge Ziegler lifted his head, extending his neck like an old tortoise, but said nothing.

'I think the man was beaten with a stone,' Eder said.

'Why?'

'He want to smash his head,' Eder said.

'I mean, what makes you think he was beaten with a stone?'

'I found a stone with blood and hairs on it.'

'You made a thorough investigation,' Hohenleitner said.

'The witness is not an expert,' Pessler said, 'and he cannot have made an investigation. It is properly called interference at a crime scene.'

Hohenleitner stepped up to the jury box. 'Herr *Vorsitzender* will recall that this murder took place high in the mountains. We are lucky to have men in our country like Josef Eder, who take charge in such remote places until professional help arrives.'

Ziegler's head looked as though it could slam down on the bench at any moment. He blinked quietly but didn't speak. Franz Josef above him remained stoic, too.

'The man did not just fall. That was clear,' Eder said. 'I thought to myself that the boy was telling a lie. I began to think he had done this.'

'Done what?'

'Killed the man.'

'And when young Halsmann returned to the crime scene, you took action,' Hohenleitner said. 'What did you do?'

'The son returned from Breitlahner with Dr Rainer, a medical doctor who was hunting with Prince von Auersperg's party. Dr Rainer also could see that this was murder. We agreed that the son must not be allowed to escape. Since also there were several beaters from the hunting party who had come, I gave strict instructions that they should guard the son. They took him back to Breitlahner under their guard.' Eder leaned sideways to look at Philipp. His mouth was a wire-thin straight line across the weathered face. 'He insisted that the body be carried away. Then I said to him, "I forbid this. It is a custom here in Tyrol that in such cases we wait for a commission." He asked me, upset: "Who are you to forbid that?" I responded: "I am from the secret police, and who I am, you will sure find out." He said, "But what should I do? I have to tell my mother what happened." I answered to that, "Go to Breitlahner. You can make a phone call from there." But I made sure the beaters would guard him and would not let him leave Breitlahner.'

'What happened to the rucksack of the dead man?' Hohenleitner said.

'The accused has taken it with him. But he doesn't carry it himself. He has given it to one of the beaters to carry it,' Eder said.

'The state thanks you for your service as an exemplary citizen.'

'So you told Herr Halsmann that you are a member of the secret police?' Pessler asked.

Eder put his hat on the table and hung on to the brim with one great red paw. 'Yes, I did.'

'And are you in the secret police?' Pessler asked. 'Or any other kind of police?'

'I keep the order around the Dominikushütte,' Eder said.

'Are you employed by any city, province, or nation as a police officer?'

'Not anymore.'

'Have you ever been employed as a police officer at any time in the past?'

'No.'

'Okay,' Pessler said. 'But you felt that someone needed to serve as a police officer under the circumstances?'

'Yes, I did.'

'So when you told Philipp you were a police officer, it was not true. But you said it because you felt there was danger and you were trying to help. Is that right?'

'Yes, that's right.'

'You also told Philipp that he could call his mother from Breitlahner, but this wasn't true, because you had told the beaters from the hunting party to keep him completely isolated – so that he wouldn't escape – and he was not allowed to use the phone. Correct?'

'Yes.'

'And you told everyone you could that Herr Halsmann had committed a murder?'

'If they know a murder has happened, any good Tyroler would know what to do,' Eder said.

'Did you tell the constables that you knew who had committed the murder?'

'Yes.'

'And you told Dr Rainer. You said, "Watch out, he could shoot."'

'I thought he might have a gun.'

'Well, now you are before the halls of justice in the Innsbruck Landesgericht, Herr Eder,' Pessler said. 'So no more lies, not even well-intentioned ones. Agreed?'

'Yes.'

'Am I correct when I say that you had one reason for believing that Philipp had killed his father – that he seemed to have lied about what happened. Is that right?'

Eder stared.

'You did not see Philipp carrying a gun, an ax, a stone, or any weapon. You did not see blood on Philipp's person, his clothes, his belongings. You did not know Philipp Halsmann, and so you knew of no reason he would or would not wish to harm anyone. You did not witness the assault on Max Halsmann. You did not speak to anyone who claimed they witnessed the murder. But Philipp said it was a fall, and there was blood on the grass and a bloody stone on the trail. That is the reason you believed Philipp had committed a crime, and that is the only reason. Because he seemed to be lying. Correct?'

'He said it was an accident,' Eder said. 'There was blood filling up the place everywhere and a stone full of blood. No one else was anywhere around. The Zamserschinder is a faraway and lonely place.'

'You mentioned your dog. I understand she was most helpful that afternoon.'

'Yes, she was.'

'It was the dog who discovered the blood, yes?'

'Yes. And she found the rock.'

'And you trained this dog yourself?'

'Yes.'

'You must be proud. The dog is a faithful guardian, a hero.' Eder smiled. He was proud.

'If you hadn't trained such a clever dog, the murder might not have been discovered in fact, isn't that right? Because several people had arrived at the scene, but no one saw the blood on the grass or the bloody rock until your dog sniffed it out and called it to your attention. Correct?'

'Right. I give her a good bone full of fat.'

'Did Herr Nettermann have a dog with him that day?'

'No.'

'And did he discover the blood?'

'No.'

'Did Herr Schneider, Herr Riederer, or Dr Rainer have dogs with them that day?'

'No.'

'And did they discover the blood?'

'No.'

'That's how important your dog was.'

A slight smile, like a little electric current, continued to deflect the edge of Eder's wire-thin mouth.

'If not for your dog, no one might have known about the blood. And did Philipp Halsmann have a dog with him that day?'

'No.'

'Did he show you any blood, or mention any blood, or a rock?'

'No.'

'And did you show Philipp Halsmann the bloody rock?'

'No. I didn't want him to run.'

'And you ordered a stretcher laid on top of the blood stains to hide them from Philipp, yes?'

'That's what I did. To keep him calm so he wouldn't run away,' Eder said.

8. On the Stand

I ask you as a human being, and not a policeman. Do you
think it possible that I killed my own father, that a son can
murder his own father?

PHILIPP HALSMANN to the arresting
constable, sometime before midnight at the
Breitlahner Inn, 10 September 1928

At the end it was allowed that Karl Meixner would examine
Philipp himself. Hohenleitner called it a special demonstration by an expert in forensic medicine. Pessler, who called it
'illegal,' was threatened with contempt of court, and Meixner
replaced Herr Hohenleitner at the *Staatsanwalt* table.

'From the accused's diary,' Meixner said, peering down at
the leather-bound book through half-glasses. Liouba and
Mama had picked out the little diary from a bookshop in
Dresden. It was embossed on the front with the image of a
tiny tree. Meixner had inserted throughout it long strips of
paper. He flipped to one of them and read:

8 June 1922
I resolve not to lose my temper with him ever again.

13 October 1922
Read at least one book per week! Do not be lazy. No more
naps after school! Stop wasting time before bed and go to

sleep earlier so you will not be tired. Remember to think of the other person. Shift the topic of conversation onto others and away from yourself as soon as possible.

9 January 1924
Silence is your watchword. Don't ever argue with Papa. Let him think he's right even when he's not. Let him think he's in control of everything while you rule in your own mind. If you keep silent, you are the victor.

'The entries were made by the accused at ages sixteen to eighteen. What we see here is the longstanding conflict between the son and the father. The son is not as strong a personality as his father and resents his father for it. He struggles to suppress the tempest that boils below the surface. Civility does not come naturally to him; he must effect it with a façade of decency. These are signs of the accused's closed and unpredictable nature, sly, Machiavellian, humorless. Not like the father. Feigning respect for the father for his own purposes.

'"My Poems, 1923,"' Meixner read. '"A night of passion with the emir's daughter. She leaves her saffron robe in the sand and enters the tent wearing nothing but jewels. She presses her naked flesh against my flesh and we watch the yellow crescent of the moon impale the desert sands. The emir's daughter, flesh of my flesh."' Some people in the courtroom laughed, but Meixner did not laugh. Herr Dr Meixner was stalwart and unembarrassed before such ugly matters as corpses and diaries.

Now the *Polizist* brought out the letters. '"Dear Papa,"' Meixner read, '"the job market for electrical engineers is not good . . . I don't wish to argue with you . . . Last time, Mama had to make peace between us . . ."' A letter of 1926 from the mother to the son says, "Don't hurt Father's feelings."'

93

Uncle Moritz and Mama went out, stepping over the others in the gallery, Mama's eyes like the eyes of a rheumy old dog. She yelled out, 'Never was there a day of disagreement between them!'

Meixner continued, adjusting the half-glasses. 'A letter sent from Interlaken to Philipp Halsmann's girlfriend reads: "I don't think I'm suited for family vacations, at least not with this family." To a schoolmate during the same trip, young Halsmann says, "Help! I am being dragged across the entire length of the Alps," and says his father is "crazy." Quote: "All I want to do is find some place to sit down and read or bathe. I can't stand another minute of this forced march."'

One o'clock. The *Polizist* escorted Philipp downstairs to a locker room, dark as a bomb shelter, and gave him cold soup. The men stood around talking about ocean turbines while Philipp ate his soup and carrots. 'The "Easter Empire" is sick and dying,' he told them in Russian. 'Shut your mouths about the turbines, you stupid trolls, you know shit.' Then back up and onto the stand, alone.

He could be calm, controlled. A full planetary orbit of days in solitude lay behind him. He would make no mistakes. He would break no chairs.

Meixner regarded him with clinical detachment, much as if he were looking at a human head, or a liver. He would not get excited, no matter what Meixner said.

'Is it true, Herr Halsmann, that your father spent time on other women?' he said.

'No, that is not true,' Philipp said.

'Herr Staatsanwalt has procured an affidavit,' Meixner said, 'from a Raphael Jungelsohn, of Riga. Do you know him?'

Raphael Jungelsohn: a boy who doubted all the newspapers

94

and repeated what his father said. 'That rumor came from here,' Philipp said, 'not the other way around.'

'You still contend that you had a very nice relationship with your father,' Meixner said.

'I loved him beyond all others.'

'Maybe in Riga it is common to wander about without clothing, but in Tyrol it is not normal. Did you remove your shirt while you were hiking that day of 10 September 1928?'

'Yes,' Philipp said.

'Why?'

'My family doctor had recommended it.'

'For what?'

'He said the sunshine would cure my back.'

'Of what?'

'Acne.'

'Another peculiarity of Latvia, I suppose. And where was the shirt when you heard the alleged cry?'

'In my rucksack.'

'Where it was safe from bloodstains,' Meixner said.

'Objection,' Pessler said.

'Who was carrying your rucksack with your shirt in it that afternoon?' Meixner said.

'My papa.'

'You later gave your rucksack to one of the beaters who escorted you to Breitlahner,' Meixner said. 'You're fond of distributing your burden to others?'

'No,' Philipp said. 'I am not.'

'No? You have claimed your father fell and that he fell because he was ill. You say he had a bad heart and was over-exerting himself. Well, Herr Halsmann, if your father was so sick, why did you give him your rucksack to carry?'

'You imply that I didn't care for my father and wished him to have a heart attack,' Philipp said. 'But up to now you've insisted that he wasn't sick at all. You'll forgive me if I'm confused.'

'No, I don't imply you wished him to have a heart attack,' Meixner said, passing a great big hand over his bald skull. 'I forthrightly assert that you struck him in the head with a rock and have made up an incoherent story about his heart. If he was ill, and you were so concerned for him, why did you allow him to carry two rucksacks on the trail? That is my question.'

'I didn't want to let him. He insisted.'

'You testified before that you were not strong enough to pull your father from the water. Correct?'

'He was too heavy. I tried with all my might. He weighs more than 200 pounds, and he was fully dressed, including a rucksack, and his clothes and pack were heavy with water. Riederer and I could not move him out together.'

'And yet, there is one photograph of you where you carry your father like a child in your arms.'

'That was a joke. He had jumped into my arms. In the next instant, after the shutter closed, he fell straight back to the ground.'

'What did you do at the Breitlahner Inn while under guard?' Meixner said.

'I was not allowed to do anything.'

'No? What were you doing when the detective arrived?'

'I don't remember.'

'Were you weeping? Grieving over your father, perhaps?'

'I have already explained that at that time I had not cried for a period of ten years.'

'So you were not crying?'

'No.'

'Were you sleeping, then?'

'No.'

'But you were doing something,' Meixner said.

'At the moment Herr Kasperer arrived?' Philipp said. 'I'm not sure. I guess I was eating something.'

'Yes, you were dining on a delicious joint of pork. With great appetite and gusto, according to Kommissar Kasperer. You even asked for compote!'

'The guard was kind and offered me food.'

'Is that the behavior of a son convulsed with grief over the death of his father?' Meixner said to the jury. 'Who among you could sit down to a feast and devour it with satisfaction so soon after learning your father was dead? Who among you could think of your own belly at a moment like that?'

'I wasn't thinking of anything at all. I was unable to think.'

'And when Herr Dr Rainer from the Prince's hunting party inquired about funeral arrangements, you replied that your father could be buried in a sack. Is this true?'

'Herr Doktor misunderstood,' Philipp said. 'It's a Jewish custom to bury the dead quickly and simply. I can show you the verse in the Bible if you like. "From dust ye came and to dust ye shall return."'

'But only a moment ago, you said you were eating pork. Is this not a violation of Jewish customs?'

'It is – '

'So you are not religious?'

'We're a secular family, but there are some customs we observe.'

'Is it your custom to observe the Ten Commandments?' Meixner asked. 'Or only the first four? Number five says, "Honor thy father and thy mother." Number six says, "Thou shalt not kill."'

The rumor monster erupted in squeals and shouts and rattled the courthouse windows.

'*Ruhe! Ruhe! Ruhe!*' Under the cries of the *Polizist*, the echoing voices died back down from the high ceiling and windows, and the last few loud partisans belatedly succumbed to authority like admonished spectators at a tennis match.

When it was over, Mama came back in, and the judge permitted him to embrace her there in front of everyone. The bones of her shoulders pressed into him, and he drew back from her to avoid her fallen breasts and the spider of ribs and sternum that he could feel through the blouse.

'You believe me, don't you, Mama?' Philipp said. 'He insisted that I give him my rucksack.'

'I know,' Mama said.

9. The Defense Case

Philipp is innocent, I would give my head for that.

MORITZ HALSMANN, brother of Max, testifying
in the Innsbruck Landesgericht, September 1929

A short time afterwards a local policeman came and
told me that my husband is lying in the church. I ran to
the church to say goodbye to my husband, but they did
not allow me to lift the blanket to see him. So I never
saw my husband again.

ITA HALSMANN, Philipp's mother, testifying
in the Innsbruck Landesgericht, September 1929

'Let me tell you a different story,' Pessler said. 'You've heard a story about a devil in the shape of a boy. He is hiking with his father. The boy is strange and withdrawn. The boy is not like us. He is not an Austrian, not a Christian. He is a Jew. His people don't share our values. We don't know about Jews, but what we hear is bad. They don't like the outdoors, the health of the mountain air. They read backwards. They don't respect their elders as we do, but instead look for any advantage where money or power is concerned. They don't value human life in the same way. Maybe they kill each other over disputes like animals. The boy dislikes his father. The father is not like a typical Jew. He is friendly, almost normal. He makes friends with the Austrians. He doesn't want to be a

Jew. He wants to be an Austrian. But he knows his son has been reared in the old ways. He knows his son is particularly brutal and strange. This basic dissimilarity between father and son has caused much household strife. Things are coming to a head now. The voyage through the mountains is bad. The father fears his son will kill him to collect his inheritance and the life-insurance policy. Such things happen among Jews. But he stands by his son, because he's a good man, more like one of us. The deranged son waits until they are all alone on a remote mountain path to which no one else has access, and there he attacks his father from behind. He smashes his head in with a rock and beats him on the head until his father is dead. Now he is panicked he will be caught. He pushes the body off the trail and washes himself thoroughly in the mountain stream. He runs to the Wesendlealpe, calling for help, pretending an accident has occurred. Fortunately, Herr Eder's dog finds the blood. The boy is caught in his lie. The boy is arrested. Justice is served.

'It's a story. Is it true? How do we know? Herr Dr Kasperer says it's true. Herr Dr Hohenleitner says it's true. Herr Dr Meixner tells you it's true with the authority of a medical degree and an Institute. Herr Eder would agree with it. Is it true if enough people say it's true? Maybe. But there are many more people, more Aryans and more Christians from all across Austria, Germany, and Switzerland, who say the story is not true. Should we believe them? I, for one, believe that people are everywhere the same, but the Jewish people are not on trial today. Philipp Halsmann is. And we are not anywhere else but Austria. The values that matter here are not the values of Jews or Latvians or Russians or Poles or Swiss or French. The values that matter here are Austrian values, and we value the truth or we have nothing. We may mean well, but without the truth, we could murder our own flock out of fears of mange, when the real culprit may be a wolf.

'The story you heard is true in part. Max Halsmann was murdered. In the first trial, that is all that was proved: a crime had been committed. The blood on the trail and the bloody rock and the pattern of injury to Max Halsmann's head were the facts that proved a murder had occurred and not simply a fall. In the law, proof that a crime has occurred is called *corpus delicti*, and it is the foundation of any criminal case. The defense in the first trial did not have all the facts. They disputed *corpus delicti* and they were wrong. But the fact of a crime does not imply the author of that crime. Specific evidence must be adduced to determine who committed the crime. Witnesses to the crime are good evidence. Witnesses to the planning of the crime. Witnesses to a criminal's attempts to hide his deed. Physical evidence linking the killer to his deed – a weapon in his possession, the victim's blood on his clothes – and with modern science, we can now, by chemical tests, match a bloodstain to the blood type of the victim. A motive – that is, a coherent reason for the criminal to commit the crime, which tallies with all known facts. The prosecution has a strong case to support *corpus delicti* and almost no evidence to support its accusations against Philipp Halsmann. Someone else killed Max Halsmann.'

Pessler now began tirelessly to request many things, and when he made his requests he always did so with the expectation that they would be granted. When the requests weren't granted, which was often, he didn't fight with the judge, but always it appeared that he retreated with reason on his side. With each petition to call a witness or submit evidence, he cited a law, a principle, or a precedent, and he seemed to know in intimate detail every murder case in the history of the Alps and how it had been processed by the law: last year's murder in the Weisstannengebirge – two teachers hiking in the Schwarzwald, one ahead, one behind, the one behind killed and then the one ahead too, when she heard the screams and circled back; Herr and Frau Hummel, robbed and murdered on an open country road in South Tyrol, having left their friends for only a few minutes; Karl Vendt, an accountant, attacked near the Darmstatthütte, robbed, and left to die of serious head wounds less than two months ago, 13 August 1929.

The old story ceded ground to the new as the baseless assumptions and contradictions of the old were laid bare. And the new story took shape witness by witness: the boy is not strange, and he does not hate his father. His friends from the Technische Hochschule in Dresden came, and Konrad Treifen said Philipp was the best student in their class. Arwid Schulz, his high-school teacher, introduced as 'Aryan from Riga,' came in person too. 'Above all things, he was extremely honest. We read Chekhov together and he was overcome by concern for the plight of the poor.' Aunt Dora said she was specially attached to Philipp since he was a baby and she prayed her son would grow up to be like him. 'Whenever he would hear a joke or anecdote in Dresden,' his mother said, 'he would write to his father, because his father liked to tell jokes.'

Max had no affairs. There was no inheritance, and Max carried no life insurance. The Halsmann family was not especially rich. Uncle Moritz had helped to support the family when he'd had extra money, and when times were better in Max's practice, he'd shared his money with his brother Moritz. Multiple doctors had treated Max for a heart condition and for fainting spells and falls, and Max pushed himself too hard. 'Max believed he was a sportsman,' a friend said. 'His health, however, couldn't take this.' The landlord of Papa's property in Berlin came and said, 'Max was full of the joys of life and very loud.' The father-and-son arguments were much like those in other families: about careers, obedience, broken dishes, independence.

The boy is not strange, and he does not hate his father. In fact, he is worried about his father's health so much that they argue about it all over the Zillertal. Max is determined to prove his heart can withstand the exertions of a young man. He drives his son onward at a strenuous pace. The boy is exhausted. The boy is aware of other trekkers making fun of him and his father, of their equipment and their appearances; he hears comments regarding Jews, and his mood declines further. The boy and his father hike onto the Zamserschinder. They don't realize it, but they are in danger. It was assumed by Herr Kasperer that no one had access to the Zamserschinder besides Philipp and Max and other trekkers, but a road from the Dominikushütte up the Friesenbergeralpe is under construction a few hundred meters above the Zamserschinder; photographs, maps, and a private detective, Leopold Zipperer, attest. Walking paths just a few meters above the Zamserschinder connect to the new road and Zipperer and Constable Eichler confirm that numerous footprints on the paths above the Zamserschinder match patterns found at the scene of the crime. Herr Eder is made to confess that construction workers in South Tyrol come and go freely across the Italian border. They work without passports, documents, or any identification in order to avoid paying taxes. They use false names. They are involved in illicit activities, smuggling goods across the border. Eder doesn't like to talk about it, he admits, because he's afraid that reports of crime in the area will hurt tourism, but he's compelled to acknowledge that his own wife was physically assaulted at the Dominikushütte less than a year ago. There have been multiple robbery-murders in the Tyrol in the last years; this is a wild borderland and these are desperate times. A witness has said that the father smells of money. There is a hunting party in the area that day too: the Prince of Auersperg and his many well-armed friends and minions.

So the father and son are in unsafe country. The father stops to urinate on the trail. Perhaps he has another heart attack and collapses. We don't know, because Herr Dr Meixner didn't examine Max Halsmann's heart or brain for evidence of vascular injury. An opportunist has been waiting and watching for vulnerable prey. He attacks the fallen man, who cannot defend himself. Or perhaps the father is surprised by a thief and knocked unconscious by a heavy rock. The thief looks for money. Max is still alive and moving and cries out, so the thief smashes his head several more times with the rock to silence him. The thief hears someone coming and pushes the body off the trail to avoid attention, and he returns to his hiding place in the bushes above or below the trail. The boy sees his father lying below the path and rushes to help him, but can't move him. His father is still alive. He runs to the Wesendlealpe for help and is gone for thirty minutes. During this time the opportunistic thief returns to the body looking for money. The father still moves and the thief puts an end to that once and for all, smashing in the father's forehead, probably with a pickax. Karl Stooss, an Aryan Swiss, not a Jew, and a world-famous legal authority, says that the forehead wound was made by something sharp, not a stone, and cites Herr Drs Fritz and Vonbun, who performed Max Halsmann's autopsy. That it was a sharp and heavy weapon is more or less obvious to any layman looking at the photographs of the deep and narrow hole in the forehead of the victim. But Meixner has kept this out of the official report. No weapon was ever recovered that matched this wound. Stooss publishes his assertion about the weapon used on the forehead and Meixner dismisses him – the eminent legal mind Karl Stooss! – as a malicious slanderer.

The thief is interrupted again while looking for money by two more travelers, Marianne Ossana of Zell and Marie Rauch of Ginzling. He hides again and resumes the search for money when they walk on. Rauch and Ossana testify that the father's body was perpendicular to the bank and lying face down, while Riederer testifies that upon arriving with the son later, the body was parallel to the bank; someone moved the body while the boy, Philipp, was gone getting help!

What of the so-called lie? Did the boy see something through the alder leaves? Was it his father collapsing from a heart attack? Being knocked to the ground or thrown off the trail by the thief? Did he see the thief himself working around the body or leaping off the trail and imagine it was his father?

Pessler explained: 'A boy finds his father bleeding below the path and assumes an accident has occurred, a fall. Panicked, he runs for help. Later, under suspicion, he maintains, "I didn't do it. It was a fall." The prosecution chooses to characterize Philipp's words as a lie. But Philipp didn't lie – because he didn't know his father had been murdered. And he didn't know his father had been murdered because *he didn't do it*. Then, as Herr Eder has testified, Philipp was deceived by those who had already tried and convicted him themselves there in the mountains. He is foreign, easy to blame. They don't tell him about the blood they found – in fact, they hide it from him! They help to insulate him from the facts that might have modified his belief in a heart attack and a fall without any violence.'

The courtroom was quiet as a church.

'"*Bei Juden musst du dich links halten, bei Christen rechts halten.*" With Jews you must hold yourself left, with Christians to the right. Do you admit you said this at the crime scene, Dr Rainer, that day of 10 September 1928?'

'No.'

'I am told that "the left" is *Gaunersprache* – thieves' slang – for deceit. For lying. Is that so?'

'I don't know. I am not a thief.'

'Maybe not, Dr Rainer,' Pessler said. 'But you are a liar. Another question. Do you recall, Dr Rainer, making this report to the Tiroler Antisemitenbund in Innsbruck on 14 February 1920? "Those in the Zillertal are perplexed by the extended stay of a Jewish woman, Birnstiel Klem."'

'Perhaps. I was merely passing on information to those who are interested.'

'But what of the money?' Pessler said. 'Neither Herr Kasperer, Herr Eder, Dr Rainer, nor Dr Meixner ever gave it any thought because they assumed from the beginning that an established *corpus delicti* meant the boy was guilty of murdering his father. Apparently, they've never heard of Occam's razor. A robbery-murder is more plausible than a patricide and, statistically, a great deal more common. But was there any evidence that might suggest a robbery? Any evidence at all of money taken from Max Halsmann?

'Herr Nettermann,' Pessler said. 'You found a wallet lying strewn among Max Halsmann's belongings when you arrived at the scene.'

'Yes.'

'And what was in it?'

'Nothing.'

'Empty,' Pessler said. 'So maybe Max Halsmann carried around an empty wallet. Herr Kasperer. 1,060 Reichsmarks were recovered in a pants pocket of the dead man, correct?'

'Yes.'

'So maybe Max Halsmann kept all his money in his pocket. Maybe he traveled without any Austrian currency.' The *Polizist* handed the attorney a small black leather book. 'This is Max Halsmann's accounting diary,' Pessler said. 'There's an entry in it every day of the trip through the Alps. The book records every bill and every coin in Max's possession, and every debit, every day. It's been translated from Russian. 1,060 Reichsmarks, which were recovered from the pants pocket. Plus 500 Swiss franks and 50 Austrian schillings, which were never recovered. And an empty wallet.'

Philipp watched the motes of dust sliding into the small patch of sunlight up by the window, like fireflies igniting, then diving back into the extinguishing gloom. Maybe he would be free soon. He would buy Ruth an ice cream at the Brandenburg Gate.

Photographs were passed around the courtroom and the letters read out. Papa in Philipp's arms at Chamonix. Papa sitting on a slope among wildflowers, one leg thrown out, one leg pulled in, happy. They'd photographed each other a hundred times.

Papa, I wish I could make you feel better. I hate to hear you say that much of the time you're depressed. I'm sure a diversion will help, and I think it's wonderful that you're taking dance lessons . . .

Papa, I am so distraught to hear about the pains in your heart. It's not serious, is it? Don't worry about a new suit — I am embarrassed to have asked anything of you now that I know your troubles. When do you see the doctor?

The boy is not strange, and he does not hate his father. The killer leaves the crime scene awash in blood to a height of eighty centimeters, as though a bleeding pig had been dragged over the grass. He strips off his own blood-soaked clothing somewhere on the slopes above the Zamserschinder. The boy hadn't a drop of blood on him. Not even under his fingernails. You can't wash blood from the fingernails without soap. A few minutes in a stream won't do it. A stiff brush is usually necessary. And they had accused the boy of bashing in his father's head seventeen times with a rock. But no blood in his hair or caked around his fingernails? There was never any blood. And he spent a year in prison. Why? When there was never any blood on him. Why didn't they care that there was never any blood on him?

Maybe the killer didn't strip off his bloody clothes. Maybe he happened upon the prince's fallen horse and sawed its head off and drenched himself in the blood of the horse. Maybe when someone saw him on the Friesenbergeralpe road, he said, 'I helped to slaughter the prince's horse.' Maybe then he ran far away and hid among the cold pine needles of Frau Hitt for some time with 500 Swiss franks and 50 Austrian schillings in his pocket.

10. Hiatus

The Halsmann trial shows all who wish to see the massive
influence and cohesion of Jewry. The Jew is master of the
German people!

from a National Socialist German Worker's
Party placard posted around Innsbruck during
the hiatus in the second trial, October 1929

Probably one of the most famous pictures in the Jewish
press, in the newspaper *Der Morgen*, was the one after the
sentencing of Halsmann. We see the picture of the judge
and jury without heads, a mockery of the judges and the
justice system while the Jew Halsmann is hanging on the
swords of Justice as a suffering Christ on the cross. We
can see almost daily such presumptions [ridiculing the
Christian religion] in the Jewish press.
In the so-called illustrated, satirical Joke papers we can find
enough of this kind of 'jokes.' Unfortunately, people are
laughing about it instead of fighting against it appropriately.

'The Jew and the Newspapers; The Press of the World
Power,' *Der Stürmer*, 2 September 1933

Pessler would not say what the so-called experts' report contained. He only said that he had been given it just yesterday
evening and that this was illegal.

On the rainy morning that followed, Pessler was unchanged and impossible to read. Calmly, he requested that Judge Ziegler throw out the 'experts' report' by the medical faculty of the University of Innsbruck. The report, he said, had not been prepared by six professors, as the law required. The report had not been submitted to the defense eight days in advance of the trial, as required by law. Prior to his appointment to the panel, Herr Dr Gamper had publicly expressed the opinion that the accused was guilty. The law forbade such an appointment. And he had reason to believe that liaisons had occurred between the panel and the prosecutor's office during the preparation of the report, in violation of the law of 27 April 1873.

Hohenleitner said that he wholeheartedly agreed: the faculty should rewrite their report. And after a hiatus, Karl Meixner would present the revised report.

'Herr Vorsitzender,' Pessler said, not so calmly, but rather loudly, 'as you know, articles 273 and 276 of the *Strafprozessordnung* do not apply to jury trials.'

The gavel came down. The court would reconvene in a month's time.

The double doors were opened, and one of the guards stood on a chair by the door and waved the spectators out. The *Polizisten* shoved and yelled and prodded with their *Schlagstöcke*.

Pessler went to Mama. Her face was bent with rage, like a witch.

Officers pushed Philipp out with the jurors into the damp, chill hallway. They walked clumsily and too fast. Then they went out into the thin, gray rain falling over the steps and the angry faces and signs, the yelling and pushing in the rain. The jurors hid their faces under their coats, but Philipp had no coat and the rain fell on his head.

The pushing was very bad. The cap toppled off one of the officer's heads and a juror slipped on the wet steps. People started to throw wet posterboard. 'Pessler,' somebody yelled, 'we know your house on Anichstrasse!' Then a man stepped right up to the juror in front of Philipp, pulled his coat away from his face and shouted, 'You're as good as Jews if you take their money!' Round spectacles plated his narrow-set eyes like funeral coins, and he smiled a smile of schadenfreude with small inbent teeth gleaming like a row of buttered corn kernels. The *Polizisten* beat him with clubs until he was a lump of wet clothes.

His twenty-fourth winter had begun. The heat had come on in the cells, flavoring the winter air with a scent of baking sugar. It was as though an odor of childhood had escaped through some rent in time – from some bright winter afternoon in Riga with apple-pie steam curling upward from the waxed table. A little clay baby elephant, Mama's elephant, glazed blue and brown, had stood on the shelf full of dusty light in their kitchen, beside the window that looked out on the weeping birch tree. That was long ago, swept past in the river of time. 'Everything is getting older,' he wrote in his letter to Ruth. 'You, for example. And as for me, the twenty-fourth winter is bleaching my hair. Strange, isn't it?' His mother had lost twenty pounds, and he himself resembled a gaunt old man. Liouba was waiting until Philipp was out of prison to marry René. He wished no one would wait for him. But he only wrote that his old horn-rimmed glasses were lost. 'As Tucholsky would say,' he wrote, *'corpus da liegt sie.'* He was physically incapable of real humor, as if he had laughed too much and his lungs were refractory to laughing anymore.

Ruth's kittens, which she had planned to sell, were dead. Their mother, Luchl, had licked their heads, but they were not to be revived. It was a coincidence because one day three black kittens appeared in the courtyard there in Innsbruck Prison, licking dew off the cold elbow of the drainpipe and pausing on tiptoe to sniff the cool air. Philipp's cell had a door to the courtyard. They came scratching at the door and he fed them, but they never stayed there, they always ran off some place, God knew where. First the one with the wide head had stopped coming, then the one with the light stripes on the backs of its ears. Now only the pure black one remained, looking at him sadly with eyes like moonstones. With a piece of cheese, he'd taught the cat to leap into the air, straight up into mid-air to hang suspended for an instant, then back down noiselessly. They were friends, true friends, he and the cat, but cats cannot be relied upon.

The letter was finished. It would go off to Berlin, where Philipp wished to go. 'Will you not discover when we finally meet again that my letters are more amusing than I am?' he wrote. 'I will become terribly jealous of my own letters. Perhaps I've discovered a new psychiatric condition. They'll exhibit me to the medical students: "The man who is jealous of his own letters."'

He lay down and closed his eyes. The days were without end, time immovable as a dam of dead, fallen trees. He'd abandoned all his methods for breaking up each day, and much of the time he simply lay there like a crocodile, trying to read, but unable to. When he heard the kitten outside his door, he went out and called to it, and at first he was very pleased because she came right away, but then she left him when she saw he had no food. He went back inside and lay down again. Sometimes it hurt to breathe the cold air, or even to breathe while he was lying there in the warm sugar air of the cell.

Pessler had planned to get Philipp a dentist, but since the hiatus, he'd been too busy. The attorney went to Vienna every week now. He said he was not tired. But formerly Pessler's left eyelid drooped only on his visits to the cell at night, and now it drooped all the time, burdened with the weight of so many days of staring at the enemy. There was progress in finding the killer, he said – real progress – a man named Franz Platzer had information about a man in the forest with a bloody shirt named Gruber. Anyway, the tooth-ache disappeared on its own. The root had probably died.

Papa had always taken care of his teeth. In Papa's office there was a big fan from China with a white dragon on gold rice paper. There was an enormous chair bolted to the floor, an electric drill on a swivel arm, and drawers full of scary silver things with handles like scissors. It was strange to see Papa there in his white coat, as though he were someone else. But then he would sing one of those Yiddish songs from Grandma's time, and the tools remained safely in the drawer; he was a guide leading you past the danger.

Papa was never afraid. The Tsar had thrown all the Jews out of Kurland. There were cousins banished to Mogiliov who could never come back. But Papa spoke Yiddish on the streets of Riga, where he'd made his home away from the safety of the other Jews along the Moscow Road. He never got hurt. He was made of stone. *See, Philja? I'm fine.* And when Russian carriage drivers yelled at him for walking in front of their horses, or Russian boys in the market mim-icked his Yiddish accent, he didn't mind. He could embarrass himself, but no other man had the power to embarrass him. They could kill him, obviously, but they could not embarrass him. Philipp thought he would do like Papa, he would walk before the dangers of the world without fear.

Pessler had the tailor make a beanbag man who was sup-posed to be Papa in the re-enactment. Philipp had sat next to the beanbag man on the train to Jenbach, where the clouds were lower than the gables of the houses and close enough to touch. Above the clouds were no more houses, only the high mountains and the mineral air where not even trees lived. *Chi va piano va sano, chi va sano va lontano, Papa. He who goes slow goes in health, he who goes in health goes far.* Pessler had puttees and hiking shoes, but Philipp was only allowed his black city shoes. The camera lenses watched him from the snowbells like many black and arthropodal eyes, and the men yelled at one another above the roaring water of the Zamserbach while the *Schneidermeister's* freakish creation knelt beside the path on its face like a Muslim at prayer. There were shiny new railings on the trail now.

It would not suffice to have his father back; Papa would have to come back to the Zamserschinder, and they would have to tear down the railings and make it just as it was before. They would not go on, but just remain there together until more travelers came through and Papa would tell them a dirty joke. They would sit before the white mountains, veined with reflected sun, and the hunting dogs up the hillside would never bark into the din of the Zamserbach. They would go backward in time, but not ahead, not to Breitlahner, not to the drafty inn alone with the hunters, the antlers on the wall, the joint of pork. He would go back to that moment when Liouba had photographed them, when Papa had jumped into his arms. He would go back to Lago Maggiore, glittering far and wide in the sunlight. He would go back to all the museums of Europe, to the many *pensiones* on crowded, narrow streets, and to all the Friday nights in Riga, back to the day he jumped the dining-room table, when Papa had been so cross at him for breaking Mama's decanter. He would go back to the early ages of the earth, before a hostile people had inhabited these mountains, when the flowers bloomed alone before the chamois and the ibex.

The reverse of what was true: you could only go forward. You could never carry the rucksack. You could write to him to say, 'I wish to carry the rucksack,' but there would be no reply.

Before Ruth came, they shaved him again in the room with green paint on the floor. He spent the half-hour before she arrived licking the blood off his fingertips and chewing the loaf of prison bread until his jaws burned. Then he was sorry he had licked the blood because he could taste its metal and salt on his tongue and he feared it would make his breath smell. But Horst kept the cell door open the entire time anyway, and if he were to kiss her under Horst's gaze, Horst would tell people what he'd seen, and then they'd write in the paper what a godless Jew he was, like those Jews that published the godless newspapers of Vienna, which showed Josephine Baker's nude Negro breasts. They'd say he was an advocate of nudity, of Negros, of breasts, of French prostitutes and anarchists, or, worse, of jazz. They'd say he should be kept in prison so that Austria would not fall into the hands of godless Jews, communists, anarchic saxophonists, French prostitutes, or Negro breasts. 'Just be careful,' Pessler had said. There would be time for kissing when he was free.

They brought their faces close together but didn't touch – their faces like two magnet ends of like polarity slipping around one another and about to touch, but not.

'Let me hear you speak,' he said.

'What should I say?'

'It doesn't matter,' he said. He handed her *Les caves du Vatican*.

She sat on the little chair and read the French aloud in a German accent. 'In 1890, during the pontificate of Leo XIII, Anthime Armand-Dubois, unbeliever and freemason, visited

Rome in order to consult Dr X, the celebrated specialist for rheumatic complaints.'

'I'm sorry about my appearance,' he said, pulling at a loose thread at his knee, where he'd sewed up another hole.

'We'll have you measured for a new suit in Dresden,' she said. 'My sister would like to pay for it.'

'No,' he said, more to the idea of her pity than to the idea of the suit.

Her face was of an impossible clarity and beauty, her body firm and healthful, so much so that he almost believed in the supremacy of the Aryan blood stock, which was purified on glacier air and sun-flashing ice and stone water and valleys where you skied in the dusk. She had not used any curlers on her hair. It seemed impossible to him that either of them would ever die when he felt what he did. It was an elemental and immortal love from the ether zone above the trees. He wished and wished and wished and he told himself to stop looking at her the way he was, because he would make her feel ashamed, but he couldn't look at anything else. Horst would see his eyes filled with broken vessels and they would write that he was a Jewish pervert and a saxophonist and they would put him in jail to die, but he couldn't deprive his eyes of her face and even less of her clothes, whose sole function seemed to be to conjure forth the naked body which had in the first place obligated them to exist. Yet by some mysterious alchemy of wind and fire, his lust seemed to him pure and inseparable from a most altruistic and spiritual love, perhaps because the lust had been deprived for so long that it now scourged his whole skin with pain – like the sensation one gets in one's teeth when the bladder is filled to bursting. They would put him in jail to die, for sure.

11. Oedipus

The Oedipus complex, as far as we know, is present in
childhood in all human beings . . .
If it had been objectively demonstrated that Philipp
Halsmann murdered his father, there would at all events
be some grounds for introducing the Oedipus complex to
provide a motive for an otherwise unexplained deed.
Since no such proof has been adduced, mention of the
Oedipus complex has a misleading effect; it is at the least
idle. Such disagreements as have been uncovered by the
investigation in the Halsmann family between the father
and the son are altogether inadequate to provide a
foundation for assuming in the son a bad relationship
towards his father. Even if it were otherwise, we should
be obliged to say that it is a far cry from there to the
causation of such a deed. Precisely because it is always
present, the Oedipus complex is not suited to provide a
decision on the question of guilt. The situation envisaged
in a well-known anecdote might easily be brought about.
There was a burglary. A man who had a jemmy in his
possession was found guilty of the crime. After the
verdict had been given and he had been asked if he
had anything to say, he begged to be sentenced for
adultery at the same time − since he was carrying the
tool for that on him as well.

SIGMUND FREUD, 'The Expert Opinion
in the Halsmann Case,' 1930

There is the insult given on the road to Thebes, of course, but before Laius ever met Oedipus on the road to Thebes, he ordered that his infant son be abandoned to die alone on the slopes of Mount Cithaeron. So why wouldn't Oedipus wish to avenge himself on his father and return to his mother's arms?

Karl Meixner passed his hand over his enormous bald head. In Philipp Halsmann's mind, Meixner said, at that moment, he'd been just as grievously injured as had Oedipus. 'The reason he killed his father,' Meixner said, spreading out the papers of his revised expert's report on the *Zeugenstand*, 'is that he had an Oedipus Complex.'

It was dimmer than ever in the courtroom. During the hiatus the northern hemisphere had reeled out farther into the cold of space, and in the courtroom the light had grown still dimmer and paler so that it was like the weak and distant sunlight on a promontory of some Saturnian moon.

'Herr Dr Meixner,' Pessler said.

'He has an Oedipus Complex,' Meixner said, 'and he repressed the deed out of consciousness. He was fatigued and confused due to altitude sickness and these physiological conditions removed those inhibitions which would normally have prevented such a violent act.'

Pessler stood up, calm, but with his left eyelid hanging quite low across his eye.

Philipp was not like Oedipus. 'Before this, in dreams too, as well as oracles,' Jocasta said, 'many a man has lain with his own mother.' But Philipp had never had such a dream. There was that one where he was unwinding a gauze from his mother's legs, but he never finished. He was not like Oedipus in any deed, and not in any desire for his mother or hatred of his father.

'Transformed in an instant from a life of honor and high morals to a murderer?'

'Yes.'

'Because of fatigue.'

'And altitude sickness.'

'What sort of fatigue is it,' Pessler said, 'that's so extreme that it disorders the most vital principles in the mind, but does not hamper a man from beating a bigger man to death with a rock?'

'Herr *Verteidiger* should be silenced for his impudence toward a court expert,' Meixner said without looking at the judge.

'And what about the stolen money?'

'I suppose you have a witness who has been encouraged – with a financial incentive, no doubt – to say he found it lying in a neat stack beside a bloody shirt?'

'No witness has been paid,' Pessler said. 'It is you who asked the court for a payment of 6,000 Swiss franks.' Pessler looked at the judge for a long while, blinking and waiting, searching with his probing blue eyes, one of them half-fallen shut, and he said nothing. He pointed up to Franz Josef. 'Empires, cities, aqueducts have never been created by angry irrational little men. They've been created by the sovereignty of reason.'

'They've been created,' Meixner said, 'by force. Herr Dr Pessler is not much of a history student. They've been created by unanimity of will and fear of God.'

'You will lead us all into the fire.'

'May I display the victim's head now?' Meixner said, calmly, coolly.

When the jury came back from the conference room, they didn't avoid Philipp's eyes, but they did look upon Philipp in an odd and new way. They looked at him almost as though the ugly thing they'd seen somehow belonged to him or to his people; as though Halsmanns by nature had dented and detachable heads; as though Philipp had inflicted upon them the monstrous vision, whether or not he was the killer, because he was a blood relation of the decapitated thing from the jar.

Pessler petitioned the court to examine Franz Platzer about the man named Gruber with the bloody shirt. This was denied.

'Herr Halsmann may now speak before the rebuttal examination,' said the judge.

'Herr *Vorsitzender* and jurors,' Philipp said, 'I am innocent. I don't know what happened behind my back that day, but I loved my father and my father loved me.'

Herr Dr Meixner got up and came to the *Zeugenstand*. 'When you got back to your cell,' Meixner said, 'what happened? After the first verdict. Were you happy?'

'No.'

'So you were unhappy?'

'I suppose.'

'Where did the scars on your wrists come from?'

'I cut them.'

'And you tried to cut the arteries in your wrists for what purpose?'

'To end my life.'

'You tried to kill yourself?'

'Yes.'

'And why did you do that?'

'Why?'

'You must have had some reason for wishing to harm yourself. No?'

'I was devastated.'

'You were devastated, you say,' Meixner said. 'But why harm yourself? Why does one do harm to a person, any person?'

'What is the point of this philosophical discussion?' Pessler said.

'Tell me this, Herr Halsmann,' Meixner said. 'Mustn't you hate yourself in order to want to kill yourself?'

'I don't hate anyone,' Philipp said.

'That's very admirable, Herr Halsmann. So why did you attempt suicide?'

'I didn't want to stay in a world without justice.'

Meixner laughed. 'I am on the medical faculty of the University of Innsbruck, I am a criminologist, and I can tell you that people don't attempt suicide after false accusations. It would be the first time I have ever heard of it in all the decades of my professional life. The innocent fight for their honor. Those who commit suicide – those are the guilty ones.'

Pessler looked more than tired. He looked like a ragged fox, running before the hounds of the Prince of Auersperg.

12. Self-Portrait

Your letter, Gioconda, in which you speak of your stream
of feelings, touched me very deeply. My love, I feel the
same way. I am also often aware of my complete inability
to share my feelings with the one I love. It is most difficult
with you of all people, to just give of myself openly.
There is a certain shyness which prevents me from
showing my true feelings, and I try to cover them over
with humor. This is truly terrible, and sometimes I fear
the reality of an eternal reunion, although I am
sick with yearning for you.

PHILIPP HALSMANN, letter to Ruth Römer,
Innsbruck Prison, 31 December 1929

After the second guilty verdict, Philipp refused to eat for
nine days. Liouba begged him to eat. And Pessler insisted
that the appeal for annulment would succeed. A doctor from
Meran offered Mama his villa, but she refused to accept until
Philipp ate. So on the night of 28 October 1929, he ate. Horst
gave him two strips of *Speck*. In the morning, he read that the
American stock market had crashed and wondered if God
was trying to tell him to stop eating pork.

His breathing had long pained him deep inside his chest,
but after the hunger strike the pain worsened and he felt
feverish too. Schnapps Face drove him in the Dürkopp to a
doctor's office with a cracked window in the vestibule. He lay

naked on his back, shoulder blades pressed against a very cold table, while a doctor with long strands of gray hair pasted flat across his bald dome prodded him with icy fingers. The photographic plate of the X-ray machine too was cold on his ribs.

The next day the doctor told him, 'It's tuberculosis.' He pointed to a 'cavitary lesion' on the film.

'Is that a silver-halide negative?' Philipp asked. 'It's an amazing image.'

'Prison is bad for your health,' the doctor said. 'Try to get out soon.'

His mother requested a temporary leave for him, but this was denied.

As 1930 began, the weather turned bitterly cold. Mama, Liouba, and Pessler went away to Vienna. The mail thinned. Philipp often felt too weak to walk but occasionally ventured outside to try to see the sun. Only once did he witness the weak alpine star above the courtyard, hanging distant and pale, a faint jewel imprisoned in the frozen air. If he spat, his saliva froze before it hit the ground, and the warden kept the pipes dripping all night. The little black cat came to his door once, licking its hind leg on a splintery patch of ice, and never returned. He wrote to Ruth, 'I understand and share your antipathy against mountains. The strange thing about the beauty of nature is that it is also dependent upon the whims of fashion.' But writing a letter brought him to the point of collapse from exhaustion.

Ruth returned his self-portrait, as he had requested. He spent many hours gazing at it and displayed it to anyone who would stop to look. Horst and Herr Glaser both thought it a perfect likeness. Another of the guards asked him if he'd drawn it, and Philipp had said, 'Doesn't it look like me?' and the guard had said, 'I certainly think so.' It was a better likeness,

Herr Glaser said, than the 'professional' portrait of Ruth. Mama and Pessler thought it looked just like him. The photographs remained wrapped. Philipp was too tired for the ritual of setting them out and wrapping them up again in wax paper to protect them from the dust. 'I have hope for the appeal,' he wrote. 'And I hope that Austria is a just state.'

'I kiss you, Gioconda,' he wrote. 'I am not contagious yet. But the fact that I am not contagious now does not mean that I won't be in the future, especially if the court has their way. That is why I must strike while the iron is hot, and kiss you now. With this closing, I am, with love, your Philja.'

13. Stein

But despite everything, Ruth, it was a love story, and I
cannot wish that it had never happened.

PHILIPP HALSMANN, letter to Ruth Römer,
Innsbruck Prison, 1929

23 January 1930

He woke up that morning from a dream of freedom – he
had been pardoned in the dream and released. In actuality,
the door had opened a hair in the night, and frost had
bloomed on the threshold. Pessler arrived at 10:30, and one
look at his face shattered all Philipp's courage. The attorney
sat at the small table then, and he wept over the table until he
had to mop up the tears with his handkerchief.

'You did all you could,' Philipp said. He used '*Sie*' – the
formal German word for 'you,' as opposed to '*Du*,' used with
friends. Even '*Sie*,' however, had not been formal enough for
Pessler; he had required of Philipp the third person at all
times. 'I mean,' Philipp said, 'Herr Doktor has done all he
could.'

Pessler stood and embraced him. '*Du*,' he said. The calm
sea eyes were all red now.

'What about the killer?' Philipp said. There had been many
incidents like the Franz Platzer case; Platzer had written from
prison in Vienna, claiming that on 11 September 1928 a man

calling himself 'Gruber' had asked him for help fleeing to Italy. The man had blood on his shirt and said hunters were after him because he'd poached a chamois. But when Hohenleitner transferred him to Innsbruck Prison and examined him, he said Platzer was a liar and had been paid. Another time, a man calling himself Rupert Auer had come to Pessler to confess the crime and had fled before the police arrived; Auer had known about the fifty stolen schillings and other details; Pessler wondered if it were Peter Auer, an ex-convict who'd robbed and murdered in the Zillertal before. Before any of that a man named Johann Schneider had written to Mama saying he knew something, but later told police he only wanted a reward. Still another time, a man had come to Pessler and offered to confess to the murder for 5,000 schillings.

'We'll probably never know,' Pessler said. Wind was whistling through the crack in the door, which glowed in its frame with a white winter light. Pessler shoved the door firmly closed, assured Philipp that the fight was not over, and walked out into the hall of the Innsbruck Prison.

They came to take him east toward Vienna, to the big prison in Stein on 28 January. An hour before his scheduled departure, Philipp scrawled a last letter to Ruth. It began objectively and rationally, so much so that by writing he began to raise his own spirits. 'No verdict has the power to turn me into a criminal,' he wrote, 'and it means so much to me that others also believe me. And besides, nothing is carved in stone. This all just means a short pause in my life plan. *Un jour viendra*, dear Ruth, when I will avenge myself.' But as his one hour of free time dwindled, along with the white space remaining on the page, his optimism dwindled too.

He told her that at Stein they would shave his head, give him prison clothes, and allow him one letter a month. The sentence was four years. He signed as he had in the early days, *Mit festem Händedruck*, 'with a firm handshake.'

There had been a child outside the gates of Stein in lederhosen, watching the truck pass through, and the boy had run away as they passed, tossing his elbows around in a gawky and unselfconscious way. The same age as he was, Philipp thought, when he'd gotten lost chasing the butterfly. He sat down on the very thin mattress. Weird and obsessive images had been haunting him in the last month. He saw the killer, the goat man, in a white mask, eyes like dark holes in his head.

Now he saw the mountain man there in his cell in the mask with holes for eyes and he remembered the day in spring when Mama had sent him matzah. Schnapps Face had searched the box with his *Schlagstöck* and Mama's crackers all got broken. Philipp saw the mountain man there next to him and wanted the man to remove his mask, but the mask stayed on so he couldn't see who it was. The mountain-goat man waited for a long time. He waited until Philipp had begun, like Schnapps Face, to throw his belongings out into the hall. Philipp threw the broken matzah out into the hall, and the André Gide novels, the book of Morgenstern poems, the photograph of Ruth, the photograph of his father in the meadow, the photograph in which Philipp carried his father in his arms, and the sketch he'd made on the tin of candied fruits, the sketch of which Philipp had been so proud, his self-portrait.

PART III
Sauter de Joie

1. The Austrian Bloodhound

As the storm clouds which have been continually gather-
ing and dispersing above the little republic in the last three
years are becoming blacker than ever over the question of
constitutional reform, everyone realizes that one person
alone can act as lightning conductor – Johann Schober.

The New York Times, 20 October 1929

There is a story of a wine merchant who long ago ship-
wrecked in the Madeira archipelago. It is said he drank all his
cargo and was drunk for the last hundred days of his life.
There are probably many people who, if stranded on a desert
island, would drink their lives away. Many would watch the
unheeding ship lights extinguish on the horizon and hurl
themselves off a cliff. Some would probably swim out over
the reef until they fatigued and drowned. Others would make
a fire, collect coconuts, and promptly die of dehydration.
Philipp's sister Liouba would have replaced the wine with
letters and filled the ocean with a thousand bottles.

Liouba was just twenty years old when Philipp went to
Stein, and with her dark hair pulled back as she often wore it,
she looked perhaps five years younger. She had a gentle face,
without any scars, and, though tall and outgoing, radiated a
childlike innocence; her fiancé, René, a Parisian Jew, sometimes looked too old for her. Yet it was this young girl, Liouba,
who had marched up to the doorstep of any and every man

of influence. She'd written a thousand letters and traveled all of Europe on Philipp's behalf, recruiting the support of Paul Painlevé and the French League for the Defense of Human Rights in Paris, Einstein in Berlin, Romain Rolland in Villeneuve, Thomas Mann in Munich, and many others.

The convention of the gods took place on the rainy night of 30 April 1930, in the presidential loge at the Théâtre des Champs-Élysées. There Johann Schober, the new Austrian Chancellor, sat with Paul Painlevé and Berta Szeps-Zuckerkandl, looking down at the musicians in their tuxedoes.

Schober hadn't been to Paris in some time, and when he was comfortably seated in his loge, he remembered why Paris and Vienna had remained close through all the troubling years of the last decades: music. The sound of the Vienna Philharmonic tuning filled the warm, dry dimness of the sumptuous Théâtre to its ceiling. There, chrome spokes burst from the sepals of an art-nouveau flower, illuminated from above by a hundred bulbs and a lid of mother-of-pearl. The nacreous, reflected light fell below on the inner walls of a cupola frescoed with classical and pastoral themes – the Greek figure on the façade outside had supposedly been modeled on Isadora Duncan – and below the cupola, just above the third tier of loges, an engraved gilt legend banded the hall all around with Latinate V's. The theater below was upholstered in red and matte gold – red carpets, red muslin curtains, and red velvet seats, gold railings and gold paint on the swooping balconies.

Having recently secured diplomatic victories in Holland and Italy, the chancellor carried a feeling of peace that evening. He was confident that the French would give him the loans his debt-ridden country so desperately needed. Furthermore, he was a devotee of classical music, and loved to hear an orchestra tuning up. Before the concert, each musician was in his own world, ignoring the others, sending up sounds into the air to mix at random: high C's from a trumpet, like an announcement at court, low chuffing notes of a bass, sudden thumps from the kettle drum, a flute ascending the scales and descending in a short sprinkling of notes like flower petals. The pleasing disharmony would end with a flourish, Schober knew, when Clemens Krauss emerged with his baton and all would applaud and hush. The musicians would then merge into one great instrument. Schober would not talk politics with his hosts, or even with Frau Zuckerkandl, until after he'd properly enjoyed Mahler's Symphony No. 3 and Beethoven's *Missa Solemnis*.

With his arced pince-nez and stiff band collar, his snow-white handlebar mustache, and close-cropped white beard and hair, Chancellor Schober struck quite a figure. The Austrian Bloodhound, as he was known to friends and enemies alike, looked every bit the police chief he'd formerly been, when he'd earned the praise of leaders the world over and the scorn of Viennese liberals. It was he who had crushed the socialist riots of 15 July 1927, leaving close to ninety people dead in the streets. And it was he who later threatened the Heimwehr with the might of his formidable state police in order to forestall a fascist putsch. Many of the leaders of Europe considered him Austria's last hope of avoiding civil war, financial ruin, or subsumption by the German Reich.

Frau Zuckerkandl, who sat to Schober's left, was a handsome Jewish woman in her sixties, impeccably dressed, with black hair, a squarish jaw, and slightly tired eyes. She wore a gown of apple-green georgette, a black silk wrap embroidered with green stones, and, as if to represent in her hairdo all the great artists who'd orbited her Vienna salon, her still-lustrous dark hair swung wide about her head like a cloud of gas around a star. It was miraculously unsupported apart from a large green comb at the back, dug in with gold teeth. Sandals of black leather and damascened gold peeked out from below the green georgette, revealing a row of painted toes, naked to the air. (In Paris, Liouba said, women had been wearing sandals to the theater already for more than a decade.) Zuckerkandl had once been one of the great salonières of modern art and music. In fact, it was she who had introduced her friend Alma to Gustav Mahler, whose music they heard that night, and it was she who'd given Schober an introduction to Painlevé. She cared every bit as much as the chancellor did about the future of the battered little Austrian state.

Painlevé, who sat to Schober's right, still had the mildly rumpled appearance of a Polytechnique mathematician. He wore his dark hair combed aside neatly like a schoolboy, a thick dark mustache, and below his basset-hound jowls, an old-fashioned ribbon of dotted red silk. He breathed somewhat laboriously, due to a worsening heart condition, and looked as though at any moment he might drift off to sleep. He was former premier of France and now held the exalted title of French Minister of the Air. Like Zuckerkandl, he had defended Alfred Dreyfus thirty years before.

Liouba understood why a couple of old Dreyfusards would help, but she never completely understood about Schober. Maybe it happened when the stage had emptied of musicians, when they followed the *ouvreuse* and gendarmes downstairs. As the people crowded before the *vestiaire* to collect their umbrellas, overcoats, and hats and the *ouvreuse* pushed her way past to the exits, perhaps Painlevé asked Schober for the pardon – as a token of the Austrian commitment to liberal democracy, he might have said, as if it were a trifling matter. Then Schober would get his loans.

Perhaps to Painlevé, who had built the Maginot Line to keep out the Huns, and to Schober who faced 300,000 unemployed Austrians at home and a Heimwehr militia of 50,000 half-trained peasants, the theater seemed like an oasis of calm and civilization. The most violent thing the theater had ever known was Stravinsky, who had caused a riot there in 1913 with *Le Sacre du printemps*. Maybe the two statesmen felt optimistic about the future of Europe as they walked out to the motorcade waiting in the drizzle on Avenue Montaigne. Or, perhaps Schober had simply agreed to do what was practical and best at a time when the storm clouds had hidden the right choices in shadow, when the buffeting of a hundred different forces undid half of everything done. It was his last act as chancellor: to pardon the Latvian Jew. His coalition collapsed and he would have to carry on his fight for Austria as foreign minister.

Of course, neither statesman would ever know about the next war or even about the *Anschluss*. By 1934 both the Austrian Bloodhound and the Minister of the Air would be dead.

2. The Weisse Rose

... after Halsmann was released Dr Saxl was the first
person who had a chance to talk to him ... [Halsmann]
sees that the only real purpose in his life now is to
prove legally to the world ... that he didn't commit this
terrible crime and that instead he has suffered a terrible
miscarriage of justice.

Neue Freie Presse, Vienna, 2 October 1930

In the street outside the Weisse Rose, Philipp saw a man dying
of consumption. He recognized that cough, the death rattle
that begins dry, then goes wet with mucus and blood, when
the bacteria have eaten through the flesh of the lung. He'd
seen a man fall down dead in the middle of a coughing fit, and
each time Philipp had a fit of his own, he feared the wall of a
major artery was about to give way and he too would faint and
die with blood pouring from his mouth and nose. While lying
in his hospital bed, he'd observed to the doctor that the cure
rates in Stein sanatorium were not as advertised in the bro-
chure. The doctor's face was a statue. Philipp's heart wasn't in
the telling anyway. At the time, the nurses had dumped him
onto his aching left side in order to change the sheets.

Philipp grew light-headed and saw splinters of purple and
green light from the effort of walking down the street. His
uncle helped him past the man kneeling and retching into the
Obere Landstrasse gutter. The *Polizist* did not help.

Inside, Philipp lay on the cool, clean sheets with his eyes half-open. Beside the open door to the adjoining room, he could see one table with a chipped porcelain tea set on it and a candle holder with a partly melted yellow candle. There was one chair, a peeling washstand, and a bureau, and the bed had little green flowers on the spread and a slightly damp bolster. An oval mirror hung above the bureau, reflecting the dark and distant cracked paint and one end of the bolster and headboard. On top of the bureau were two electric lamps with shades like coffee filters. The lights clicked off by themselves after a few minutes in the bed. The detective showed no reaction at all, merely leaned his shoulders back against the wall in the corner and watched Philipp breathe.

'We thought we'd go shopping on the Ringstrasse,' he heard his mother say through the open door. Then a muttering of indistinct voices in Russian – *canceled the Hôtel de France,* he heard. *He isn't allowed to go to Vienna.*

Is there a toilet here?

Down the hall, with a pull-chain up above. It's cold water only in the bath. Can't afford the gas, I suppose.

Philipp didn't care about the Hôtel de France in Vienna. He wasn't sweating in a hospital bed; neither was he gluing paper bags in solitude in Stein prison or waiting to empty his bedpan, so the little inn felt incomprehensibly opulent. Only the name, Weisse Rose, was somehow a disappointment. The entire purpose of a rose was its color. But up here in the bloodless Alps, things lost their color.

He sat up and reached for the handerkerchief on the table beside the bed. '*Nein,*' said the detective, reaching toward him with imprecatory fingers outspread. If the Austrian authorities had anything to do with it, the *Polizist* would lie in bed with him for the rest of his life.

'I would like to blow my nose,' Philipp said, pointing to the handkerchief.

'*Ja*,' the detective said, lowering his hand slowly like a sorcerer who had been moments away from transforming him into a pig.

The sweat was already coming, earlier than usual. The sheets would get wet like the sails of a capsized boat.

In the other room, Uncle Moritz was talking and talking nervously to Liouba. Liouba began to tell about Einstein. *He said, it may be of small comfort that Hitler hates us both. He said, the bandits killed Rathenau. He said they published a book called 'A Hundred Authors Against Einstein.'* Professor Einstein had heart troubles too, but maybe he wouldn't die. Apparently he lived on Haberland Strasse. Philipp had held Ruth's hand under a poplar tree in a little park on Haberland. Birds had been singing. It was a quiet, crooked little street in the Schöneberg district near the zoological garden. *Yes*, Liouba said, *he wrote on our behalf to the French League.*

Someone pushed the door half closed and the voices grew dimmer from the room where the candle flickered. *They say there's a law of 27 July 1871. It's because of the law, they say. No, he will not be able to go to Vienna.*

It was easy to hear Uncle Moritz's voice, going nervously on about Schober. *Schober's very last act, last of all! Well, they'll never get their hundred million with the Christian Socials in power. Maybe from Rome, but not from Paris or London.*

Mama: *We have nothing to thank him for.*

It was the church that brought him down in the end.

Someone then pushed the door almost completely closed. An old green sweater was hanging on a hook there, one he hadn't seen in years. Mama had brought it for him all the way from his bedroom in Riga.

Philipp asked the detective's permission to go to the washstand. The detective granted it, but offered no help as Philipp stood up, listing slightly from vertigo. He went to the washstand and splashed water on his face, a numbingly cold water like the waters of the Zamserbach. He remembered his father drinking the water from his hands on the last day. 'It's cold,' Papa had said, blowing onto his hands, and when he replaced his gold-rimmed glasses, they were all fogged up. 'Good for the spirit! Good for the heart!' The guidebook said not to drink the glacier water.

Philipp got back into bed and, gurgling in his chest, began to fall asleep.

The door opened. Mama's silhouette came and stood in the wavering candlelight of the doorway. Then she turned and disappeared again.

3. The World Resort

There no wicked Northwind enters;
No evil Southwind wreaks its powers;
How fair the unturning center flowers –
The place to go – especially in winter.

CHRISTIAN MORGENSTERN,
from 'The World Resort,' *Alle Galgenlieder*

The Villa St Hubertus in Meran was a grand house that stood at the top of a hill. The Jewish doctor from Innsbruck had lent it to them for free. Meran was quite nice. The street and hotel names were German, but the city belonged to Italy since the War. There were palm trees, just as in Lugano, but no lake. Instead there were radon springs and terraced hills whose sunny trellises were loaded with purple grapes. The autumn cure in Meran was called the grape cure. Wisteria and grape vines grew up the yellow stucco on the face of the villa, curling around the giant lichened urns of birdfeather-blue gentians and tracking over the marble balustrade. A cobblestone drive in front circled around a running fountain where three bronze-black cherubs tiptoed in its rainy pool.

From his chaise Philipp could see on one side the vine-yard, on another, beyond the balustrade, a flight of crumbly steps twisting down between the palm and oleander. Even bougainvillea grew there, as if the sea were just nearby. But there was nothing but mountains all around, mountains that

140

began the day dark and cold like the Brandjoch outside his cell window, then mellowed in the rising sun, lightening and receding as the sun revealed the grade of the valley slopes. Elevation, Philipp supposed, had much more to do with climate than proximity to the sea; Meran was in a basin at the meeting of the Vinschgau, Etsch, Passeier, and Ulten valleys, and it was green and mild as the Mediterranean Sea.

Before dinner, he hung onto the cypress tree, which shot up to the sky like a pillar and he swung himself around and called out, 'Look, Mama! *La donna è mobile!*' And he belted out as much of *Rigoletto* as he could remember, which was fortunately not much, and then he nearly collapsed with green stars in his eyes.

'You're feeling better!'

'I'm feeling better!' He refused to touch his chest where it felt the blood might spurt out.

'Hurray!'

They ate at the end of a long, long table in a room full of mirrors. His mother did nothing but cook. (It was like those days when she taught him to read in three languages, except that those days had been special and filled with love and the excitement of unknown horizons.) Sometimes he thought that the seat way down at the other end of the table was Papa's seat, that he was there but for some reason they were all observing an oath of silence and would not speak to him or look at him and Papa would not speak to them. Philipp knew he should take care of Mama and Liouba now, instead of the other way around.

'Why don't you go?' he said.

'Why don't I stay?' Liouba said.

'But you do stay,' he said. Every time he tried to make a joke, all he could think of was everyone waiting and listening to him.

'What?' she said.

'Why do you hate the mountains?' he said.

'I don't,' she said.

'Why don't you hate the mountains?' he said.

'We would never have taken the hiking trip but for my asthma,' she said.

'So?' he said.

'So, everything,' she said.

'It's your fault?' he said. 'And all this time they thought I did it!'

'That isn't funny at all.'

One night he heard her weeping in her room, a horrible groaning like a sick animal. He did not go to her.

In the mornings he would walk beneath the poplars down to the *Kurpromenadene*. One entered the *Kurhaus* through a curved colonnade festooned with geraniums and crowned by a white tympanum with an oculus window. Atop the tympanum, three marble figures danced in a ring, robes flowing, and, still higher, beyond the tympanum, a cupola of gleaming windows rose before the snowy peaks. Inside, all was bright and clean, quiet as a monastery. Marble floors shone. People whispered. Sometimes Philipp sat in the great empty Hall of Mirrors. He never read, not a newspaper or even a book.

He saw a doctor from time to time at the Kurhaus, but the old man offered only the slightest direction. Herr Dr Trebitsch had a curved spine and couldn't turn his head or bend his neck. He called it his 'spondyloarthropathy.' Though a mild-mannered creature with thinning hair and a reedy voice, his condition forced him to walk stooped forward, with his head lowered and his hands linked behind his back like some miserly overseer of a fortress or a mine, surveying his armaments or his diamonds. 'Airs, waters, places!' he would say to

Philipp, rolling his eyes to their outer limits in order to see up from beneath his long, gray eyebrows. 'It's been true since Hippocrates. Now carry on.' Dr Trebitsch would then go loping down the corridor to the radon baths, where he appeared to spend most of his time, with no appreciable benefit.

Philipp had declined the vaunted grape cure, which didn't sound at all scientific, but the medicinal water and temperate air did seem to help his breathing, so he took a steam bath every day in a dim wood-paneled room and inhaled a vapor of eucalyptus oil. Some days, he went to the little Italian woman who rubbed his chest with peppermint. (In her own way she was rather beautiful, but he preferred her to the other masseuse less for her beauty than because she didn't talk.) After the steam bath, he would lie in the open air on the Kurhaus sunning deck and gaze out at the mountains and cloudless sky. Afternoons, he would walk up the steps from Galilei Strasse, and then he would follow along the Tappeiner Weg, a garden path lined with magnolias, olive trees, and flowering cactus. He made a mental note each day of the exact tree or the exact cactus where he'd turned back, and the next day he would make sure to walk farther by at least thirty paces. He continued doing so each day until he could walk all the way to Gratsch, looking down on the shell-colored rooftops of Meran among the green leaves. Occasionally, the thought would enter his mind to leave the path and eat the white oleander petals, which he knew to be poisonous.

One day, when he returned from the Tappeiner Weg, he saw Mama on the veranda and she said, 'You look fit. They weren't able to harm you. You're too strong. Just like Papa.' She smiled at him, but her eyes were not part of the smile.

'God damn it!' he said. His fingers curled into vibrating

claws, and his neck muscles pulled at his mouth and quivered like the cordage on a ship, and he showed all his teeth.

'What's wrong?' Mama said, crying.

'Don't look at me that way,' he said and shook his fists at her as though he would strike her. She hadn't done anything. He knew that. But her words were meant to assuage her own fears and not his. 'Go to the Kurhaus!' he screamed, so loud he thought he would rupture his pulmonary arteries. 'You weigh eighty-five pounds!'

'You're behaving strangely,' Mama said.

'I'll be here for you,' he said violently. 'Don't you worry. I'll be here for all of you. I'll be the last one to complain. What do I have to complain about?'

Liouba was there in the doorway and he couldn't meet her eyes.

'Don't look at me that way,' he said. 'I know how undignified I am. What a nothing I am.' Mama and Liouba looked at each other as though he were crazy.

He thanked Mama for the eggs, and apologized to them both. He kissed his mother's hands, though he hated her and her stupid grammar lessons in the kitchen in Riga with a stubborn hatred that sent him reeling down the maze corridors of hate and self-hate.

It was into this unsettled situation that Ruth came without warning. She arrived, it turned out, on a Wednesday afternoon. Philipp came up the steps of the Villa St Hubertus, and there she was, standing in the open French doors with a solicitous expression that bore no resemblance to the portrait in wax paper. He climbed up the stairs faster than was comfortable. He grasped her shoulders and kissed her on both cheeks. She seemed to expect a different sort of greeting, and there was a near-collision of chins.

'You look so well!' she said. He was just a pile of loose clothes standing on end and his hair had not yet fully grown in.

'So do you!' he exclaimed. He had learned his lesson with Mama, and would from now on be a passionless automaton.

She reached out and sadly touched her fingers to his temple.

He took her valise and carried it through the double doors into the hall, set it down at the foot of the winding staircase. 'It's coming back,' he said cheerily, and patted the back of his head.

With her short, straight hair, lack of makeup, and indifferent clothing choices, there had always been something partly boyish about her – she was wearing another of those slightly outdated blouses with toreador shoulders that Liouba would never have worn. It was the sort of dress a tomboy wears because she doesn't know any better, and on such a beautiful girl it was interesting to his senses to an alarming degree.

Ruth looked up the staircase. 'It's like the staircase in the Museum Johanneum,' she said.

'Well,' he said, 'you'll have to write me about its new exhibits, as I won't get to go there myself.' *Be a machine, Halsmann.*

'I know,' she said, looking somewhat afraid of him. 'I heard the Technische Hochschule wouldn't take you back. It's horrid.'

They were alone in the hall. Mama and Liouba had disappeared and the place suddenly seemed quite desolate without them.

He just stood there and watched the white curtain blow into the empty parlor behind Ruth. She took a step toward him and retreated. It was so spastic, her chin knocked against her breastbone. He had never seen that before. She had always moved as if she were in a ballet.

'Let's go sit down on the veranda,' he said.

A scent of oleander blew in through the open windows there. They sat on the veranda together for a time without talking.

Ruth straightened her skirt on her knees and looked out into the valley. Her legs were still lean and strong. Philipp looked where the chaise had drawn the skirt back a bit too far against her thigh. 'It's a lot like Lugano,' she said. 'Do you think?'

'But no lake,' he said.

'No. No lake.'

He grabbed her hand, and squeezed it. 'I thank you, Ruth.'

'I've missed you so much,' she said.

'The great *cause célèbre*.'

'No.'

'Where are Mama and Liouba?' he said.

'They said they were going out to buy some sheets,' she said.

'So tell me about your boyfriends,' he said. 'There must be someone in Berlin!'

'Boyfriends?' Ruth looked horrified. Then she said, 'The book of letters has been published.'

Published his love letters in a book. You lie like Mama.

'I thank you for everything,' he said, 'I thank you for coming to see me here. Gioconda.' The name turned his tongue to wood. The idea that he was hurting her was beginning to awaken in him the old urge to harm himself, and he mustered all his energy for a counterfeit smile.

'I died from want of your letters,' she said. 'But today is like a dream.'

Her words caused the facial muscles winching open his fake smile to pull even tighter, until his face was so contaminated with emulation and falsehood that it actually quivered. He felt queasy and salty in his stomach.

'Liouba says you're much better. How do you feel?'

'Oh, I'm quite fit. I can actually walk up one flight of stairs now.' He wasn't funny anymore.

'I brought something for you.' Ruth rummaged in her messy handbag and pulled out several smudged pink tins of makeup, brushes, and a folding oval mirror caked with reddish powder.

'Thanks, I've already applied three layers of pancake,' he said.

She withdrew a little gray box tied with a blue ribbon.

'Oh, Ruth,' he said, 'I can't accept it.' But the look on her face when he said that compelled him to take the box from her and pull the ribbon. It was a silver fountain pen.

'It's inscribed. There.'

'You spent too much on me!' he said. He gazed adoringly at the pen and what he thought was: *You'll never be a husband or father to anyone* and *what a foul, pathetic, self-pitying creature you are, you deserve to die for your craven self-pity and suicidality and Ruth would not love you anymore if she knew your thoughts* and *just eat the oleander without a note and disappear from this world of paradox.*

Philipp and Liouba were supposed to play tennis, but Liouba said Ruth should take her place.

'I have to write to Monsieur Hertz,' Liouba said.

'It's all right, Liouba. Ruth will be here for a while. She doesn't want to disrupt our routine.'

'I don't have any clothes for tennis, anyway,' Ruth said.

Philipp got two racquets out of the hall closet and gave one to Liouba.

'You two play,' Liouba said. She handed the racquet to Ruth. 'You can borrow some clothes.'

Philipp spun his racquet a few times, then held it out to Ruth. 'No, it's all right,' Philipp said. '*Le Journal* arrived today.

I think Mama needs help looking through the classified ads. Besides, it's no good on my lungs.'

Mama came in. 'Oh, a tennis match.'

'Philipp says you're busy this afternoon,' Ruth said, 'but you're welcome to play. I don't have my whites.'

'Busy with what?' Mama said. 'I might like to watch a tennis match. I could use the fresh air.'

'No, Mama, I'm a bit tired.'

'Are you ill?' Mama came near to inspect him.

'No, Mama, I'm just tired.'

They played tennis without him. Afterward, Ruth came out to the deck all flushed and perspired. The tennis dress was too small and, damp as it was, it showed off her athletic figure very well. 'She's a liar!' Liouba called through the doors. 'If she's no good at tennis, then I must be terrible!'

Ruth sat beside Philipp and took his hand. A garnet sun was sinking into the mountains, shining darkly on the palm leaves while the blue mountains entered again into the darkness.

'I'm going for a bath,' she said.

At dinner, you could hear every clink of the silverware on the plates. You could hear ice melt. When Liouba announced the flavors of the gelato in the icebox, her voice boomed into the quiet like a bullhorn.

After dinner, Mama said that he and Ruth would probably want to go for a walk since the evening was so mild.

'Do you want to?' Ruth asked.

Philipp suggested the four of them play *Skat* instead, as it suddenly seemed very lonely to him not to play those old family games, but Liouba escorted him and Ruth out and swung the French doors shut behind them.

Ruth laughed. Philipp looked at the glass doors and manufactured a look of serenity. Ruth took his hand, and they walked around to the deck. An arc of moon had risen over the mountain. He almost remembered those days in Innsbruck Prison when he would have given away food and air to stand before the moon with Ruth. But in Stein there had been no moon, no letters, and no Ruth.

'How is your *entrechat* these days?' she said.

'If I *entrechat* here, I think I will go over,' he said and pointed out at the palms and oleander with a mock laugh. Then he punched his own wrist, hard, right on the stupid scar. The act of hitting was so melodramatic and shameful that he hit himself again.

She held his wrists firmly. She was stronger than him now. Moonlight shone down on the terraces loaded with grapes.

'How do they grow so many grapes in the midst of a depression?' he said. 'I guess grapes don't know any better.'

'You're not so happy to see me,' she said. She had taken the blue gentian out of her hair.

'Why would I be happy?' he said. 'Why would I want to see someone who greets me at the dungeon exit and is only concerned whether I'm happy to see her?' He pulled his arms away from her.

'Who is that talking there?' she said. 'Is that Philja?'

'I don't know.' For some reason the name Volker Kopp lin came into his mind. Some friend of Pessler's who died the war.

'Can I help you?' she said, but she was remote. He h that remoteness, though he had caused it, and he hated self for causing it.

'I don't know what's happening inside me,' he said. 'T told me a story once, about an inspector from Sty investigated the murder of cows. I feel crazy.'

'Look at the moon,' she said. 'How beautiful.'

'I shit on the moon,' he said.

Ruth looked out at the city lights and the terraces. 'I was reading that book on suffering you sent me a long time ago, the Freudian one,' she said. 'I was wondering if you had a hardship or a trauma.'

'I don't remember the book anymore.'

'It says that when hardship ends, mental life and development resume as before, but with a trauma, the consciousness of desire is afterward endangered.'

He didn't listen to what she was saying, but something in him softened anyway at the idea that she read the book. 'I love you because you read,' he said. He noticed suddenly how majestically beautiful and upright her breasts looked in the wine-colored dress. 'There has really been no one else?' he said.

'No,' she said.

He led her off to her bedroom, right past Liouba and Mama, and he didn't give a damn. And when he reached the door, he remembered something else Pessler had told him: *Death plays tricks in the mind.*

Her naked body disappointed neither his eyes nor his fingers nor his lips, but he couldn't figure out how to please her, and she couldn't help him. There was no crushing of grapes. Instead, when the final moment arrived, Ruth cried out in fear and pain.

Afterward, she whispered in his ear, 'I told you to stop.'

'You told me to go.'

'I mean after we'd begun,' she whispered. 'When it hurt. I asked you to stop.'

'I wanted to stop,' he said. 'Didn't I stop?'

'No.'

She had also told him when they began, in a voice small ith fear, 'Be gentle.'

Be gentle. Stop. He stood over her on the bed and covered himself with the blanket and said haughtily: 'I didn't think that there were such words in German.'

'Philja. You are never nasty.'

'I can be nasty. Germans taught me in prison. Go to Stein for a year and see how gentle you are when they bring you out on a stretcher.'

'I shouldn't be cross with you now,' she said. 'Let's be old-fashioned like Adam and Eve, remember?'

'Adam and Eve are a fairy tale.' He was like an angel on a rooftop in Rome, who removes his wings and hurls them from the top of the Spanish Steps. She just wasn't the same Ruth as the one in the little portrait he'd wrapped in wax paper each night in Innsbruck prison, and not the same as the Ruth of Lugano, Dresden, or Berlin. He felt himself closing again like the balustrade gentians at night.

4. Der Lichtaffe (The Light Monkey)

Among all the many misfortunes to which we are heir, it
is only fair to admit that we are allowed the greatest
degree of freedom of thought.

ANDRÉ BRETON, *Manifesto of Surrealism*

It took just a few months for his body to heal. Before school
started, the hair had come back on his head and his lungs
had ceased to hurt him in any way; Liouba saw how hard his
chest and stomach were again and he could outrun René
with ease. But his efforts to become a Frenchman had not
gone well. He'd watched the girl in saddle shoes reading Gide
in the Jardin du Luxembourg, but hadn't actually spoken to
her. And it turned out she was American. He'd visited all the
landmarks, the Eiffel Tower, Notre Dame, the Louvre, but
that only made him feel more like a tourist. And at the Eiffel
Tower he'd haggled with a Moroccan over a pen like a dirty
Jew and the Moroccan had stopped and looked at him with
watery eyes, as if to say, 'Do you know how many children I
have, you dirty Jew?' And at Notre Dame he'd sat before the
Coustou Pietà and at the Louvre he'd sat before the Avignon
Pietà, and he'd gone back to the little room at the hotel near
the Sorbonne and thought about pietàs.

He'd thought of the American girl with her saddle shoes
split wide apart in the air, and he'd thrown the handkerchiefs
back into the opaque white water in the sink before they

could stain or even stiffen, and then he'd thought about the pietà again. He didn't punish himself with push-ups anymore; Paris presented more beautiful ways to self-flagellate than prison did.

The Quarton painting was supposed to be different from the other pietàs because Mary is not touching Jesus, or grieving. Instead, she's praying and looks a hundred years old. Mary Magdalene may be weeping, with the gold lining of her red robe pressed to her right eye. But the Virgin Mary is not weeping; a flood of tears has already passed from her body and left it withered as an ancient scroll. John removes the Crown of Thorns from the spokes of light around Jesus's head slowly, like a physician disentangling his patient's brains from a bombshell.

But the Quarton isn't any different. It's a lie, like the others. (Just ask a dirty Jew.) Mary's hands are a steeple pointing straight at heaven, but the steeple of her body is listing to the right, enough so that her head has become dislocated from the halo embossed on the wall, and the wall is bleeding. It's merely another tale of a mother destroyed by grief; Quarton just shows the grief later on in its natural history, after a passage of many aging tears from the body of the mother, when the ruination of her beauty is already complete.

It was impossible to relax with the pietà in his mind. But it was also impossible not to think of the American girl wearing nothing but her flyer jacket. So he defiled his handkerchiefs and then did his penance in the sink.

His own mother liked to lean on him, to be comforted by him, to see that his ribs didn't show anymore like Jesus's ribs. She liked him to be perfectly upright, not listing before the bloody embossments of the Quarton wall; to see him upright caused her to sleep better. To see him leaning caused her to go into the kitchen and cook briskets while making happy predictions – what a thing to see a pietà cook briskets and make happy predictions! So he didn't tell her anymore about engineering school at the Sorbonne, where he had failed in being French worse than anywhere else. And he told Lucien he would go with him and the other boys to Sainte-Chapelle. They said they would show him the famous chapel because they had gone to Catholic school and because it would make him French. But he said he already knew all about Sainte-Chapelle.

When they got there, the sun was glittering on the Finding of the True Cross and the Translation of the Crown of Thorns. Philipp marched around and pointed and spoke a bit too loud, and he told the Sorbonne engineers that in the mornings the sun lit the rose window of the Apocalypse. But when he pointed to the ark of bulrushes, Christophe farted and Pierre laughed and swatted Christophe on the head and told him to keep his ass closed in the sight of God, and Christophe punched Pierre. Pierre said, 'Stop! Philipp is trying to tell us about the glass!' But then Christophe grabbed his nose and shouted, 'You mean before the nose of God!' And Pierre chased Christophe around the baldachin, and then the boys ran down the stairs to the lower chapel, shushing each other and yelling about cigarettes.

Lucien remained behind and stared up at the creation of the world on the north windows. He was better looking than the other boys and the only one of them Philipp had ever seen with a girl. 'What do you expect,' Lucien said. 'They're rejects from the Polytechnique.'

'Are they?' Philipp said.

'Yes,' Lucien said. 'I'm one of the rare cases who has turned down the Polytechnique. The Sorbonne gave me too much money.'

'I see.' It was quiet again, and organ music could be heard faintly from somewhere below – a Bach fugue.

'You said you are a student of French art.' Lucien waved his arms around at the tall panels of colored glass.

'Yes, I've been here before,' Philipp said.

'I come here to think sometimes,' Lucien said. 'But not with them.'

Lucien was from the provinces, like Pierre and Christophe, but it seemed to Philipp that he too wished to prove himself, and that he was smart, if not yet a Parisian. 'The French have the best educational system in the world,' Philipp said suddenly.

Lucien laughed, maybe at his bad French. 'I agree,' he said. 'But I've never studied anywhere else. You?'

Philipp said nothing.

Lucien headed for the stairs and Philipp followed him. They descended through the chapel of the Virgin Mary, where the organ music was somewhat louder, past the tombs of the dead canons, and out into the sunlight, where the boys were smoking in the cobblestone road next to a big empty packing crate.

Lucien pulled a box of cigarettes from Pierre's jacket pocket and tapped it against his palm, then he opened the box and knocked one of the cigarettes out. Pierre and Christophe were smoking solemnly and quietly, trying hard to look as though they'd lived in Paris all their lives.

'Do you have a partner for the solenoid lab?' Philipp asked.

'Me?' Lucien said. He lit up his cigarette. 'Where did you come from, Philipp?'

'Latvia.'

'Latvia?' Pierre said. 'What is that?'

'What religion are they in Latvia?' Christophe asked.

'Same as here,' Philipp said. 'All.'

'Right,' Lucien said. 'But you must be Christian. You know so much about the Rose Window.'

Philipp created a smile.

'It's expensive to come to France now,' Christophe said, 'unless you have money. The prices are terrible.'

'I don't have a choice about the money,' Philipp said. 'I'm making a new beginning here.'

'There aren't many scholarships these days,' Pierre said. 'We're not all so lucky as Lucien.'

'I don't think luck has much to do with it,' Lucien said, blowing smoke up into the air.

'We all work in the library,' Christophe said. 'Even Lucien pushes carts in the library. I never see you there.'

'I prefer to study in the cafés,' Philipp said.

'He means you don't push carts,' Pierre said. 'For money.'

'No.'

'Ooh, did you get that chill?' Christophe said. 'There must be a breeze out here. It just got a few degrees colder.'

'Do you plan to stay in France when you're done with school or go back to Latvia?' Pierre said. His tone had turned clinical.

'I'm French now,' Philipp said.

'Are you really?'

'In my heart.'

'Good,' Pierre said. 'I mean no disrespect to foreigners, but some of these wealthy foreigners, they come to France and have no allegiance to France and take her education and leave with it and go back to their home countries. Poof! I'm only saying that French education is meant to invest in the future of France.'

'Of course,' Philipp said.

'And then there are the Jews, who have no allegiance at all,'

Christophe said. He seemed to be examining Philipp's face and Philipp saw how bad Christophe's teeth were. He displayed the bad teeth brazenly, as if they were evidence of the malice done to him by the Jews.

Pierre flicked cigarette ashes over the stones and watched them fall. 'Christophe thinks the Jews have made a social experiment out of France,' he explained. 'The socialists. But we have a Jewish friend in the army who isn't a socialist at all. Roger. He's Jewish isn't he?'

'No, he's Russian,' Christophe said. 'But did you come from Latvia, truly?'

'Don't ask him that,' Pierre said.

'We heard you came from Austria,' Lucien explained.

'I spent some time there,' Philipp said and unbuttoned his jacket to let in some of the cool river air.

'Look, Christophe,' Pierre said, 'Halsmann is taking off his clothes. You must be ill, Christophe. It's not cold.'

'What were you doing there?' Christophe said. 'They say you already passed your engineering exams. You were studying?'

'No. I was traveling.'

'Ah, I thought so,' Pierre said, 'a man of leisure.'

'No,' Philipp said.

Lucien offered him a cigarette. 'You look nervous.'

'He's understandably afraid of Christophe's anus,' Pierre said. 'It can go off at any time.'

'I don't mean to pry, but I hear things being passed around, some fantastic rumors,' Christophe said. 'I assume they are rumors.'

'Don't assume,' Philipp said. 'Notions being passed around are called rumors.'

Pierre said, 'He doesn't need to know, Philipp. It's none of our business. It's just that Christophe studies too much and

157

he can't slow his brain down sometimes for days at a time. That's why he has to fart so much, to relieve the heat of his overactive imagination.'

'But haven't you been cross-examined by Halsmann? He's a real detective,' Christophe said. 'Why can't I do the same? We're all equals here.'

Lucien leaned his head back and blew a spout of blue smoke up into the air. 'People say you were in prison,' he said.

The three boys looked down at the cobblestones and smoked quietly.

'My father fell,' Philipp said.

'You don't seem like a criminal,' Lucien said. 'I think you should have the chance to set the record straight.'

'Well,' Philipp said, 'I must go to meet my sister.'

'Look, Philipp, I'm a straight shooter,' Lucien said. 'You seem very bright. And I for one believe you're not haughty. You're just shy. Aren't you? But I hear things like "Oedipus Complex" and "Freud" and "killed his father" and "buying a pardon" and I think you deserve a chance to set the record straight.'

'I must go to meet my sister,' Philipp said. There was as little point in talking to the French Heimwehr as in talking to a packing crate.

He left them in the cobblestone road, smoking beside the packing crate, but he didn't go to Liouba. He went instead to the Conciergerie, to the cells – squat little pigeon cages, now dry, swept, and empty. They had once been dark and dirty. They had once terrified Marie Antoinette and the Cour des Femmes with rats and centipedes in wet straw and the waiting for death. He didn't want to be in there at all, to be anywhere with a door meant to lock people in, but he felt compelled to gaze at the tiny empty floor until he could be sure the boys had deserted the Île de la Cité.

You could look through the picture into that meadow. A camera was a kind of time machine. There Papa was, sitting in the meadow, happy, with his back turned, refusing the lens, refusing to be captured, refusing to be dead. Ah, well. Remember other things, better things, the pie, sweet, warm, on the windy Altmarkt, under an umbrella. '*Entrechat!*'

The American girl was there under the same crooked plane tree. She didn't look up at him. She had curly brown hair tucked into a striped woolen cap and a clear face, saddle shoes with thick socks, a long brown skirt, and a leather flyer's jacket. Always there in the Jardin du Luxembourg on the same bench under a leaning plane tree, reading *Les faux-monnayeurs*. Big breasts and soft white skin that would remain a secret to him, but not to somebody, someday.

He hadn't spoken to her, but he had asked that waitress if she'd read *Der Prozess*. '*Non*,' she'd said. She was probably an aspiring model, one of those giraffes without any money to pay for real clothes. '*Je ne lis pas des livres*,' she'd said, as though she were quite proud of the fact. Really. You simply don't read books, even French ones. Then she'd walked away without filling his coffee cup and ducked under an advertisement for Modiano cigarettes.

Sometimes he got out the photographs of Ruth in Paris, the nudes, and filled the sink with white water in the small bare room with the cathedral radio that stood on a shelf by the bed. Then he studied himself in the mirror, where he saw a nose that now seemed big and scarred, a knob on which his history was written. He had taken after his mother before, but now it seemed that he looked more like his father.

Liouba said to answer Ruth's letters. 'You were happy.'

'It was my last attempt at *joie de vivre*,' he said, thinking he should throw away the dirty photographs of her.

'She loves you,' Liouba said.

'One can't love a *cause célèbre*,' he said. He was lying on the rug in Liouba and René's bedroom.

'You were meant to be.'

'Nothing is meant to be,' he said. 'The End. Bedtime story brought to you by the second law of thermodynamics.'

'It's unlike you to talk such nonsense,' Liouba said. On the wall beside the master bathroom Liouba still kept a photograph of Philipp and Ruth at the Place des Vosges.

He didn't answer anyone's letters, really. A few of his old friends persisted, but not out of love, it seemed.

Pie, sweet, warm, on the windy Altmarkt, under an umbrella. That was far away now, across a sea of time. Instead of wet, warm, sugary lips very close to his face and Ruth's hair blowing into his face in the cold wind, there were diamond saws now, and Audion tube receivers, background radiation, squiggles of wire, crystal receivers, and unreadably small chalk numerals. Before that had been the airless charnel smell of dead fish and pigs in Stein prison – the glue. He used to lie in bed and wish for the smell to go away. He'd give up his firstborn to make it go away, he sometimes thought, but it never went away. It followed him from the room where they made the bags out into the low passages, into his cell. *First you fold the bag on this side, like so. Then the other side. Then place the paper weight here. Then one line of glue and another, here. Are you listening? Komm Schon!* He'd wish and wish for the glue to turn back into pigs and fish that could run and swim away. Philipp walked out of the lecture on Zepp antennas. The boys asked him about it at lunch. They sat in the long hall that smelled of dirty dishes and echoed with dish piles and silverware crashing into wet bins.

'This doesn't interest you, Halsmann?' Lucien said. 'It's going to be on the exam, you know.'

'I know,' Philipp said. 'Since when do they examine us on anything interesting?'

'Who lit the fire under Philipp's ass?' Christophe said.

'He doesn't care about the future, remember?' Pierre said. 'He's a man of leisure.'

'Did you see the Andréossy Prize is a thousand francs?' Christophe said.

'That money is mine,' Lucien said.

'Oh, I forgot, they only offer these prizes for Lucien,' Christophe said.

'He wants the money for his grandmother,' Pierre said. 'Remember?'

'What? Oh, the cancer,' Christophe said.

Lucien released smoke slowly from his nostrils like a dragon.

'Still,' Christophe said. He was the sort to insist he could win a prize he was not good enough to win. He could never fail enough times to convince himself he was no good. But Pierre knew he would never win any prize in his life, and so he laughed.

Lucien tried to show them he was bored of them by talking about the construction of the Maginot Line. The Polytechnique, which, as he had frequently reminded them, he had been admitted to, was shaping the future of France, he said. The engineers. He was not one of those Frenchmen like his father, he said, who had given up after the Great War. He was of a new generation that would carry the ancient strength and splendor of France onward and upward into the future. Cancer did not belong to him; war injuries did not belong to him; they were the afflictions of another age.

Pierre and Christophe never talked politics. Christophe batted his box of cigarettes across the table at Pierre.

'The times are changing,' Lucien said. 'But France will live. The strong survive.' Lucien knew nothing of wars, nothing of hard times, and nothing of death. But he clapped Philipp on the back and said, 'Isn't that right, Halsmann? The strong survive.'

'Halsmann, do your trick with the cigarettes,' Christophe said.

'It isn't my trick,' Philipp said.

'Pierre, then. Balance your cigarettes in Halsmann's hair.'

Pierre examined Philipp seriously. 'Yes, his hair is looking very bushy today. I think I can do seven cigarettes today if the patient is cooperative. Hold still, now, Halsmann.'

Pierre reached for Philipp's head and Philipp knocked the cigarettes out of his hand.

'Ho, ho!'

'Ho, ho!'

'Oh *la vache!*'

It was true that only the strong survived. Papa would have agreed with that – Papa, storming up the Schönbichlerhorn at six A.M. and drinking glacier water with a red face. But Philipp didn't tell them about his father, or that he would rise where his father had fallen and dedicate to his father all the glories he would never witness. He didn't tell them of the recompense he would have from the mountain. It was not heroic to show one's hand that way. He didn't tell them that the Jewish nation would again appear as warriors *and as horse-men, so shall they run*. He didn't tell them either about Papa in the kitchen, cleaning the glass tulips with a rag, standing on the ladder not talking, examining the glass and refusing to look at him even once. Or about the time he'd given Philipp that anatomy atlas and Philipp had given it away and then

Papa discovered it at a used bookstore with his own hand-writing inside it that said 'To Philipp'; Papa had pretended he wasn't hurt and then refused to speak to him all through their vacation at the Blue Lakes.

Philipp would not ever again mention Papa in their midst. He would not allow the delicate image of his father to be sullied in their rude Gallic minds. He would encircle Papa like a fortress wall and he would flatten these French boys with his mighty Jewish brain like Gideon with his trumpet.

Lucien, he knew, was going to build the mechanism of a Valjoux 23 wristwatch. Philipp didn't know what he would build for the Andréossy, but he knew Lucien was nervous about it because Lucien had asked what he would build with an affectation of insouciance, and because Lucien had said, 'They say you were first in your class at the Technische Hochschule,' and because he reminded Philipp of the cost of bedsheets and his grandmother's copious need for them, owing to the cancer, and because he lent Philipp a pencil during the solenoid lab when he had never before helped him with anything.

The idea for what to build came when he was thinking about the American girl in saddle shoes. He was looking out the hotel window at the Seminaire du St Esprit. The shadow of a bare plane tree was rising in the cold light on the rectory wall as it did every afternoon and the sink had already been drained and the wet handkerchiefs lay dripping. (Shameful to do it in the afternoon.) But he had seen the American girl again in the Jardin du Luxembourg, *still* reading *Les faux-monnayeurs*. When she had got up to stretch beside St Bathilde, the unseemly narrow eyes of the men on the benches turned after her like glinting stones, and two boys stopped to talk to her there by the white marble statue.

One had balanced on one foot and shrugged his arms at the sky like a clown and she had laughed with her hand self-consciously against her cheek. Philipp had followed her all the way to the Fontaine Marie de Médicis.

When he was back at the hotel, alone, he thought how nice it would be to photograph that girl naked as he had photographed Ruth, and to keep her naked photograph. And he thought about how wonderful photographs of girls really were – something akin to flowers and stars. He drew the shades, filled the sink, and went through the ritual of the sink, and then he went to the closet. He was ashamed, so he thought: *Feel your terrible freedom, Halsmann. Yes, you, YOU, the miserable ex-convict, actually have a closet. The miserable ex-convict has been graciously supplied with an entire closet, including a door, doorknob, and light bulb that can be extinguished and even illuminated at will.* And he got out the camera from under the itchy blankets, his father's old Ica. He felt the dimpled cool black leather fitted over the steel, felt the edges, where the chafed leather now sprouted rough and undyed. The camera weighed slightly more than a steam iron and smelled like something his mind could not name, like the velvet-lined cases where Papa kept his pipettes, or like a shirt with oxhorn buttons, or the drawer in which such a case or a shirt would be kept. Philipp opened the lid and drew out the lens, extending the leather accordion along its steel carriage, where the oil had acquired a hairy coat of dust. A plate above the lens read ICA under a row of fractions, decreasing in magnitude by halves, and the lens itself was covered with dust like an eye with a cataract.

He rebuilt the Ica with nervous hands, as though he were rebuilding his father's brain, did it right there in front of Lucien, in front of the judges, sweating under the hot desk light in the theater where terrible student actors put on their plays. His hands trembled because of the ghost of his father but also because they were the hands that would strip Lucien's grandmother's deathbed of its bedsheets. But he had no choice in the matter; he was inhabited by the ancient horsemen of Israel. He had prepared like a Jew and the ticking of the clock on the judges' table, like a ticking of the cold, indifferent machine of the universe itself, was insubstantial against his Jewish preparedness. He even forgot about the clock for a while and enjoyed himself. He enjoyed thinking of the camera as an artificial eye, and of the eye as a machine designed by the genius of four billion years of life on earth. Without lenses, in a blind universe, every object shattered light rays into chaos. But a biconvex lens captured the light rays and reconstituted them on the retina, which had evolved in exact congruity with the lens's focal length (or in his case, a little short of his focal length – hence his need for those meniscus lenses that were at that moment slipping down his sweating nose). It was true of all the eyes of the earth, shining like jewels in lizards and birds and fish and tree monkeys like himself, seeing all that might be seen. And that was all a camera was: an eye, with a retina of ground glass. And it remembered not with a brain but with the chemistry of silver halides.

He had enough extra time that he derived the lensmaker's equation for the sheer pleasure of it and wrote it out on his graph paper. The inverse of the focal length is equal to the refractive index of the glass minus one, multiplied by the sum of the inverse radii of the lens surfaces and that funny thickness term, which looked so redundant, but was really so straightforward when you thought about it. Philipp put his head under the dark cloth and adjusted the focal length until he could see Lucien perfectly, standing by his desk with a renewed air of Gallic confidence. He too had finished within the time limit.

The professors, Salty Old Beard and Big Hard Belly, both of them humorless minds steeped in the history of machines back to the wheel and lever, marched out among the desks, all heaped with bolts and wires. The scraping of toolboxes echoed under the high ceiling where the pitiful actors dressed in order to butcher the malignantly dull works of Racine. Salty Old Beard licked his lips and Big Hard Belly scratched below his ribs. Lucien's Valjoux 23 didn't work. All its many little parts lay within the watch casement still as dead birds. Christophe's phonograph looked like an exploded trombone, which he somehow attributed to the terrible lighting. And even though the Ica worked perfectly, Philipp made sure not to smile at all.

Beard and Belly conferred and then stood in front of the desks. 'The winner is the Valjoux,' Beard said. 'The camera is complete,' he added, looking at Philipp as if to forestall his objections. 'But a camera is a crude device. This is not what was asked of you. We asked of you the future.'

'His doesn't work,' Philipp said.

'We don't know if your device works,' Belly said loudly, 'because the film must be developed in order to tell. The camera was not a good choice at all. A good engineer executes, but he must also think creatively, of the future.'

'The Valjoux,' Beard said, 'displays quite honorably the ingenuity of modern French engineering.' With a look of conviction that nothing more of relevance could be said about the matter, he waited for Philipp to speak.

'If I had only understood the future of France,' Philipp said, 'I too would have built a watch that doesn't work.'

'Get out!' Beard yelled. 'And take your German lightbox!'

Lucien stared straight ahead, unwilling to embarrass him by meeting his eyes.

*

Philipp went out to the gardens every day for seven days and waited with the Ica. He would not have been able to wait for eight days, but the American girl appeared again on the seventh day. The horsemen of Israel were still running in his mind and the edges of the frosted pane of glass were still sharp in his mind as if he'd actually broken the window that said ENREGISTREMENT. (The old shadow man behind the glass was only too pleased to purge him from the books.) The world seemed to Philipp outrageous and comical and suited for lies, and so he lied and said he was a fashion photographer. The American girl blushed and looked into the pages of *Les faux-monnayeurs*, but she looked right back up with a readiness to believe. That is a secret of people who blush: they hate themselves too much, but consequently they also love themselves too much. He said he would tell her some interesting things about André Gide. And he took her to the café where the surrealists banged the silverware on the tables.

Before the week was through, he'd bought a photoflood lamp and a used enlarger from a fat Russian who tried to cheat him. ('Watch this,' the fat man had said in Russian to his fat wife, 'here comes M. Sorbonne with Papa's checkbook. He doesn't know the cost of a loaf of bread.' Philipp had told him he was a fashion photographer and needed the lamp for a pretty girl, а **красивая девушка**, as they say in Russia.) And so, for a reasonable price, he photographed the American girl in the nude in his hotel room, leaning on the empty sink. He'd asked her to bring something glamorous, so she leaned against the sink in an opened fur coat and pearls borrowed from her friend's mother. She fanned her chest where the warm blood had risen to the surface of her white skin and formed a faint red delta. It heated her perfume and scented the warm air of the entire room with gardenias. She seemed to think she might be famous very soon, and that it was only logical Philipp had found her, but she was nonetheless very thirsty and drank up several glasses of water from the sink. He photographed her from the left side, which was the more beautiful, and painted her undulating skin with a stripe of silver light, and lit her from below so that her pale eyes burst out of the darkness like illuminated jewels. And he developed the photograph there in the middle of the night, with a red lightbulb screwed into the socket over the sink, and tacked the pretty naked girl up on his wall like a captive spirit in the lair of a sorcerer.

In the morning the warm air still smelled like the American girl's perfume, even his bedsheets (which she had not touched) smelled like gardenias, but he went back to the Louvre and sat alone before the Avignon Pietà. He could never tell his mother that he'd left school. She'd ask him immediately what he would do now, what he would be now, and she would start making happy predictions and cooking a brisket. He felt that there was something not right inside him, something frivolous and morally lax that would have disappointed his father, something the boys at the Sorbonne had smelled on him, even without knowing where he'd come from and why. He wouldn't tell his mother. He'd never tell her about school just as he'd never told her how the paper bags cut his fingers. One life. One time only. Mistakes written forever in the code of time. Did Nietzsche say that?

When he went to the café by the old church for breakfast, he couldn't eat. There was a girl on the *terrasse* in a Beaux-Arts beret and a green scarf, writing in a little book. The cold had splotched her cheeks like ripening apples, and he felt intensely the heat of her thinking, her intelligent gaze onto the paper, the heat of her blood, and all her rich and intricately perceived history there in her brain awaiting him like an unknown treasure on a sunken galleon. He wished to tell her he was a fashion photographer and to invite her to his room and to do much more, but the tree branches in front of the church were twisting back and forth in the wind like a man shaking his head no. The plate smelled like the glue. The bacon-scented air pouring out the glass doors smelled of preservatives, nitrates, bad, like that glue that was made, they said, of the bones of fish and the skin of pigs. The bacon lay on his plate untouched, and he aligned the knife and fork straight on the napkin, like the hands of the Virgin Mary of Quarton, perpendicular to heaven.

5. The Minister of the Air

Everything about this animal, a victim of contradictory
forces, suggests that it has disguised itself to escape, and
in warding off the fiercest fates, it carries away the most
diverse and unexpected possibilities.

JEAN PAINLEVÉ on the seahorse, *L'Hippocampe*

The problem was desire. He had had designs upon the girl in
the beret and green scarf, and he realized that it wouldn't be
possible to ask for photographs were he really asking for
something else. When he began to photograph other girls, he
did so as a kind of existential exercise. Without desire, it was
easier. And when one of the girls got an acting job with his
headshots, then it felt less dishonest to tell the girls on Boulevard Saint-Michel he was a fashion photographer. Without
lies and without desire, he found pretty girls often who
wished to be photographed, at Café du Dôme or at the Select
among the painters, and he experimented on them with his
lamps. Photographic beauty was all about the lighting, he
noticed. He found the prettiest girls at the Tuileries and the
most interesting ones in Saint Germain among the writers; at
Les Deux Magots, while he showed girls his portfolio over a
café complet, the surrealists would yell at one another and
pound the tables so that the silverware jumped.

He never tried to touch any of the girls, even when one of
them had put her hand in his pocket while he was leaning a

mirror against the bed to alter the light. He resigned himself to living a lonely and meaningless existence and put the girls' photographs up on his wall over the sink and filled the sink and did his penance. He turned his father's picture facedown, so he couldn't see the forlorn meadow while he did his horrible deeds, and then he went to see his pietàs, and he went religiously to visit his actual living mother at Liouba's apartment by the Place de l'Opéra. (His mother's predictions had become frantically, unnervingly happy, and her brisket production was such that he and René had to work all Saturday afternoon sawing at the mounds of beef and sweet onions, eating until they actually sweated.) Many times when the camera seemed too utterly stupid and wasteful of his time and potential income, he haunted the solemn places – like the Church of the Madeleine at the end of Rue Royale, where Saint Luc had been beheaded by a German bomb – and as he walked he revered every Great War *mutilé* on the street and every child, those sad midgets clunking along the windy sidewalks in wooden shoes and black aprons with white collars. Even a pleasure as small as a visit to the Maison des Amis des Livres in the Rue de l'Odéon demanded penance because of his meaningless way of life.

He knew it was all gravely and terribly wrong, but the days stretched out empty before him, and to interpolate something between himself and his own death, he kept snapping pictures. Photography had become almost like a tic, and he asked every person in the hotel: 'May I take your picture?' He brought the camera everywhere and photographed everyone. (Animals interested him not at all, things even less.) How strangely eager people were to be photographed, as if it could bring them fame or immortality. So there were many photographs to take, and there was much penance to be done. He would not touch the girls and he would not make friends with the people of this foreign land. He would just take photographs and saw up his mother's briskets.

The invitation from the Minister of the Air arrived as a gift in these days of self-hate. For such a man, Paul Painlevé, the former premier of France, the Polytechnique mathematician who had revolutionized the study of differential equations, could never understand the idea of photography. His name was printed in textbooks that cared nothing for history, but were obliged to his eponym by solutions and equations he'd created new under the sun. This was the man who'd built the Maginot Line. This was the man who had rescued him from prison. And this was the man to whom he would confess that he'd dedicated his life to making pictures of pretty girls. Somehow it seemed to Philipp that this act might relieve his sense of unaccountable guilt. Perhaps Painlevé would regret his intervention with Schober and return Philipp to prison. He went on a Tuesday afternoon.

Though the father had invited him, the son Jean answered the door.

'I'm in the wrong place,' Philipp said, leaning back to look at the number on the door. 'Sorry.'

'Another apologizer,' said the young man with the long equine face. 'What's with you mathematicians and your apologizing? Come in.' Jean Painlevé was not at all happy to see him. Sighing, the younger Painlevé thrust his left arm into the front hall and looked up with incompletely disguised impatience, like a concierge who has calibrated his false smile precisely in order to indict you for requiring his labor when you are not a king, after all, and should open doors for yourself. 'I told my father he should live here if he prefers to entertain here,' Jean said wearily.

Philipp walked into the bright salon. It was not the furniture of a thirty-year-old man – Louis XVI chairs and tables, all very stuffy, except for the large film projector standing in the exact middle of the room. Philipp handed Jean a bottle of red wine and began to recite what his neighbor had told him about the grapes, but Jean raised his hand and clanked the bottle down on a marble-topped buffet.

'Tell him,' he said, pointing over his shoulder with his thumb. 'When he wakes up.' Jean then went into the kitchen and put on a tall, white stovepipe chef's hat and resumed cracking clam shells.

Philipp sat down on a settee beside a tall mahogany clock. The minister's son was somewhat famous. Not only had his father been premier of France, but René said that Jean was well known for racing cars. Jean's chin was pinned to his chest as he frowned at the clams. He was unshaven, and his dark hair was slicked back over the top of his head, hanging out the back of the chef's hat.

'Do you know my father from L'École Polytechnique?' Jean asked, so grudgingly that Philipp hardly felt like giving an answer.

'No. I dropped out of school not long ago.'

'Oh?' Jean said in the same weary, distracted tone. 'But you don't know my father from the Polytechnique? You look like a mathematician.'

He felt the danger he had felt outside Sainte-Chapelle, but a friend had just that morning won a part in a film using Philipp's headshot, and this fact of Philipp's growing powers seemed to offer some magical protection against the danger. Plus, he was there to confess. He said, 'Your father rescued me from an Austrian prison.'

Jean put down the clams. He came to the door of the kitchen. 'Oh, yes. I remember now. Philipp Halsmann. Welcome to France. Are you enjoying yourself here?'

'Immensely.'

'And what do you do now?' Jean asked.

'I am a photographer.'

A slight grin broke across Jean's face.

Philipp was not going to be laughed at by this trivial person. 'And I have heard you are a race-car driver. But perhaps you're a chef.'

Jean smiled widely and pulled the white stovepipe hat from his head. 'I am a filmmaker!'

Jean wiped his hands on a rag and crossed the salon to a door at the opposite end. There he stopped and signaled for Philipp to follow. Through the door, there was a small sitting room, and there among many pillows and blankets sat an old man asleep with his legs up on the couch. 'Your guest is here.' The old man opened his eyes.

'Bring me some coffee, Jean,' Paul Painlevé said. 'My heart causes me a great deal of fatigue.' At that moment his eyes sank shut, and he breathed heavily. Jean left Philipp there with the sleeping man and for a few minutes his breathing was the only sound apart from the chiming of the Normandy clock in the salon and the perking of the coffee and the distant cracking of clam shells. Painlevé opened his eyes again. 'But I assure you, not a single neuron has expired.'

At the mention of Painlevé's brain, Philipp instantly began to sweat. Wanting to seize the opportunity while Painlevé was awake, he began fumbling around: 'What can I say to you? You saved me.' He held up the wine bottle and began to expound about the grapes, but the senior Painlevé wasn't interested either.

'Tell me about your studies.'

Philipp coughed into his sleeve and wiped the sweat from his forehead. 'Monsieur, I have become a photographer.'

Painlevé's eyes opened a bit. The heavy lids reminded Philipp of someone.

'How do you find the time?'

'I have left the Sorbonne.'

Jean returned with the coffee and cream on a sterling tray, which he placed in his father's lap.

'He's like you, a dropout,' Painlevé said, looking up at his son. 'Halsman, in a few months you can have your engineering degree, and you want to become . . . a photographer!' He shook his head, perplexed as though he were grading a particularly bad student's math exam.

'The older generation!' Jean said. 'With education from them, we only have to re-educate everyone anyway.'

'Science gave us the aeroplane,' the older Painlevé said, as if he were beginning an argument, but the argument seemed instantly to tire him. Again his lids were falling. 'Tenth October 1908 at Camp d'Auvours . . . '

'Papa,' Jean said.

Paul Painlevé's eyes fluttered open again. 'Young people always like to hear about the day I flew with Wilbur Wright.' Philipp nodded as obsequiously as he could, but the old man continued in a somewhat rehearsed voice, as though he needed no audience at all. 'It rained that morning,' he said. But that was as far as he got before dozing off again. He slept for a little and when he opened his eyes again he shouted, '*Soixante-quatorze!*' as if the number were of special significance, and added, 'Conquerors of the air!' The eyelids then sank shut with finality. He was soon completely asleep, breathing noisily through his nostrils.

Jean lifted the tray from his father's lap and carried it back into the kitchen. He asked Philipp somewhat sheepishly, 'Would you like something to eat? Or something to drink?

Or . . . ' He tapped his finger against his lips as though trying to think quickly of something to do or say.

'May I photograph you?' Philipp asked.

'Ah!' Jean said, with evident relief. 'Come to my laboratory in the morning!'

Philipp said he would come, and saluted to the slumbering Minister of the Air. But he thought he would rather go to the Tuileries and find the prettiest girl and ask to photograph her, and see what beauty he could capture for his lair. The confession was done. Now he had only to wait for that feeling of sin to lift. In truth, the attempt at expiation had not completely failed. And this buffoon in the chef's hat had somehow been of service.

6. The Seahorse

The subsequent development of the little ones offers just
as many marvels. We see offspring who slowly substitute
themselves for their parents by resorbing them; elsewhere,
we see parents decompose in their children. We witness
organs of propulsion becoming jaws, an eye passing from
one side to the other or fusing to the one next to it; in
some, all the organs disappear . . . Indeed, a dully colored,
carnivorous larva might grow into a dazzling colored
vegetarian who, when fully grown, no longer has a mouth
and fasts until its death.

JEAN PAINLEVÉ,
'Mysteries and Miracles of Nature,' *Vu*

After his visit to the Minister of the Air, Philipp dreamed
of flying with Albert Einstein into the sunset. The great
man wore flyer's goggles and held a shiny pocket watch.
And there was another part of the dream, with an eye
behind a curtain of mail, and the links were drawn back to
reveal an eye that changed color from blue to brown like a
precious stone turning back and forth in a spotlight to
exhibit one facet, then another. There was some wish in it,
or some premonition of change, something important,
but it was forgotten. All he knew was that he would like to
earn some money with his photographs in order to show
his mother he was not a fool. It would be a great benefit to

add to his portfolio the photograph of a famous man like Jean.

He felt depressed and foreign as he walked along the icy Rue Armand-Moisant with the heavy Ica view camera slung over his back. He couldn't find the place and he didn't know where he was. Nothing on the street looked like an institute, and no sign identified the Institute of Scientific Cinema. There was, however, a movie theater playing American movies with sexy movie posters on the wall. The day was sunny and cold, with bright low clouds flowing through the blue air over Paris and a more sluggish layer of clouds higher up. Reflections of the warped old glass in the windows above the movie theater spangled the dark façade across the street with funny light. 'Look for the marquise,' Jean Painlevé had said, but there was no institute anywhere around it. Philipp asked inside the theater, but the manager couldn't understand him and had never heard of it. On one side of the theater was an apartment building with the number 14 on the glass above the door. On the other was a narrow fish-smelling alley, where he found a brown door with an opaque grate. He tugged on it, but it was locked. Across the alley was a building that said number 10. Philipp was looking for 12. Finally, Philipp went back into the alley and banged on the silent grate.

He was about to give up when a muffled voice came from within. The door then shook, as if it were about to fall off its hinges, and swung out into the alley, forcing Philipp back against the opposite wall, which caused two rats to flee down the alley. A man in a gray uniform leaned out from behind the door and looked Philipp over suspiciously. Philipp stated his business, and the man continued to examine him with hostility, shivering in the cold with great drama as if to emphasize what an imposition it had been to answer the door. Then he barked, '*Attendez ici!*' and pulled the door shut again. Inside, Philipp heard a loud bell ring. He waited. The rats crept back to the garbage heap. Philipp watched the long fall of water drops from a drainpipe overhead.

The door opened again. Philipp stepped inside. The man in the gray suit was sitting on a stool by a little table with a lamp, reading one of the gossip rags. From the tiny vestibule, a steep flight of stairs led down to a landing with a bare bulb hanging over a lidless garbage can. Jean Painlevé came up to the landing from steps deeper still and hailed him – 'Halsmann!' – then disappeared.

Electrical wires of all colors snaked along the ceiling, drooping in places, so Philipp lowered his head as he lugged his heavy view camera down the stairs. He'd never liked small spaces, but now, because of the prisons, they terrified him, and he felt a squeezing in his chest and knocked his tripod against the bricks, causing dirt to crumble from the wall. It was a stairwell like that leading down to *der Keller*, and he wouldn't have been at all surprised if Horst were to step out of the shadows with a lobotomized smile and lock him up.

When he reached the bottom, Painlevé came out again. On Philipp's left, behind a gate, wet laundry dripped in the dark over a field of empty wine bottles. 'What's wrong with you?' Painlevé said.

Philipp couldn't speak because of the claustrophobia.

'You're a free man now,' Painlevé said. 'Let's have some fun.' He led Philipp into the 'Institute.'

Philipp opened his father's camera up before an empty aquarium and drew slow breaths to calm himself. All he wanted was a photograph, but there was hardly room to move among all the wires and cables; the place was like the inside of a submarine. On one wall stood bookshelves packed with microscopes, Petri dishes, camera parts, journals, stacks of filter paper, and jars of turbid water, some with soil at the bottom, some containing what appeared to be worms, some seaweed. 'Eel grass,' Painlevé called it. There was a spasm of movement inside one of the jars. In front of the bookshelves sat a slim young woman at a microscope, a cigarette clamped in her mouth. Across from the shelves were rows of aquariums and basins covered with mesh lids – a menagerie of toads, eels, crabs, octopi, urchins, anemones. Several spotlights were trained on one of the aquariums, reflecting so brightly it was difficult to look. A camera was suspended over the tank by a complex apparatus of vises and rods, its motor running, and the camera lens was pointed straight down into a glass box submerged in the water. 'Acera,' Painlevé said, pointing to the tank, 'a bisexual mollusk.'

The whole place made Philipp feel as though something bad were about to happen to him, as though the rods and jars, the moving eel grass and bisexual mollusks, were meant for some malign experiment to be conducted upon him by Dr Meixner. But Philipp continued to set up his shot in obedience to that urge for expiation through money. There were no real lamps in the studio, so he aimed a spotlight at the white ceiling to obtain a dimmer reflected light. It would be a terrible picture. He had no idea what he was doing, or why he took photographs at all. He just wanted to get on with it and get out of there.

'Geneviève,' Painlevé said, 'help this man,' and he stooped to square up some papers stacked on the floor of the lab. 'Help introduce him to the mutable life of the seas. He is a man who needs an introduction.'

The woman at the microscope continued to stare through the lens. She had short dark hair, and her buttocks were thrust far out on her chair and her knees thrown wide apart and low to the floor. 'This is Geneviève Hamon, my principal scientific collaborator,' Painlevé said, shoving a box across the floor with his foot. The woman looked up momentarily, nodded curtly to Philipp, turned back to the microscope, and adjusted one of its knobs. She had a rather unusual wide face with wide thin lips, and there was something sure and commanding in her bearing. She didn't seem to like him. Painlevé told Philipp that if *Vorticella convallaria* and *Amphileptus anser* could withstand the light and heat, they might film for the first time commensal relations among surface plankton. One organism could become encysted inside another, he explained, only to re-emerge later. 'Uh-huh,' Philipp said, as he set down his photographic plates on a barrel. He thought he might vomit from the smell of the dense subterranean air. He opened the shutter and pointed the camera at Painlevé, who was half-turned to push aside an empty beaker.

'You must mind your background,' Painlevé advised.

It was better to enter the universe of another person's mind when he felt this way, so Philipp ducked under the black cloth and said, 'Tell me more about your films.'

'Ah! That is exactly what you need to know.' Painlevé explained that he'd made strictly scientific films on the stickleback's reproduction and on vibratory cilia, and popular films – art films – on the octopus, the daphnia, the sea urchin, the hermit crab, sea spiders, shrimp, and many others. The stickleback, Painlevé said, was unusual in that the male created the nest for the eggs, then tended the nest by himself. The male Mallorcan midwife toad, *alytes muletensis*, did the same. Male seahorses actually carried the eggs in a pouch and gave birth to them. 'Of course my films are not popular in the sense of people actually going to see them,' Painlevé said, 'but artists love them. Do you know Marc Chagall?'

'You're interested in androgyny,' Philipp observed from under the cloth.

'No,' Painlevé said, 'in mutability.'

Philipp came out from under the cloth. He closed the shutter, withdrew the ground glass, and was about to insert the film, but he saw that Painlevé's posture had shifted and he looked hunched and small, nothing like the Gallic, equine face he'd intended to photograph, the giant among his sea creatures. Painlevé was now bent and peering into the acera tank. But perhaps he would soon move again.

'It was a relief to meet your father,' Philipp said. 'My mother thinks I'm very tardy in thanking him. Does your mother make you feel such guilt?'

'I never knew my mother,' Painlevé said, turning back to Philipp's camera. 'She died just after I was born.'

Geneviève looked up. The movie camera ticked over the acera tank.

'You're an only child?'

'Yes,' Painlevé said. 'She died two months after I was born.' He added, stumbling a bit on the sticky medical words, 'Puerperal fever.'

'And your father never remarried?'

'No.'

Again the ticking of the camera over the tank filled the room. 'You were raised by a stickleback,' Philipp said. The claustrophobia was beginning to lift and he was beginning to breathe easier now.

Painlevé frowned. 'No,' he said decisively, and it seemed that more words might be forthcoming, but the filmmaker's mouth hung open, and no words followed. He clasped his hands together, raised his index fingers into a steeple, and rested his chin on the point, frowning. Philipp drove home the film, pulled out the holder, and released the shutter. It would be a good portrait after all. He would have to remember to interview his subjects like that.

'I'm sorry about your mother,' Philipp said.

An octopus was looking out at them seriously with red eyes, lower lids half-drawn up. Its head alone was the size of a watermelon and its legs were coiled and still beneath it.

'Is it alive?' Philipp asked.

'Of course.' Painlevé's face abruptly brightened. 'She's purple when she's happy. Maybe she likes you. She has a color for every mood, like Geneviève.' Painlevé challenged Philipp to pick the animal up. Philipp declined, out of pure terror that any contact with the animal would cause him to vomit on something expensive.

'You film all of them alive?' Philipp said.

'Of course, alive.'

'And afterward you return them to the sea?' Philipp said.

'Afterward,' Painlevé said, 'we eat them.'

'Even the octopus? I heard they are smarter than dogs.'

'Especially the octopus. I salt it everywhere and then braise it in red wine.'

'Geneviève, do you eat octopus?' Philipp said.

'Yes,' she said, still peering into the microscope.

'Is this light too bright, Ginette?' Painlevé said, pressing his thumb against a corner of the glass. 'The tank is scalding hot.' To Philipp, he added, 'The glass can shatter under the lights.'

'We need every watt,' Geneviève said, still looking into the microscope. 'Don't call me that in front of him.'

'Sea creatures don't like the light,' Painlevé told Philipp. 'They withdraw or refuse to mate. They don't like to be watched, so it's very difficult to catch them as they really are. You must work with instants.'

'To catch the organism in a moment of unguarded truth,' Philipp said.

'Exactly.'

183

Well, this man was not Lucien. That could be said for him. And his girlfriend was not that skinny bitch who hung on Lucien's every word. 'Let me photograph you, Geneviève,' Philipp said.

Just then, the glass exploded with a bang and the sea and the sand and the bisexual mollusks rushed out onto the cellar floor amid big shards of glass. Painlevé tumbled backwards, bleeding from the forehead.

'You see, Philipp,' Painlevé said, 'photography is a very dangerous game.'

'You can call me Philippe,' Philipp said, and hauled Painlevé off the floor. For the first time since Sainte-Chapelle, and quite suddenly, he was feeling French, if also slightly nauseated. Painlevé lifted up a shard of hot broken glass with a towel, and the three of them commenced searching the floor for the lost mollusks, to see if they might be saved and encouraged once more to mate.

7. Ty an Diaoul

The tragedy suffered by Philipp Halsmann, namely the
destruction of his youth through a two-year prison slavery,
cannot be corrected by any authority. But it is the honor-
able duty of the state to eliminate the stigma of public
guilt still attached to an innocent person. The means of
accomplishing this are obvious, as are the reasons.

JOSEF HUPKA, Professor of Law,
University of Vienna, *Der Fall Halsmann*

When the weather was growing warm, Jean and Geneviève
invited Philippe, as he now called himself, out to her family's
country estate in Brittany. The estate was called Ty an Diaoul,
'the Devil's House,' and Geneviève said it was just the place
for him to learn to have fun again. The witches and fairies
would bewitch him there with good magic as they had
bewitched her throughout her life. Jean considered it a fore-
gone conclusion that Philippe would come out with them
and come out again too, as if they had known each other for
years. 'Raised by a stickleback!' he said.

Philippe told himself he would go in order to photograph
more famous people and build his portfolio; Geneviève's
parents, Augustin and Henriette Hamon, were the principal
translators of George Bernard Shaw in France, and they
knew a great many famous artists and writers. That also
meant money and a great many opportunities for Philippe to

expiate his sins. 'What's all this talk of sins?' Augustin asked him by the old carriage house. Augustin and Henriette wore nearly identical thick round glasses, as if in reading so much side-by-side they had developed the same focal correction. Augustin's glasses were nested in a mane of soft white hair that engulfed his mouth and completely encircled his head, except at the top, where it had thinned into a swaying plume. They were anarchists.

The first evening Jean, Geneviève, and Philippe played poker with green beans in the dim little interior room that Jean called 'Le Cabinet du Roi,' since Augustin Hamon used it as his private redoubt. The scholar's pipes lined the shelves of the enormous glass case beside the door.

'This is fun, no?' Jean said. He sat before a wire man on a bicycle that Alexander Calder had made for the Hamons out of a radio antenna. Beside the Calder were three candles, the only lights in the room. Jean laid down three aces.

'What do you do for fun?' Philippe asked.

'Do you mean fun or do you mean joy?' Geneviève said.

'What do you do?' Jean said.

'I take photographs of beautiful women,' Philippe said.

'But you say this causes you guilt.'

'I was supposed to be an engineer,' Philippe said. 'And before that, my father wanted me to be a doctor.'

'Do you fall in love with these girls of yours?' Geneviève asked. Geneviève said that what he needed was very simple: it was love.

He explained that it was only possible to ask the girls for their photographs, not for their love.

'What about asking for their pussies?' Geneviève said. 'That would be fun.'

'But not joy,' Jean said. 'Or, on second thought, maybe joy.'

'It depends on the pussy,' Philippe said.

'I don't think you have ever been in love,' Geneviève said.

Philippe blushed in the dark.

'Well? Have you?' she said.

'Watch, Ginette,' Jean said. 'There are skeletons there that do not wish to be disturbed.'

'He is not a skeleton,' she said. 'Whatever has happened.'

'I have been in love,' he said. *Lugano. Love. Does it mean you're 'in love' if that's what comes to your mind? I think it's wonderful that you're taking dance lessons, Papa. Love, your Philja. P.S. The dead betray the living.*

'Then you know how to do it,' she said, throwing a handful of green beans into the middle of the table and drinking the last of her wine.

'It's not so simple,' he said.

When the candles had been snuffed out and they had gone to bed, he heard Jean and Geneviève loudly screwing in the bedroom upstairs.

He returned to Ty an Diaoul around Easter time, and Geneviève brought her friend's cousin Amandine, an art student at L'École des Beaux-Arts. 'Ginette intends for you two to fall in love before dinner,' Jean said.

They had a lunch of goose eggs, asparagus newly risen from the earth, and Ginette's homemade mayonnaise. 'So, the photographer!' the girl said. She was attempting to be coy, but she was simply too young to pull it off.

'This will be easier if you drink, Philippe,' Jean said, but Philippe would not drink. He had never drunk. 'There is a very serious side to you, Philippe,' Jean said. 'But we'll forgive you for now because you are a victim of fascism.'

They went out onto the heath behind Ty an Diaoul to look for toads. The air was wet and made Philippe's sweater wet.

To prove to them that he had a sense of humor he told them the *savoir faire* joke, and they laughed, especially Amandine, who was leaning decorously against a haystack. In the evening, Philippe consented to drink a little red wine in Le Cabinet du Roi and as soon as he had, Geneviève and Jean retired.

'Let's you and I go too,' Amandine said. She led him by the hand away from the dining room.

'The dishes,' he said.

'Don't worry,' she said. 'Geneviève explained to me about you. I'll take charge of you.'

Amandine must have found something very romantic in Geneviève's story, because as soon as they got to the bedroom, she got up on his bed and took off her clothes, and she showed him the rose bushes on her brassiere, the rose bushes that would unite them forever like Tristan and Isolde, she said. She had had a lot to drink. Philippe had had too much as well. She was pretty actually, but her lower teeth were somewhat crowded, he noticed, with one little tooth in front of all the others, and one of her breasts was slightly larger than the other – he couldn't help assessing her as though he were going to make a photograph.

Did she really think they would be united forever?

'Of course not,' she said. But she was herself studying photography a little, she said, and her family were Bretons; they believed in fate, and somewhat in ghosts and mermaids. She shielded her breasts from his gaze now, whether to hide the rose bushes or the asymmetry he did not know.

Geneviève and Jean were at it again upstairs. The only other sound was the ticking clock. Philippe put a hand over his mouth and laughed. But Amandine crawled across the bed toward him with a look of renewed seriousness. She touched his hand and asked, 'Was it very hard?'

He said his father fell. The clock was ticking furiously. He remembered summers in Latvia, and his great lack of concern with time then, as if it were limitless, as if time were a slow tide from the sea to the bay and back out to the sea, just a harmless expansion and contraction of the universe. But when Ruth came to visit in Dresden, then he was aware of time. Now he was aware of it every moment, even in his sleep, a post-exilic ticking of the clock.

Amandine said she was always fighting with her own *père*, a stingy bastard who ran a saloon in Camaret. She was only twenty. Having experienced almost nothing, she was one of those people who expected everything to go according to plan, who assumed that death happened only to other people. She didn't understand why he left the bedroom.

Philippe sat in the dark hallway and felt the floor hard underneath him like the floor of a prison cell. It seemed that the photograph of Ruth was there in the dark with him, leaning against the opposite wall and wrapped up in wax paper. Where was La Gioconda now? Riding horses without a thought of him. Riding with a German, that moron Andreas, a salesman, a man of directness and light, and no complicated letters, no questions, no repetitions, no fear of pity and no need for it, either.

In the morning, Jean came to find him in his room.

'Don't worry, Philippe,' he said, 'we'll cure you yet.'

'When I was here the first time,' Philippe said, 'there were daffodils in my room.'

'Yes, they don't live long,' Jean said.

'They're still there, in the closet,' Philippe said, 'in a sack. They're not alive anymore. I saw one of the dried-up petals on the floor, so I thought the daffodil plant would be there inside, but when I opened it, it was somehow much deader looking than I expected.' Philippe's eyes filled with tears long held at bay. 'No green in it at all, and the stems plastered to the side of the pot like wet hair.'

'You'll be all right, Philippe,' Jean said. 'We'll set you straight.'

'I don't think so,' Philippe said, speaking in a scientific voice despite his wet eyes. 'Times are changing. Bad times are coming to Europe. This is a bad time to be in love.'

'Nothing can happen now, Philippe,' Jean said. 'You're in France. It's 1932.'

8. The Vaneau

Neither vengeance nor pardon nor prisons nor even
oblivion can modify the invulnerable past.

Jorge Luis Borges, 'A New Refutation of Time'

It did not remain 1932. It became 1933, and as soon as it did
Hindenburg made Adolf Hitler the chancellor of Germany.
And 1933, too, yielded to time, as did Jean's father Paul.

Philippe didn't go to the funeral.

'Of course you will go,' his mother said.

He had stopped listening to his mother. Each time he took
out his calendar to mark the funeral that last week in October, something else presented itself and the funeral withdrew
from his mind like one of Jean's sea squirts withdrawing
from the light. He told himself that Jean would understand:
he had not attended his own father's funeral. The date passed
and Philippe photographed a girl in a Côte des Blancs vine-
yard for a maker of cheap champagne. But he thought of
Paul Painlevé on his way to the Vaneau.

André Gide's library at 1 bis Rue Vaneau was empty and
quiet except for a typewriter clacking and ringing somewhere.
It was not Gide in the adjoining room but a younger man,
bowed over the typewriter, and when Philippe peered in at
him, the handsome young man kicked the door shut without
lifting his eyes from his work. Then Philippe was alone with
the bronze alligator that climbed up the side of the beech

staircase – or rather looked like it was climbing, frozen as it was there on the bright wood, staring at a white sconce it would never reach.

The girl in brown gauchos came in. 'Grandma is here,' she said. 'La Petite Dame.'

A very small woman with short white hair came into the study. 'You look confused,' she said. 'Welcome to the Vaneau.'

'Is she yours?' he said.

'I like to think so.'

The woman with the white hair pointed to the piano, and when Philippe turned, there was Gide installed behind the instrument as if his entrance had been choreographed that way. The great man was imposing as an oak door, and very unhappy looking. But then Philippe knocked over the tripod and Gide grinned slightly.

Philippe knelt and examined the wood boards, then looked up at Gide. He couldn't see him due to the backlighting from the window behind, as though rays of blinding light emanated from his bald head. The typewriter continued clacking faintly behind the closed door.

'Leave us my dears,' Gide said, and the girl and the white-haired woman left. 'I have heard of you, Philippe Halsman.'

'You have heard of me?' Philippe said.

'Don't look so disappointed,' Gide said.

'Is it from the French League?'

'I don't believe in leagues,' Gide said. 'I heard of you from André Malreaux. And I saw your photograph on his book jacket, with his pinky finger across his chin like a Corsican gangster.'

Philippe stood up the tripod.

'Aha!' Gide said. 'Now you are happy again.'

'I'm just fine,' Philippe said. He opened his bag and began

to set out his floodlamps while the old mandarin of French literature watched.

'There is nothing to fear here,' Gide said. The typewriter rang one last time and then went silent.

'Am I afraid?' Philippe asked, looking into the light through his extinction meter. 'Shall we photograph you at the piano, then?'

'As you wish,' Gide said.

'I'll need you to turn this way,' Philippe said.

'Okay.'

Philippe moved the tall floodlamp to the other side of the piano. 'I'm a great admirer of *Les caves du Vatican*,' he said.

'Why thank you.'

'I had occasion to spend a great deal of time with that book.'

'Yes?'

'The unmotivated crime,' Philippe said.

'Yes, the unmotivated crime,' Gide said.

'But I think Lafcadio has a motive.'

Gide lifted his face up to regard Philippe from a new angle. 'No, the unmotivated crime is an unmotivated crime. Why do you think I am in such trouble with the Church?'

Philippe did not meet Gide's eyes, but looked out the window through the extinction meter and said, 'I think he murders Fleurissoire in order to punish him.'

Gide smiled. 'But he does not know Fleurissoire when he murders him.'

'When they ask Lafcadio what grudge he has against the virtuous Fleurissoire, Lafcadio says, "I don't know. He didn't look happy. . . ." So Fleurissoire is the criminal.'

Gide laughed. 'The crime of unhappiness. Yes, that is a crime.'

The floodlamps and reflectors were all set up now. 'Unhappiness, but also, well, you know.'

'I don't know,' Gide said.

'He isn't true to himself.'

'In what way?'

'You know.'

'But I don't.'

'Fleurissoire? He's gay. But he pretends not to be. Isn't that why you had him killed?'

Gide lowered his eyelids almost until his eyes were shut and they became strange and dark, and he lifted his head again as if studying Philippe. 'You speak French very well, M. Halsman.'

Philippe attached the cable release to the camera and the click caused Gide to stare at the photographic equipment as though he were about to undergo a medical procedure.

'Do you feel different from others, too?' Gide said.

'Oh, I'm not gay.'

'I mean that it must be very lonely sometimes, taking photographs. Like writing. You do it alone. And you are new to France. And then there is the terrible thing that happened.'

Other people were happy, while Philippe was not happy. He was a criminal, whom Lafcadio would have thrown off a train.

'Some people speak of "finding oneself,"' Gide said in an evident effort to ignore the camera pointed at him. 'But most people don't know what that means. They think of themselves as a mystery to be found out. But no one is a mystery. Everyone is what they always were. The courageous thing is to be who one always was and to find in the world those people and places that are like oneself!'

Philippe walked around Gide and closed the drapes. 'I think we'll make a beautiful photograph today,' he said.

When he ducked underneath the dark cloth and focused the camera, however, he saw Gide nervously pat down his hair (of which there was hardly any) and tug at his tie, and sweat began to shine at the top of his magnificent head.

'Are you ready?' Philippe asked, watching through the lens.

The muscles of Gide's face tensed horribly. Philippe came out from under the cloth. 'There's nothing to fear here, remember?' Philippe said. 'There's nothing to fear because I'll stay until we get the true Gide.'

'But you can't tell,' Gide said, his face now relaxed again. 'They may all turn out badly.'

'If they do, I will invent a new camera,' Philippe said.

'How could you do that?'

'I'm an engineer.' Philippe removed the ground-glass plate and drove in the film. 'Hold still, M. Gide. But remember, we're about to throw M. Fleurissoire from the train. We are about to murder him for pretending to be like everybody else. We're going to throw him from the train to punish him for the sin of unhappiness.' A glimmer of pleasure appeared in Gide's still face and Philippe tripped the cable release. He photographed Gide with his bifocals on, so that the reading lenses arced over his kindly cheekbones like a pair of crescent moons. The shadow of the frames fell directly on his eyes and made it seem, Philippe thought, as if he were an oracle who knew the secrets of the gods.

André Gide's bonhomie stayed with Philippe after his visit to the Vaneau, like a shot of some good medicine. For a time, he felt that Gide was the most benevolent creature on earth, for if his old fear had not quite departed him, then it had been tamed and it sat idle beside him while he did his work, at which he excelled even on a bad day, and when he was sick or tired or depressed. The agency had new portrait requests for him every day now and he crushed the other photographers who lined up in the gray office of *Vogue* looking out onto the smokestacks; the amateurs paid no attention to the direction or quality of the light, and never coaxed anything, man or beast, out of his shell.

When his work appeared in *Vu*, *Voilà*, and *Vogue* all at once, then he rented a new studio. Liouba sewed the drapes for it and he turned on the radio in Liouba's kitchen and danced.

'You dance just like your father,' Mama said.

'Mama, next weekend I'll take you to St Cloud.'

'Oh Philja, will you?' she said, flushed like a young girl. He could almost remember the old Mama. When he was ten or so, he'd once taken her out to dinner by himself. She'd dressed up in a hat and earrings, just like she were going out with Papa, and ordered wine, and at the end of the evening had hugged him to her warm breasts. 'Now, when people ask me what you do, I tell them you are a photographer! And you have done the book jackets for André Malreaux and André Gide!'

'Mama.'

'I do!'

'At the gallery they asked me how I became a photographer and I said it happened as a girl sometimes becomes a prostitute – doing it first for herself, then for friends, and finally for money.'

'No.'

'That's probably what Papa would have thought – that I'm like one of those men pasting ads on billboards.'

Mama had got out the coffee press and she set it down now and looked somber and mad. 'Why do you say things like that?'

'Mama, how is René? Is he any better?'

'You have to ask me, how is René?' Mama said. 'You don't ask your sister? She's working very hard for you.'

'Can he keep down his food yet?' Philippe said.

A key turned in the lock.

'Here she comes. You can ask her yourself.'

Liouba opened the door and shuffled in with her hair in a mess. 'I called Alliance Photo, Philja. The schedule's all straightened out now.'

'Thank God.'

'You're working too hard,' Mama said.

'There's lots of work to do,' Liouba said. 'Philja can't be his own secretary.'

'The baby is still asleep.'

'Liliane must get up now or we'll never get her to sleep tonight.'

Liouba and Mama went into the baby's room and Philippe spread *Le Petit Journal* on the table by the radiator in the *salle à déjeuner*. After a time, Liouba returned with Liliane, who blinked drowsily with arms clamped around her mother's neck, and Liouba set the baby beside the coffee table, and went to the kitchen. Liliane wobbled, then plunked down on the floor and began to cry.

'I'm washing the diaper!' Mama called.

'I'm boiling the milk!' Liouba said.

'She wouldn't take the bottle!' Mama yelled. 'She's going to starve!'

'Let me try again!' Liouba said.

So Philippe went to the coffee table and clucked at Liliane as though she were a puppy or a cat. He lifted her up but she continued to howl. Mama came back in. 'That's no way to hold a baby,' Mama said. 'Come here, pumpkin.' And Mama took the little girl in her arms and they went away into the baby's room and shut the door.

Liouba passed through the salon without looking at him. 'Can you look at the radiator in there?' she asked. 'It's gone cold again, and I can't turn the valve.'

Alone again in his room overlooking the Seminaire du St Esprit, Philippe watched the shadow of a bare plane tree rising in the cold light on the rectory wall. How much more spiritual to think that the light falling on the quiet rectory was consecrated to a star instead of to the Holy Ghost, or to think that the Holy Ghost was the light of a star.

He was good at what he did, whether it be prostitution or advertising, he was good at it, and no one could take that away from him, could they? But how many chances did one have in life? How many hearts?

9. The Pontoise Swimming Pool

One would not be going too far in saying that the son
occasionally had strong disagreements with his father, but
that he was not successful in emerging victorious against
the stronger personality.

From the Halsmann psychiatric report,
medical faculty of the University of Innsbruck, 1929

Captain Yves Le Prieur, who admired a fascist of any nation,
was not bothered that summer of 1934 by the 'Night of the
Long Knives.' When Hitler executed eighty men, electrifying
the news services of democracy, Le Prieur threw a party of
the Club des Sous l'Eau and became quite angry with Philippe about his girlfriend's missing necklace.

'Martine!' Philippe said. 'Stand still.' He didn't like to yell
at a model, even a drunk one, but he was running out of film.

'This is the last time,' Captain Le Prieur said.

'I would like it to be the last time,' Philippe said. 'That's the
point.'

'This is the last time,' Captain Le Prieur repeated. Then he
added to his friend, the one who liked to squish fireflies on
his forehead, 'The Jewish attitude is very pushy, isn't it?'

'I would like it to be the last time, but you said she would
like to be in *Vogue*. It must be a beautiful photograph to be in
Vogue, not just a woman at a party.'

'A beautiful woman at a beautiful party.'

'Yes, she is beautiful,' Philippe said. 'It is beautiful.' He took the diamonds from around Martine's neck. She could not hold herself upright and the light on the diamonds exploded unpredictably every time she listed left or right.

The photograph would be what it would be. He had used up most of his film. 'Your necklace, Martine.' He dropped it into her hand and began to pack up his equipment. The captain and his drunk girlfriend wandered off through the archway toward the pool.

But before Philippe had stood the heavy case on the hand truck, Captain Le Prieur came storming back through the archway. 'Why did you remove the necklace?' he shouted. 'You just had to see the diamonds, did you?'

As Jean and Philippe emerged into the Pontoise courtyard, where the swimmers were splashing and dancing in the pool to crazy banjo music, Jean said they ought to write their play about guilt. 'Don't you see the irony,' he said, 'of a man who's publicly branded with false guilt, and though he's exonerated, he can't forgive himself?' Jean was at his most philosophical, and least helpful, at a party. He looked off into the crowd distractedly, as if looking for someone else.

'People aren't interested in guilt,' Philippe said, peering into the darkness under the banner that read CLUB DES SOUS L'EAU. A few of Jean's fireflies still spun around in the darkness there, where Philippe had photographed them, but Le Prieur's army friend had mashed most of the fireflies to make warpaint out of them.

'The play could still be surreal,' Jean said, looking off into the crowd with his face lowered to the drinking straw. 'Surrealism is the answer to guilt.'

'Help me find this necklace before Le Prieur has me executed and submits my body to the medical school,' Philippe said, bowing down to look into the darkness under the banner, as if by looking harder the diamonds might suddenly appear. But the last firefly there shut off its light, and when Philippe turned around, Jean had vanished too.

The party went on heedlessly. There was something uncomfortably Roman about the formally dressed waiters stooping down to the men and ladies in the pool and walking briskly through the puddles to refill their platters. Le Prieur had brought in truckloads of food from the Halles Centrales: hanging sides of veal; pyramids of onions, tomatoes, button mushrooms, celery, carrots, truffles, and chocolate; gleaming sole, cod, oysters, and mussels on cracked ice; hog bladders and plucked partridges; sacks of mint and chervil, coffee beans, sugar, and flour; crates of Madeira and eggs; enormous wheels of cheese; tubs of butter, beets, and caviar; barrels of peaches, apples, and pears. All this paid for out of the Prieur family coffers, and consumed by revelers without a care for tomorrow, for the employment rate, the cost of food, or the Night of the Long Knives across the Maginot Line. They talked about such matters as if they cared, but they didn't care. They had the juice of crushed fireflies on their foreheads. Such people could not help him.

Probably, Captain Le Prieur was at the bottom of the pool, demonstrating yet again the breathing apparatus he'd invented. But he would resurface, demanding the necklace with mean eyes that flashed like darting fish.

Philippe went back once more to the site of his shoot with Martine under the archway and got down on his knees on the wet tile and felt for the diamonds on the gritty tile and wet grouting at the base of the wall, which already smelled of mildew.

Look at him, Philippe Halsman on his knees — the greatest portraitist in France.

This was what he'd meant when he'd told Jean it was a bad

time to be in love. It was a bad time to be anything with all these fascists on the loose with their bad teeth. He'd already learned the lesson of the fascists from the mountain. That is, you think you're in control, but you're not. You think you're in control until you fall, and then the mountain teaches you that the mountain is in control, and you are not in control. Your mind may deceive you into believing you are in control, but the bones cannot be deceived. The mountain teaches the lesson to your bones. Then you learn just how good you have to be. You have to be nimble on the mountain and you have to run like a dog. And he'd done that. He'd become, in his mother's words, 'a success.' Though the fear crept over his subjects' faces again and again before the camera like moss creeping on a stone wall (it was, underneath, just a fear of the mountain), he conquered it again and again. And what was it worth? A 'success,' on his knees looking for some lost diamonds. The last lone firefly winked on again for a moment and winked out.

Jean returned, more distracted than before. 'I could tell the octopus a thing or two,' Jean said. 'She wants the lights off, I wish to have them on. She wants to go, I want to stay.'

'Le Prieur is back up,' Philippe said. 'I see him there.' The captain was dripping like a sea monster, taller than everyone else by a head.

'You know,' Jean said, 'there is a book on the cartilaginous fishes I sometimes dip into, and every time, I think I will dip into it in a new place and look for a place I have not opened it before, and every time I open it to the same exact page, page 273. One is mutable and not so mutable. But perhaps the binding is cracked there.'

'Jean!'

'Will you stop worrying about him?' Jean said. 'He goes off now and then, like a geyser, and then falls back down into the mud.'

'Have you heard him talk about the riot at the Place de la Concorde? He's *Action Française*! And he deported his maid!'

'Who is he?' Jean said. 'A retired army captain. He has no power.'

'He's coming.'

'What will we do with you, Philippe? Maybe you're right. I don't know if I can save you.'

'Don't say that.'

The captain greeted them with a false smile and placed a dripping hand on Philippe's shirtsleeve.

'What's all this nonsense about the necklace?' Jean said.

'It was found,' Le Prieur said, still smiling the false smile with water drops dripping down onto his teeth. 'But I don't know about him.' He clapped his wet paw on Philippe's shoulder again. 'Martine says he took it from her, and forgive me, but I always listen to Martine.'

'Martine is drunk,' Jean said.

The captain glared.

Jean gazed distractedly out at the crowd. 'I think it's now time for serious business, Yves. Thanks to your genius apparatus, Philippe and I are going to make the first photograph in the history of mankind of a man bicycling underwater. Show me to my diving gear.'

Le Prieur smiled the false smile, lining up his teeth on purpose. 'This, I would like to see.'

'It's just a matter of the light,' Philippe said. 'It always is.'

When they had assembled all the floodlamps and the tanks and masks and the bicycle and the little man who was going to ride it across the pool floor, Philippe suggested a photograph of the Club des Sous l'Eau founders, and Jean and Captain Le Prieur stepped into the hot light of the floodlamp beside the fern.

'Captain,' Philippe said, 'you look as though you were made of stone.' He suggested to the captain that he pretend the camera were a man, but this was of no help. Then he suggested to the captain that he pretend the camera were Martine, but this seemed to bring the incident with the necklace into his mind and turned him more deeply, more resolutely, to stone. 'Pretend you're shooting down the Kaiser's spy balloons,' Philippe said. But Le Prieur squeezed his eyebrows imperiously at these obsequious words from the mouth of a foreigner and a Jew. So Philippe heaved the captain's tank of compressed air off the deck and the captain rushed to protect the tank from his grubby Jewish hands, but once Le Prieur was holding his invention against his chest, he smiled as though he were holding his very own baby. It could not be helped that Le Prieur had a face like an old tree, but it would otherwise be a nice photograph.

'Sometimes, in order to relax the subject, you must supply, rather than remove, the mask,' Philippe said as Jean attached the belt around his waist.

'And sometimes, you must only remove the mask,' Jean said.

Philippe could tell that Jean was irritated with him, but he said, 'Don't be cryptic.'

'I'm going to start writing tomorrow, early,' Jean said.

'I have a shoot tomorrow morning,' Philippe said.

'Too bad for you. It begins: "The man is free from jail, but he can't forgive himself his crimes."'

'I thought you said the man was innocent.'

'I mean he can't forgive the crime of existence itself,' Jean said, looking over the edge, down into the pool.

'That's vague,' Philippe said. He looked down too. 'I will need two large mirrors down there.'

'Why?' Jean said, and he kneeled down and began to rummage in his gear bag before the lake of fire created by the floodlamps. A firefly wandered by with its light off.

'They've slaughtered all your fireflies, Jean,' Philippe said. 'And no one even to mourn them. Very sad.'

Jean was busy in the gear bag.

'I'm sorry we brought them here for a stupid photo shoot,' Philippe said.

Jean was ignoring him.

'Don't be disappointed with me, Jean.'

'I'm not disappointed with you,' Jean said, neutral, but not neutral, like a witness for the prosecution on the *Zeugenstand*.

'Remember,' Philippe said, 'I am a stranger here, and I'm losing my hair.' He tried to joke, but he couldn't completely banish the anxiety from his voice. Jean didn't look at him. Philippe tried to make his voice cool and clear and said, 'Aren't you upset that these cannibals have killed all your beautiful fireflies?'

Jean sat back on his heels and looked around, thought for a moment. 'No,' he said. And he went back to rooting around in the gear bag and pulled out a silver reflector.

'A reflector won't be strong enough down there,' Philippe said. 'It must be a mirror.'

They argued about this for some time.

'I know about light,' Philippe said.

'But you don't know your own reflection,' Jean said.

In the end, they pried the mirrors from the lavatory walls, and, in so doing shattered one of them. They lowered the mirrors into the pool with fifteen ropes and cantilevered the floodlamps over the pool by a complex system of ropes, rods, vises, and mosaic tiles scavenged from behind the unfinished lavatories. They filled peach barrels with green mosaic tiles and used the barrels to brace the mirrors. They exhausted two tanks of air in order to obtain Philippe's desired angle of light, and when Philippe finally sank to the bottom with the camera in its special glass housing, his fingers were white and wrinkled and his eyes burned with chlorine. Finally, the man rode across the bottom of the pool, into the path of the light and past the table with its bottle of water on it, and Philippe took the picture. They wouldn't know whether it came out until he developed the film, but when Philippe broke the surface of the water and pulled off his mask, Jean applauded and so did the rest of the Club des Sous l'Eau.

Le Prieur gave Philippe his hand and helped pull him up out of the pool. 'You have the work ethic of a Christian,' the captain stated with pride, as if it were a baptism, and went away to put Martine to bed.

10. Rue Delambre

Strangely, our mind often overlooks the most obvious
solution. It is like searching for a secret lock in a jewel box
instead of simply lifting the lid.

Philippe Halsman, 'The Rule of the Direct Approach,'
Halsman on the Creation of Photographic Ideas

The morning of the booking with the young French actress,
Philippe decided that Jean was right. He had a problem,
because if he listened to reason, there was no cause for
worry. France was safe. The Maginot Line was nearly complete and the Germans might walk all over Europe but they
would not walk all over France. And now he was so busy, and
had so much of 'success,' that he could not see why he should
be ashamed to be a photographer. He was surrounded by the
most beautiful girls in Paris on a daily basis. The art often
came to him naturally and he felt that light was like a paint-
brush. But there was that nagging feeling that something was
wrong, and the thing now was to take an action, a bold action
that would change everything. Geneviève said that love
would conquer all, but love would not arise on its own. It had
to be wrested from the inimical forces of fate by violence, if
necessary, by bold and dramatic action. If only one of these
models were smart enough, and deep enough, then he could
begin that course of action now and leave his past behind
him.

His first bold action of the day was to wait, without any coffee, for over an hour. When he met the new assistant at his studio in the Rue Delambre, he was not in a nice mood.

'What's your name?' he said as he coiled a cable release.

'Yvonne Moser?' she said, as if she were unsure he would recognize her name. She had a good, symmetrical face, with startling blue eyes and wavy, dark hair, but she'd carelessly pinned it behind her head as though she had little regard for her own appearance. She held herself at the elbows with long slender limp fingers and her watch was loose on her wrist and had slipped so that its face looked down at the floor.

'Bring me that spotlight here, would you?'

'Pardon?' she said. There was something depressing about the girl. It turned out that she was a music student at the Conservatoire Russe, a pianist, and had only a little knowledge of photography.

The actress, meanwhile, on whom he'd pinned his hopes, had no instinct whatsoever for male arousal. She was young with big breasts, but she'd brought only a nightgown with a pattern like an old curtain and looked chronically ill, with her nose somewhat pinched like a person smelling dirty socks on a radiator. After changing camera angles many times and cajoling her in a hundred different ways to let desire and not foot odor play upon her features, he gave up. He went to the bed and just grabbed the neck of her nightgown in both hands, and tore open a big *L* in the fabric, completely exposing her naked breasts. Then he tripped the shutter.

Yvonne came to the young woman and wrapped her coat around her shoulders. Then the little pianist went back to her post against the wall. She said nothing and did nothing while the actress got dressed, and didn't help him clean up.

*

The next week, when Philippe was on deadline and had still to develop all the shots he'd taken at the fair in Chartres, he again called Alliance Photo, and again Lehfeldt sent her cousin Yvonne.

When he opened the door the girl was smiling, but when she saw his face she stopped smiling. She strode past him into the studio and began looking around at the tall strips of gray hanging paper with an air of false confidence.

'Maria told me to bring my own pictures,' she said, 'so I can learn how to develop.'

'You don't know how to develop,' he said.

'No,' she said, 'but I don't think it's as complicated as Bach.'

They spent the afternoon in the darkroom, developing the film she had brought with her – shots of her father in a *cristallerie*, taken with a thirty-five-millimeter Leica. She was not as confident as he wished her to be, and her arms looked thin in the dim red safelight. But her hand with the tilted wristwatch moved slowly and intelligently over the dark glistening trays, reaching between the bottles and funnels for tongs or the thermometer.

'Don't judge me too harshly,' she said as she leaned down to try to see her father's image on the contact sheet.

'I'm not judging,' he said.

'When they're enlarged, you'll see how clumsy they are.'

'Not at all,' he said.

'Well, my father will hate them.'

But the photographs were rather nice. She picked up the contact sheet with tongs and pulled it slowly from the developer. The clotheslines suspended red blinking stars above them on strips of shiny film and on the 9 x 12 centimeter negatives from the actress shoot: the dark torn nightgown and dark bare breasts with nipples like two white coins.

'Check your timer,' Philippe told her. The warm, dark air smelled like vinegar. He had never been in a darkroom with a woman before. Her face was not so exotically beautiful as Ruth's face, but it was impossible not to stand close to her in the little room, and, in the half-darkness, he felt free to look her up and down. She was only twenty-three and her body was that of a healthy twenty-three-year-old, with an ass in fact of such perfection and excitement that a palace ought to be constructed in its honor. But it might have been an effect of the darkness. 'Why will your father judge you?'

Her father had been forced off the board of Moser Glass, she said. Her father had been the last of his brothers on the board. The Germans in the Sudetenland had smashed a vitrine and fifty bowls of Alexandrit glass on the pavement outside the *cristallerie* in Karlovy Vary. In days past, she said, they'd designed glass for popes and kings. Now the Moser family was ruined.

She stirred the bath in silence for a while, then said, 'My father pretends that he's not a Jew. He still works for the company here in Paris, even though the Germans have taken it from him.'

Philippe thought of the little dictator born on the Inn River and of the Maginot Line and the Minister of the Air. He hadn't even gone to Paul Painlevé's funeral. He mopped up some spilled hypo and threw down the rag. 'I won't talk about politics anymore,' he said harshly.

'Sorry,' Yvonne said.

'Hitler makes no difference to me,' he said. 'Some things can be relied upon. We're safe here in France.'

'I'm not sure,' she said.

He regretted all his desire for her ass and her sturdy twenty-three-year-old legs. She was weak. She could not help him overcome the mountain and his desire for her went out of him. 'Let's finish this,' he said.

The timer rang.

'The contact sheet,' Philippe ordered.

She fumbled around and turned off the timer, and he pulled the sheet from the development tray and slipped it into the stop bath. 'I prefer to overexpose and underdevelop,' he said harshly. He stirred the acid with the tongs, then pulled the sheet out and moved it into the next tray, stirred around the tips of the tongs in the fixer, and slipped the sheet into the final tray labeled L'EAU. Almost immediately he pulled it out again.

'You're suddenly in a hurry,' Yvonne said.

Philippe hung up the contact sheet with clothes pins. He wanted to shut her in the darkroom by herself, but instead he stood still and looked up at the negatives of the actress with the bare breasts. 'You were disgusted when I tore the girl's nightgown,' he said.

Yvonne said nothing.

'I knew it.'

'You don't know anything,' she said.

'What did you think?'

'I'm a Parisian girl, you know.'

'So.'

'To be honest, it excited me.'

Philippe thought about that for a bit. He stood up and stepped up close to her body in the warm vinegar-smelling darkness. She didn't move, and couldn't have even if she'd wanted to since there was nowhere to go. He grabbed hold of her and hugged her warm body against his and looked into the dark with the red stars wavering on the negatives above. She didn't hug him back at first, and then she did. That caused something to stir in him and he stepped back from her, but kept his hands on her body, and because of the darkness, his thumb touched the side of her bra. Philippe could feel her breathing. The end of his thumb was just touching the soft bulge of her breast. He felt another question rising up out of him, but he decided that statements must replace questions at the moment of bold action, and that all statements at present would be made with his hands.

11. Octopus

Someone must have been telling lies about Joseph K., for
without having done anything wrong he was arrested one
fine morning.

FRANZ KAFKA, *The Trial*

Philippe allowed Yvonne to assist him on another shoot that
week and they went into the darkroom again for another lesson. They kissed in the dark, and without meaning to, he
called her 'a little ladybug.' She lifted her hand to her face and
pretended to scratch her nose. The following week, she came
back and they went into the darkroom three more times.

Fall seemed to come early, and they went around Paris
together in high, chilly winds. The sandwich bags blew away
and flew over the white sands around the fountain and on
somewhere into the Jardin trees.

'What were you laughing about at breakfast?' he said.

'I'll tell you,' she said, and started laughing again so she
couldn't get any words out.

'You like to have a private joke with yourself.'

'You're the spy,' she said.

'Who am I spying for?'

'I don't know,' she said. 'You wouldn't be a very good spy
if you let me know that.'

'And you want to know my secrets.'

'God forbid.'

'They're not secrets,' Philippe said. 'They're just things I don't talk about because no one would understand them. I don't understand them.'

'Try me,' she said.

'Maybe I will,' he said.

'Here,' she said. And she pulled a piece of gray yarn out of her pocket. 'I knit,' she said. 'And somehow this ended up inside my pants, like this.' She pulled aside her coat and pulled up her blouse and pushed the thread of yarn into her pants along the young naked skin of her lower stomach. 'I kept pulling it out and tried to wind it discreetly around my finger, but it kept coming and coming!'

'I like that you knit,' he said. He liked schoolmarmish women who cited Balzac and knitted and understood suffering and showed him their naked lower abdomens. 'But perhaps you should try knitting with your pants on to avoid such entanglements!'

'No, knitting in the nude is so much more fun,' she said. She was still pulling open her own pants and looking inside them, seemingly unaware of what response this might create.

'Like the Ancient Greeks did it,' he said.

'Yes, nude knitting. Like the ancients. Oh, look! What a coincidence!'

A ladybug had landed on the sand in front of Yvonne's feet.

Almost by an involuntary movement, Philippe suddenly crushed the insect under his foot.

She stared at him.

They were both quiet. They sat and watched the three children playing near the bench. The blond one had a ball, but the other two – both smaller, with brown hair – didn't want to play with the ball. The blond boy said, 'Do you want to play?' but the other boys ran off.

'Have you ever been in love?' Philippe asked.

'Yes. With Bach.'

'But really.'

'I guess once or twice I thought I was. Have you?'

'I'm not sure I know anymore what love is. What is it?'

'You told me you fall in love with your models,' Yvonne said. 'So you tell me.'

The boy with the ball stood up and called to the other two boys. The brown-haired boys came near again and stood before the blond boy, considering. 'Let's get away from him,' one said.

'Yeah,' said the other. They ran away again, all the way to the fountain.

'I think attraction is always to that which you cannot have. I never loved so well as I did when I was separated from everyone I loved.'

'When were you separated from everyone you love?'

He said nothing.

'The spy returns,' she said.

The two boys came back and started to hit and kick the boy with the ball. The boy with the ball laughed.

'That's only how men love,' Yvonne said.

'Hitting and kicking?'

'No, always hungry for something else.'

'That's how everyone loves.'

Now the two boys were kicking and hitting the other one in the stomach harder than before. The blond boy stopped laughing and cried out in surprise, 'Ow!'

'Let's take his ball,' said one.

'Yeah,' said the other.

The first boy wrestled away the blond boy's ball and smashed him over the head with it. Then the pair ran away with the ball and the blond boy yelled with all his little power, hands clenched in rageful fists, 'I'm going to punch you two in the eyes!' The other boys yelled far away, by the fountain, and danced with wild screams and shouts.

'But I don't think I would fall out of love,' Yvonne said. She looked at the unhappy little scene of the three children and added, 'Where are their mothers?'

Now the boys returned, one of them with the ball upraised in his hand, about to hurl it at the blond one.

'No!' Yvonne said, standing up. 'No hitting. No throwing balls at people.' The boy dropped the ball and the blond boy retrieved it, and all three ran off in different directions without another sound.

Philippe stood up and looked in the dust for the dead ladybug. 'I shouldn't have killed it,' he said.

It was time to do more than kiss, but they hadn't done more than that when Philippe invited Yvonne to *L'Hippocampe*, Jean's movie about the seahorse.

The main feature would be a film by Fritz Lang called *Le Testament du Dr Mabuse*, he explained, as though he were still giving photography lessons. Dr Mabuse was supposed to be Hitler, he said.

Philippe might have known it would be a strange evening when he found that one of the stars of *Mabuse* was an actor named 'Karl Meixner.' And when the lights on the high ceiling went down to barely glowing bulbs and Jean's *chevaux marins* began swimming through the dusty half-light, he felt still stranger, because Jean wasn't there. He hadn't spoken to Jean in a month or more and he felt a powerful longing to be near to him, an actual artist, the first living human being he had seen make art before his very eyes, with tools and instruments that had never made art before. Somebody shouted rudely, 'Give us Mabuse!' and Philippe wished to stand up and shout back, but Jean's quiet voice went on speaking the carefully wrought poetry on the life of seahorses. Magnified, the little aquariums from the institute under Rue Armand-Moisant now looked like a sea, with big particles of sand or scales twinkling in the water like motes of dust in sunlight.

When *Mabuse* began, Philippe felt stranger yet, as he saw the basement laboratory, almost like Jean's institute, thrumming, shaking with the rhythmic sound of marching boots or a locomotive slowly starting down the tracks: the counterfeiters' printing press on the floor above shaking the lanterns and the bottles on the crate, swaying the rope hanging beside the door. March. March. March. March. Philippe sensed instantly that someone or something was hiding in the room. It concealed something. And, in fact, someone was hidden in the basement – a terrified man. The character's name was Hofmeister. The man sitting behind nudged Philippe, then pointed ahead into the dark: 'Karl Meixner.' But the actor looked nothing like the Innsbruck pathologist. Hofmeister hid behind a crate like a nervous mouse, a pistol against his chest, then ran.

Nature calls, Philja. You go on ahead, and I'll catch up.
Nature calls, Philja.
Nature calls.
The wall of alder leaves
Plum, plum, plum.

He suddenly imagined a giant seahorse sitting where Yvonne sat. If you listened closely to your own mind, you found things like giant talking seahorses. He shivered. 'Why is it so cold, M. Cheval Marin?' he asked the seahorse. 'Is there something wrong with the heat in this theater?'

'It's because of death, Philippe,' the seahorse said. 'Only time separates us from death, and time is melting away. The cold of death is merely growing stronger as the seconds slip away between now and death. Another war is coming in Europe, you know, so death may come quite soon to all of us.'

A seahorse looking at him with one bulbous, lidless eye.

Philippe wanted to say something to Yvonne, but he didn't know what to say.

The male seahorse bears the young. And do you know about the octopus? Once the eggs are laid, the mother never eats again. She watches over the young till they hatch, then promptly dies. The father can live only a number of weeks after mating. When the young hatch, the father is already dead or wandering the reef as a ghost in the terminal phases of its short life.

If he thought hard enough, he could sense his father just there, just beside him in a movie theater, breathing loudly through the mouth, sniffling from a cold, as he had the last time they'd gone to the theater together, in Berlin. His thoughts were an octopus that grabbed its tentacles around anything pleasant. It had released his nudes and his photographs now that he was a 'success,' now that he made money, and now the octopus had laid its arms around this stupid little date and filled his mind with that rotten fairy tale: his father's head floated in a jar off in the laboratory of an evil scientist who experimented on the dead.

Herr Vorsitzender will recall that this murder took place high in the mountains. Dr Rainer standing so close he could see the pores on his nose. *It looks like rain, you can tell by the wind, better hurry to Breitlahner.* The innkeeper with the alpine hat tufted with gray chamois wool clapping the doctor on the back. Papa would not have minded the man. *We have a train to catch in Mayrhofen.*

'You know, murdering one's father is a very serious offense,' the seahorse said.

'Or even hurting his feelings, really,' the octopus added.

'Don't you read the newspapers? It's the Austrian courts that are under trial now, not me.'

'Your father's feelings were badly bruised,' the seahorse said. 'It's serious to hurt your father's feelings, because we only live once in this life of ours. And what's once said to a mother or father, or even an aunt, uncle, or cousin, cannot be unsaid. I always send my father a tin of candied fruits at Christmas. Easy and tasteful, I think, without great harm to the pocketbook.'

'I didn't hurt anyone,' Philippe said.

'But, you didn't go to Paul Painlevé's funeral,' the octopus said. 'That's why Jean doesn't like you anymore.'

What had he said? What were the last words before he'd heard the little cry through the alder leaves?

A dull pain was aching in Philippe's side. Could he be bleeding? Tubercles in the lung could remain dormant for years and then bleed again, they said. That was it. He was bleeding. He would die right there and then.

'Are you all right?' Yvonne said.

She was looking at him in the dark. Up on the screen, Dr Mabuse was making a vitriolic speech with Hitler's hand gestures: two fists rising in unison up the sternum and together down! Back of the fist smashing into the open palm. *L'empire du crime*, he said. *Herrschaft des Verbrechens*. The Empire of Crime. 'Yes, of course,' Philippe said. *Ruhe, hier ist Justiz! Hier ist Verbrechen.*

Philippe remembered just then a dream he'd had the night before. Karl Meixner had imprisoned him in an amphitheater deep under the Prison de la Santé. The pathologist had been dissecting corpses, and there had been a little seahorse there lying on a gurney, dying of dehydration in a circle of alpine roses.

Meixner had said to him: 'I see you take an interest in the changes of the dead.'

He put the images out of his mind. The girl would think he'd gone mad.

Yvonne was watching the film again. Philippe too tried to focus on the images in front of him: Kommissar Lohman, fiddling with his pocket watch, rocking it back and forth like an open clamshell on his desk blotter.

He had composed himself by the time they came back into the lobby of the theater. Yvonne looked at him again as though trying to divine some secret. They stood on the red carpet as the people streamed around them and out the glass doors. She was waiting for him to act, and yet he felt as he did when Frederick the Warlike's electoral sword hung above him in the marble gloom.

'I liked the character of Kommissar Lohman,' she said, 'his cigars and his booze and his lust for life. It reminded me of what you said about living without fear.'

He led her out into the chilly air. It was unseasonably cold, like winter. 'I must go on to my studio,' he said. 'I left some proofs there.'

'That's OK,' she said. 'It's on the way to my place. But, are you all right?'

'Yes.' He could see that she intended to come with him into the studio. 'I'll get the proofs tomorrow,' he said.

They got into a cab and traveled in silence. When they reached Yvonne's apartment, she invited Philippe upstairs for some wine.

'I don't drink,' he said.

'Oh,' Yvonne said. She looked as white as Jean's octopus the day he'd fed her a rotten egg. She got out of the cab.

Seahorses. Mountains. Pitons. Foreheads. Do not let Papa

down. He slid across the seat after her and shouted, 'But tonight I'm quite thirsty!'

Together they climbed the creaky staircase and walked along the stained brown carpet in the hall. In the apartment, there was almost nothing but a huge piano and a little table with a bottle of cut red tulips. There seemed to be little heat in the place, though a radiator was somewhere clanking, and the air was cold. The door to her bedroom was open and it appeared that the bedroom was not much larger than the bed. He could see a violet bedspread on the bed and a white afghan folded at the end of it.

Yvonne put a record on. 'You can dance the java to this. Do you dance?'

'In fact, I'm a very dangerous dancer,' Philippe said. 'I'm no longer allowed to dance in several European countries.'

'You step on girls' toes?' She brought him a glass of water.

'No, it's because my dancing is so outrageously beautiful that all the girls – and boys, too, really – swoon from sheer awe and they smack their heads on hard objects. This is considered manslaughter in Austria.' He felt like crying for some reason. He remained seated at the table with his glass of water, as Yvonne danced a few steps by herself.

'When's the last time you danced?'

He couldn't remember a time, besides the day in Liouba's apartment, when he'd danced with his mother. 'There's a *bal musette* near the studio I've been to.'

'The *bals musettes* are for kids,' Yvonne said. 'I'll take you to one of the *clubs de nuit* if you pay for the drinks.'

'I have no sense of rhythm,' he said. He felt those old tears in his throat.

'It doesn't matter,' Yvonne said. 'I can't afford nice clothes anymore and that's a much worse offense at those places.'

'Perhaps we could help each other, then,' Philippe said,

still wanting to cry. 'I'm good with women's clothes.' A chill passed through him and rippled the skin on his arms. 'Maybe we should go back outside – it would be warmer.'

'Yes, the bedroom is the only warm place in the apartment.'

'Right,' he said.

It was as though one part of him had split off and was standing aside and carrying on the conversation. The doppelgänger had some wit, it seemed, but not much strength. It could not climb mountains.

'How do they punish you for dancing in Austria?' Yvonne said.

'Four years of Austrian cuisine. Oh, and you must glue 400,000 paper bags.'

He sat at the table and she danced self-consciously by herself until the record ended. Then she kicked off her shoes and went to her bedroom and climbed into the bed. 'This is how I get through the winters,' she said.

He untied his heavy shoes and went to the bed. When it grew warm from their bodies together under the covers, Yvonne pulled her clothes from underneath and, one at a time, laid the undergarments on top – the black bra, stockings, garter, panties. She lay on her back, and the violet bedspread sank down between her parted knees.

He didn't move.

'You look like you want to cry,' she said.

'The fascists will get us,' he said, and tears did start to spring from his eyes.

'I'm sorry I upset you that day in the darkroom,' she said.

He told her that his father fell, that they had accused him, that it was anti-Semitism. He wept a long time, a great cleansing gush of tears. Then he calmed down and breathed slowly in the dark. 'I photographed him with a third of a second,' he said. 'There's my father looking at me for a third of a second. That's all I have left, a third of a second.' *Would you enlighten the court as to what you mean when you say, "an Oedipus Complex"?*

Yvonne was very gentle with him, and he was very grateful. It was not a bold action when he lost his virginity again – for it had been so long, that was just how it felt. And when it was done, he was the octopus, flushing with unexpected moods. *Les amours de la pieuvre.* When it was done, he noticed once again how thin were her arms, and how solicitous was her gaze. How weak.

'Philippe,' she said, 'you've showed me something very special with your camera.' Her lips were drawn nearly together as if she were about to ask some question that began with *quoi*.

'Well?' he said.

'Do you need an assistant?' Yvonne said, finally.

'I can't pay for one,' he said.

'You wouldn't have to pay me,' she said.

She was disgustingly weak, not like Geneviève. There was no joy in such a weakling. There was nothing to report to Jean and Geneviève, and no victory over the mountain. He felt a sudden urge to hurt her and he told her she ought to have more ambition.

She didn't raise her head from the pillow, but opened her eyes up wide.

'Don't define yourself through me,' he said. 'Show some independence.' Then, as if his words had so far failed to injure her sufficiently, he added, 'You have no courage.'

Yvonne flung away the bedspread and stood up naked in the cold air. 'Who made you my critic?' She began pulling on her clothes. 'I have skills of my own. I am a pianist.'

'I know that,' Philippe said. The color of the octopus was again shifting. This was not what he'd wanted.

Yvonne looked around the bed for her clothes and began to cry. 'Go away,' she said, and he immediately felt wounded as if it were she who'd first injured him.

He went away. When he reached the street, Philippe pulled his thin jacket close around himself. The autumn night was crystalline and dry like a night in Innsbruck; each lamp cast a pure and heatless light onto the bare trees and cobblestones. He thought of the octopus in Jean's basement, long since consumed in a bouillabaisse. They really did change color, from orange to black to blue to white – the color of their displeasure. He thought of an octopus's baggy white head arisen suddenly from the sea floor. He'd actually seen that underwater on the Côte d'Azur with Jean and Captain Le Prieur, who said he preferred German fascists to French socialists. The captain had tried to spear her, and she lifted up suddenly in a commotion of sand, tentacles, ink, and blood, that funny fleshy skirt stretched tight over her many arms, white with dismay.

12. The Courtrooms of the Mind

Strangely enough, I was not aware of any movement by
my father; it was a picture in arrested motion. I almost
don't see the incline at all. But my father is standing at the
edge. His hands clutching the straps of his rucksack. He
is at an unbelievable angle in a backwards and somewhat
sideways-oriented position. I didn't see any more.

PHILIPP HALSMANN, in a statement written for
Kommissar Wilhelm Kasperer, September 1928

He was so distraught about the whole evening that he wished
to kill himself again. He hadn't felt that since Meran, but
now he felt a terrible self-hatred – for his frivolous photography, for his nudes, for his cowardice before Le Prieur,
for his unkindness to Yvonne and his neglect of his mother,
and for his failure to live and love like Jean and Geneviève.
The mountain had conquered him because he was too weak.

He walked for a while on the spacious glowing sand before
the Palais du Luxembourg and went to the tree where the
American girl had long ago sat. There were two old ladies
there in gloves with no fingertips, playing cards. He'd never
seen the girl in the park again after that night he photographed her nude, after she'd bared herself to him with all
her flaws – the little mole under her left breast. She'd never
even asked to see the pictures.

The pietà awaited him. The subversive Quarton with its

bleeding haloes would not suffice. It would have to be the marble one at Notre Dame, stout, white, cold, stone. He went in silence out of the public garden, past the lycée, and out onto Boulevard du Montparnasse. He walked right past the many people talking, drinking coffee, reading evening newspapers, past the many beautiful women in colorful scarves, past the braziers smoldering with hot coals and the tungsten lamps shining like cold crystals. The pain gripped his side again and he had to stop and rest against a lamp-post. The pain had come and gone over the last weeks, but in recent days it had grown hard to ignore, like it was in Stein.

He breathed very small and shallow breaths. The door to the café just near him was propped open, and waiters hurried in and out of it. Faintly, the sound of violins spilled out. '*Bon soir*,' said a voice. A little Maltese on a leash was sniffing around his shoes, and the old man holding the leash gave Philippe a glittery, winking smile. The gentleman carried an acrylic glass cane, and whistled with the violins, which were playing *Eine kleine Nachtmusik*. Philippe smiled back, if only to certify that he was not insane, that he understood how merry the music sounded to the average human being, and how young he looked to outward appearances. Of course, in the brimming, floody eyes of an old man, his worries deserved no more than a wink. What could be so wrong, after all, with all the grim years of death and decay now standing before him? No, he wouldn't live out his days making phony faces at old men because of some maudlin violins. He would rather be dead. He would rather be buried today in the Cimetière du Montparnasse. The violins didn't cheer him at all. He remembered dancing with Ruth on the promenade at Lugano with the lake beside them. Now those were violins to make your heart soar.

There was hardly any point in going to Notre Dame. He had memorized the face of the pietà and in fact it now made him sick. Just now, it filled him with a boiling rage of the kind he'd felt in Yvonne's bed, a rage that physically hurt his ribs, like a tubercle bursting through his body wall. There was nowhere to go. No one to go to. The many beautiful women transfixed in his mind as on photographic plates thronged in his memory and he wished to photograph more and more of them in images of perfectly deceptive beauty and to go to the sink in the room at the hotel by the seminary. He physically ached to do it, but he wouldn't.

CHORUS:
There is no clash of brazen shields but our fight is with the
    War God,
a War God ringed with the cries of men, a savage God who
    burns us

He had rung up Jean three times, but Jean didn't answer, wasn't there. The Painlevés cared for him. But the minister was dead, and what could Jean do for him, anyway? Jean would hate his suicidality and self-pity, that weakness on the mountain to which his family line had succumbed – his foolish father, never knowing if he were being laughed at, telling Philippe to trek without a shirt, to show the pimples between his skinny shoulder blades to the uncircumcised shepherds and guiltless drinking men of the mountain, his father smiling away and all the while pushing and pushing on his weak rotten heart until it broke. God damn Jean to hell.

OEDIPUS:
Hark to me; what I say to you, I say
as one that is a stranger to the story
as stranger to the deed

He couldn't go to Liouba and Mama in the Place de l'Opéra, either. It was too far to walk with his side hurting him the way it did and he had no money for a car. He wished to go to Liouba and joke with her as he used to, staying up talking beside a candle. There was a code, he remembered, whereby they could communicate without Mama and Papa understanding them. They used it on trains. The first letter of the first noun in the sentence. *J'ai cassé le vase . . . Quel est l'amour parfait? . . . C'est une goutte d'eau dans la mer . . . Êtes-vous un ichtyologiste? . . .* Right in front of Mama. They would laugh and laugh. But if he went there now, they would hurry around in their robes solicitously. They would tell him it was all just fine, they would lie and lie. Hiding among women. That was no way to avenge himself on the mountain.

> *OEDIPUS:*
> *So I stand forth a champion of the God*
> *and of the man who died.*
> *Upon the murderer I invoke this curse —*
> *whether he is one man and all unknown,*
> *or one of many — may he wear out his life*
> *in misery and miserable doom!*
> *If with my knowledge he lives at my hearth*
> *I pray that I myself may feel my curse*

God damn Jean. Where was he? A man was needed now, not a crying woman, strength was needed, and truth. *I'm sorry I failed to find your killer, Papa. You were right about my loud mouth. I'm sorry I let those Austrians defeat me with my loud mouth. I'm sorry I let Mama hire a Jew the first time and screw it all up. I'm sorry we were all so weak. I'm sorry I failed you. And I'm sorry you dragged me all across the Alps and I'm sorry you left me behind to rot for two years in an Austrian prison. I'm sorry that I hate you, Papa, you stupid corpse.*

TEIRESIAS:

I say you are the murderer of the king
whose murderer you seek

The pain in his side was so strong then that Philippe sank
onto the pavement and twisted his ankle. Jean was right.
They should write that play, the one about the man who is
falsely accused, who gets out of prison and can't forgive
himself for being alive. *Agenbite of inwit*, as he'd read in the
Maison des Amis des Livres.

At three in the morning, he turned the key to his apartment door. He was too tired to wash his face, and after
pulling off his clothes by the closet, he buried himself under
the blankets. When he'd closed his eyes, unmoving faces,
arms, legs, people materialized on the dark mirrors of his
retinas and then, as if stung by an adder, slowly swelled until
they filled his eyes with their distorted shapes.

'Good as new,' the little man said. He polished Philippe's
glasses with a chamois and handed them across the dusty
plank, which was piled with boxes of lenses and heaps of
tangled frames.

One of the hinges had separated. When he'd lifted his
glasses from the nightstand that morning, the temple came
right off the frames, and though he'd spent a half an hour on
his hands and knees, peering with a flashlight at the dust
bunnies under the bed, he couldn't find the tiny screw.

'Come back for an exam,' the man said, handing him a card.

'*Opticiens Fauvel et Fils. Depuis 1930.* I see. Thank you.'

'I'm the son.'

The man seemed very happy to be working with his dad,
and unaffected by the desperation that haunted the shop-
keepers these days. Imagine that, working with one's father.
When he was thirteen or so and having his teeth examined,

Papa had pointed out that the office next door was for rent. The old doctor who worked there for many years had just died. So should Philippe one day want to come back to Riga and practice medicine there beside him ... Yes, then they could always be there together, just the two of them, side by side, forever. They could wind down the passage of time to a dead stop.

Philippe went out into the bright sun. He could see again. Dozens of automobiles careened on the stones around the Arc de Triomphe, leaning on their wheels and making sporadic noises from their tailpipes like volatile bursts of inhuman speech.

He looked past the swerving and careening cars in the traffic circle to the Arc. The structure looked beautiful today with the hot light on its white stones. He suddenly wanted to climb to the top of it and survey all of Paris in the light of this stupendous day. And he jumped off the curb, over a sewer grate, and walked out into the circle of cars.

He was winded when he reached the stairwell, where a scary woman accosted him from within her heap of ragged sweaters. She had a dirty bicycle with an unraveling straw basket on it, and the basket was full of folded white pamphlets, two of which she held up to his face in fingers that were black under the fingernails. He took one, dropped a sou in her palm, and ran up the stairs. There were just a couple of tourists there, an American man with a little girl, and the view was better than he'd imagined: light warmed the cold slate rooftops all across the city and illuminated all the streets, the twelve astral spokes around the Place de l'Étoile. The Eiffel Tower, across the river to the south, was drenched in light. How many wondrous things had happened in this city, and how many more wondrous things were to come? A few empyrean clouds were stationed above like great monuments, like mountains in the air. He unfolded the pamphlet in the flapping breeze, the same misspelled sort of document on cheap paper that he'd seen outside the churches. He'd forgotten that Napoleon built the Arc after conquering Austria and taking its archduchess for his bride, and forgotten too that the Arc's eternal flame was the first on earth since the vestal virgins were thrown out of the temple. The pamphlet had educated him after all. He looked down over the railing and saw the ragged woman with the dirty fingernails lying down beside her bicycle on the stones. His side was still hurting him, but he felt better in his mind and disinclined to kill himself.

Things were changing fast in Europe. Yvonne read the newspapers and understood perfectly what was going on over there, across the Maginot Line. Because of that, and because he was a man of bold action, it took him only a little while to telephone Yvonne's father. He did it first thing in the morning, and it seemed to make his side slightly worse. In fact, it tired him to cross the room, and he felt vaguely feverish. (There was no denying it now; he would have to see a physician.) He took a warm bath, anointed himself with perfumed soap, and dressed in a newly pressed shirt and pants. He waited till five o'clock, then he headed back out into the cold autumn wind.

He met Yvonne's father, Gustav, at a little bistro across from the Opéra Comique.

When Philippe entered the bistro, Gustav was already seated and consuming a white loin of pork with cabbage leaves. He was in a more unpleasant humor than usual. 'Sit,' he said, dabbing at his gray handlebar mustache with the napkin and then swishing some red wine into his mouth. 'What do you want to eat?'

'It's too early,' Philippe said. 'I'll just have coffee.' Beyond the restaurant windows, the Opéra glowed under a granite sky.

'I'll order you the pork then,' Gustav said, without looking at him.

'Thank you,' Philippe said.

'Did you hear about the riots on the Kurfürstendamm?' the weary-looking little man said. 'You read about them, yes?'

'I did.'

'A taste of what's to come,' the old man said. 'They'll be here on Boulevard des Italiens soon enough.'

'I've come to ask your permission,' Philippe said, 'to ask Yvonne to marry me.'

'I gathered that,' Gustav said. He put his elbows on the table and leaned his face forward beside his interleaved fingers, long and delicate – Yvonne's fingers. 'Life is short, Philippe. What do you do with your time? Go to parties? To this club of yours, the Club des Sous l'Eau, you call it, this silly club of atheists and drunkards?'

Philippe methodically chewed up the pork and swallowed. 'What is your reply?' he said.

'Yvonne is free to marry whomever she chooses. I have no money to withhold from her anyway.' He laughed bitterly. 'Just remember that her youth is short. And so is yours, shorter than you think. Respect death in this decision of yours.'

Somehow the voice of the prosecutor, Hohenleitner, entered his mind: *The family can sue you. For what? For charades. For reckless endangerment of the girl's future. For breach of promise. They used to sue for it all the time in the last century. Do not play with this young lady's fortunes as you did with the last girl. Her eggs are jewels.*

When he got to Yvonne's apartment, she was just coming down the front steps with her camera slung over her shoul-

der, and was very surprised to see him. It was almost dark by
now.

'You're all perspired!' she said. 'Are you ill?'

'No,' he said, though it winded him to stand upright beside
the iron railing.

'You're ill,' she said.

She took him to the doctor, a young man with long hair
who listened to his chest and told him immediately: it was a
recrudescence of the tuberculosis. A logical punishment for
falling in love.

Philippe rested for a month, during which time he had
three more fevers. He had to tell himself repeatedly that
fever had nothing to do with love and was connected to his
wedding only in that magical insane old cathedral of his
unconscious mind. But during the last fever, he dreamed of
Karl Meixner again and the amphitheater deep below the
Prison de la Santé.

Philippe was alone with the dead seahorse and two human
corpses in the collapsing lecture hall. He had killed the people,
and in the dream, murder was a pleasant deed, like eating pork
loin. But then he'd been caught by the Austrian police, and the
murders no longer seemed pleasant. Now everyone would
know what he'd done. Now he was ruined. Meixner interro-
gated him there on the stage at the bottom of the amphitheater
and instructed him to water the body of the seahorse. And he
cast a magic spell over him to command him to remain there
and obey, and then he exited through a low blue door, like the
door to a garden shed, and locked it behind him. Philippe did
for a time continue to douse the seahorse's body with water
from a flask, as though it were his last hope of absolution. But
it occurred to him that absolution might mean being there forever – that is, until his death – and soon enough, his love of
the upper world prevailed over the dank vast emptiness of the

amphitheater. He leapt up to try to grasp the ledge at the top of the theater wall, but it was too high. So he dragged the two corpses to the base of the theater wall and piled the headless man on top of the beaten, bruised woman. He ran toward the wall and, planting one foot on the back of the man, vaulted upward. He wondered if the Nazi magic would stop him, but nothing did. He climbed up easily into the aisle. He glanced back at the little seahorse on the gurney, circled with red flowers, and it occurred to him that that freedom from magic which had allowed him to climb up was the very same unconstrained and immoral freedom that had allowed him to kill the two people in the amphitheater. He was infected with an unfeeling, murderous freedom. Yvonne woke him. He was screaming in his sleep. He sat in bed for a while with human bones in his mind, his own skeleton, as if viewed from behind, and the indelible stain of murder guilt. But he was able to go back to sleep then, because the dream began to relax its hold on him, and he slowly remembered that he had not in fact killed anyone.

PART IV
The Leap

1. News

BERLIN – A wave of destruction, looting and incendiarism unparalleled in Germany since the Thirty Years' War and in Europe generally since the Bolshevist revolution, swept over Great Germany today as National Socialist cohorts took vengeance on Jewish shops, offices and synagogues for the murder by a young Polish Jew of Ernst vom Rath, third secretary of the German Embassy in Paris.

The New York Times, 11 November 1938

The final meeting of the Club des Sous l'Eau that summer of 1938 was so pleasant it was hard to ponder world affairs. They had convened once again at the villa of Captain Le Prieur on the Côte d'Azur. And though St Raphaël was eerily quiet – the prices had driven the tourists away – the villa itself thronged with tanned young women in sleeveless white dresses and men in fedoras and white linen shirts. Yvonne's pregnancy was just beginning to show, and she lay peacefully beside him with bare legs extended on the chaise, eyes closed in the sun. On his other side, at the foot of the white stucco wall, sat an enormous cactus in a white pot. How pleasant it was to sit on the bright patio, then swim, then sit again with damp hair until the sun had dried his skin; or, later in the day, to retire indoors and relieve his sunburn in the shade. How nice to feel crisp clean linen on his sun-bitten skin and to roam the tile floors amid baskets of pale-yellow immortelles.

It was almost sunset when Jean, Geneviève, Captain Le Prieur, and Louis de Corlieu returned from their dive at the sunken Roman village. Le Prieur had encouraged Yvonne to join in the *plongée*, but Philippe forbade it. Now Le Prieur aligned on the patio all the dripping shards of Roman pottery, some of it hairy with seaweed, and several slick black fish glittering with blue stars and dead. They had each been neatly perforated in the middle by Le Prieur's speargun, which lay on a chaise beside a row of air tanks.

'Congratulations!' Le Prieur said. 'When does he – or she – arrive?'

'Not until the winter, I hope,' Yvonne said.

Dimly, Le Prieur could be perceived to be grinning under his colossal nose. He was a giant and, though his limbs were lanky and unmuscular, Philippe had seen him lift six air tanks at once. 'Ah. After the war has begun, then?' Le Prieur said. 'If the communists have not completely destroyed our will to live.'

Philippe and Yvonne said nothing. Yvonne preferred to talk about the Germans, but Philippe preferred silence.

'Get dressed for dinner!' the captain commanded, and pivoted on his heels. 'The leeks are fresh – the idiots have finally repaired the highway.' Then he strode into the house, leaving long wet footprints behind and calling out, 'Martine!'

The light had suddenly grown severe over the Spanish tiles on the villa's roof. The other guests had already withdrawn and a great quiet had befallen the mountainside: above, the Estérel Massif, the purple volcanoes where they quarried the blue porphyry for France's roads, and below, the golden light on the tiny boats, whose rigging clanged like distant bells. The scent of pine was sharp in the newly cool and shadowed air.

*

Fascism continued to be a difficulty, especially in the bedroom. Sometimes Yvonne began talking about the offices in Karlovy Vary right in the middle of things, when he had already half-prevailed over her, and he was studying her beautiful bare legs in the partial light inside the mirror on the bathroom door. She would choose that instant to tell him that Henlein's goons had bashed her Uncle Leo in the head with a clock and painted swastikas on the Moser family linens. He would touch her in the darkroom, and she would ask him whether there would be a war over the Sudetenland. Then he would wonder if Frau Hitt and the Brandjoch would finally defeat him after all.

But there were several surrealists at the villa, and surrealists, if nothing else, made excellent dinner companions. Philippe enlisted Georges Hoyningen-Huene, another photographer for *Vogue* and an aspiring Dadaist, in the fight against lugubrious conversation. Jean could not be relied upon for this purpose anymore; he had lately been arguing with Le Prieur at every opportunity about Hitler and the Action Française, and Philippe no longer saw as much of him and Geneviève as he had when he was single.

So, while the servants brought shrimp canapés to the long table and set them down between the candles, Georges did his best to regale the guests with stories of his experiments in the art of chaos. Georges had himself shown Philippe and Yvonne the false steps he'd painted on the wall of the circular stair at La Quatrième République in the Rue Jacob. His mastery of perspective was such that one drunk patron had smacked his head into the wall and tumbled down to the bottom.

'The proprietor was not amused,' Georges said. 'M. Chuzeville didn't bring out the *pelure d'oignon* again for a month!' Georges leaned over to Philippe then and said, 'You still don't drink? What's wrong with you?'

'I should, theoretically, drink,' Philippe agreed, and yawned. He didn't sleep much these days, because he thought about Germans all night.

'M. Chuzeville is a very smart man,' Le Prieur said from the end of the table, where he was peeling the foil off a bottle of red wine. 'One should invest in his restaurant now that the Third Republic is on its last legs. Have you seen the lamp-posts? Everywhere, LA FRANCE EST FICHUE.'

'France is not sunk!' Philippe said. 'And anyway, Captain, let's not discuss politics before we eat. Georges, tell us about the time André Breton set fire to your aunt's wig.'

But the captain and Jean would not be deterred. 'Dinner is my favorite time to discuss politics,' Le Prieur said. 'It's a digestif.' He pulled the cork from the bottle and began to administer the wine. 'We call this "rabbit's blood".'

'And why is the republic on its last legs?' Jean asked. If Jean insisted on talking politics, Philippe wished he would talk about the visa. He reached under the table and buried his hand between his wife's legs.

'Other than the inflation? Other than the economy?' Le Prieur said. 'Other than Léon Blum? Other than the fact that no one works in France? The landslide was six years ago and only now do they finish repairing the road to Antibes. Were you with us during the storm, Jean? Did you see the water-spout on Toulon Harbor? Amazing.' The captain began to open a second bottle of rabbit's blood.

'The Popular Front needn't worry you, Yves,' Jean said. 'Your real problem is six hundred miles to the east.'

Philippe said, 'The real problem was that Georges's aunt had so much wax under her wig.'

'It was not Breton who did it,' Georges said, but Le Prieur shouted over him.

'And why is he my problem? The fact is, Hitler has the

right idea. We'd all be better off under Hitler than under a Jew like Léon Blum!'

'You think the children in the Camelots du Roi will run this government better than Blum?' Jean shouted. Geneviève just yawned.

'I destroyed a hundred spy balloons during the war,' the captain said. 'What will the Jews and Marxists do to defend the republic? They don't care about France.'

'And Hitler,' Yvonne said, 'is not a problem for France?' Now the evening was truly lost. Philippe would never have any sex. 'It's all right with you,' Yvonne said, 'if he takes the Sudetenland as he took the Rhineland, as he took Austria?'

'They welcomed him in Austria,' Le Prieur said.

'Do you welcome him in Paris?' Yvonne said.

'At least they would fix the road to Antibes,' Le Prieur said, shoving a canapé into his mouth.

'All those unborn children of the Great War dead are starving the economy, not Léon Blum,' Jean said.

'I trust that you will not deport us from your dinner table, Captain,' Philippe said, 'for being Jews?'

'Oh, Halsman, you're not a Jew,' Le Prieur said. 'Not the kind I mean.'

'Can't we talk about something else?' Georges said. 'Let's paint. Or, better yet, let's take off all our clothes and parade naked to the bay!'

The whole table was silent. Philippe's comment was particularly awkward because of what had happened at the Pontoise swimming pool. 'Just don't deport me before the crêpes,' Philippe said, and all erupted into excessive laughter.

The corn crêpes came out, as did squab stuffed with foie gras. Georges Hoyningen-Huene drank the rest of the rabbit's blood and whispered to Philippe in Russian: 'Let's tie rocks to Le Prieur's feet and throw him off the pier.'

The dinner guests steered safely away from further political discussions, but Le Prieur would have darkness at his table in one way or another.

'Do you believe in spontaneous human combustion?' he asked. 'You know the coroners find these old ladies in their homes, in their rocking chairs or their armchairs, all burned up – nothing there but a pair of perfectly intact legs leaning against the chair, just where they'd be if someone were still sitting there, and a pile of ashes on the chair. Not even any bones. Perhaps the fat of the body burns at lower temperatures than wood, just like candle wax. But what about the bones? It's a mystery.'

And the rest of the guests went on talking about the dead almost as if dead bodies were a different species, or as if the people at the table happened to be exempt from death.

'Doesn't it hurt to be burned?' someone said.

'They are knocked unconscious from the smoke.'

'But they don't get up from their chairs?'

'They are asleep.'

'Can you imagine being burned alive?'

'Or your children burned? Such things happen in wars.'

'What do you imagine it is to be gassed?'

'1.4 million French were killed in the war.'

'And a million maimed for life, they say.'

'Imagine death on that scale.'

'We don't have to.'

What would the Romans who lived in the sunken village have said if they looked into the future and saw their city buried under the waves, a playground for fishes – and, occasionally, for alien beings with strange masks, plumes of bubbles rising from their faces, flippers on their feet, calling themselves in a language only faintly recognizable, 'the Club des Sous l'Eau'?

The Romans couldn't see the future, of course, even if they had their oracles. And the living, for now, couldn't know what would happen either. History was chaste about the future; it never revealed anything. Philippe imagined all those people in Paris during the Great War, not knowing what would happen. Something would, but they didn't know what. Philippe knew, of course, from his vantage point in the future. If he could go back in time to that moment, he wouldn't feel afraid. He'd know that Paris doesn't fall. But what would happen this time? Nobody knew. It wasn't the past yet. Someday it would be. Someday it would be written in history books. But it wasn't known now. What would happen there on the peaceful Estérel Massif, in the cork forests of Bormes and the cherry orchards of Solliès-Pont?

After dinner, Philippe took Yvonne back to the bedroom and threatened a hunger strike if she insisted on more talk of Le Prieur, war, the Sudetenland, or Adolf Hitler. And they did have sex, though he feared it would hurt the baby.

In the morning, Jean told him he had failed. Jean had written to the foreign ministry to secure French citizenship for Philippe and his mother, but where the ministry would surely have listened to the father, they would not listen to the son. Paul Painlevé was gone.

And Clemenceau, the Tiger of France, was gone. Schober was gone. Jakob Wassermann, the great novelist who'd defended Philippe in the *Neue Freie Presse*, gone too. Hindenburg, who'd once held Hitler's leash, dead, and King Albert of Belgium was gone and with him the French-Belgian alliance against Germany. All dead, gone. They were like the Romans of the sunken city: in the past now, and they would never know what came next.

'Never mind!' Philippe said. He told Jean that he had many

other angles to pursue, and though it was a lie, Jean seemed relieved. They really hadn't spoken in a long time.

'Listen,' Jean said, grabbing his arm, 'if there is war over the Sudetenland, where will you go?'

'We can go south to Cellettes, where my mother-in-law lives. But between the Nazis and my mother-in-law, it will be a tough choice.'

The two friends looked up into the sky and were silent. A plane was traveling down the coast, and they watched it approach until its shadow flashed over them.

'I'm sorry I missed the funeral,' Philippe said.

'No,' Jean said, waving his hand.

Philippe admired the handsome equine face of his friend, which was veiled in a half-light. He threw his arms around Jean.

'I think it's no good coming from a tiny place,' Philippe said. 'And a tiny people.'

'You're wrong,' Jean said. 'I'm a Jew at heart.'

That night, their last on the Côte d'Azur, Philippe looked at all of Yvonne's things there in the room – her hairbrush full of tangled-up hairs, her shoes standing alone before the closet door, her bag, her lipstick – and it seemed as though they belonged to someone who was no longer there, as though she had disappeared suddenly and left all her things.

'Why so many kisses?' she said.

In bed, he held her until she fell asleep. Then he lay awake all night listening to her breathe and thinking of the Germans and the indifferent limestone peaks, which he had studied for so many days from his prison-cell window.

Many Parisians fled south that September, only to return the following month, after Chamberlain and Daladier met Hitler at Munich. Philippe and Yvonne spread out the newspapers across the floor of the new studio at 350 Rue St-Honoré, or on the white table in Liouba's overheated *salle à déjeuner*. Since Jean had failed to win him citizenship, Philippe followed the news very carefully. They crowded into the breakfast room to listen together as voices crackled behind the console's impassive tall veneer, as its tuner wavered across remote frequencies as if in a swoon from too much information coming from too many places, too far away. René was impassive, whispering by the radio, interpreting, though everyone knew he'd be called into the army if war broke out, though Liouba had begun to chew her fingernails. At other times, Philippe sat alone by the cathedral radio late into the night and hobbled to bed on numb legs, or fell asleep in the studio office with the radio on and his head against the wall. One fact calmed him at night and helped him to sleep: his son or daughter would be born a French citizen. And despite the eerie ellipses and blank spaces on the front pages, as Liouba said, the newspapers remained optimistic.

The day the pogroms broke out in Austria and Germany, Philippe went out to the patisserie around the corner and deliberately bought two pieces of chocolate and coconut pavé with raspberry coulis. But they didn't have the appetite to prepare dinner, let alone to eat his dessert, and the little cakes sat on the table in a box tied with blue string, unopened. The light grew dim in the quiet apartment.

'Don't worry about your cousins,' Philippe said, as a man chattered rapidly on the radio about the violence in Berlin. Behind the rapid French, distant voices cried out, glass shattered. She picked up her father's Rauchtopas vase from the shelf and held it close against her chest. Neither she nor Philippe dared remark the irony of the name *Kristallnacht* and the ruination of her family's glassworks. Where was Ruth now? he wondered. Thinking of him today, no doubt.

Looking into the street from above as the store windows crashed down.

His wife sat on the sofa, closed her eyes, and silently breathed. Her slender fingers rested on her big round belly, and the loose wristwatch was turned on her wrist so it faced her feet. She waved her hands at the conservative newspapers that littered the salon floor, but said nothing.

'It's a riddle,' Philippe said. 'We Jews control the media, and the banks, and have the power to start world wars. How is it that none of us can persuade a single immigration officer to issue a visa?'

'I'm going to try to get through again,' she said.

'They won't kick me out, anyway. Who will photograph the leaders of the Action Française when they take office?'

Yvonne put down the phone. 'I won't go. But even your mother told me to go.'

'This is nonsense. Halsman always finds a way.'

He hugged Yvonne close and they held each other for a few minutes in the stillness of the early evening. It was time to turn on the lamps.

Philippe got up, plucked *Le Figaro* from the floor, and pointed to an image of a Nazi poster in Germany. 'That is why I never do photomontage,' he told Yvonne. Then he went to turn on the lights.

The world seemed to be changing in parallel with the changes in Philippe's own household. Yvonne's breasts had grown heavy and hard. Light-blue veins ran across her taut round belly and down the backs of her thighs like cracks in a retaining wall. The sight of a pregnant woman had filled him with a sense of serenity in the ignorant days of his youth, but there was nothing serene about these poor creatures whose bodies were stressed to the outer limits of natural possibility.

He worked on her red swollen feet at night. Meanwhile, Philippe's moleskin jacket, which he'd recently let out, now hung loose around him. He was shrinking again.

On 17 November, the day that Ernst vom Rath was laid to rest in Düsseldorf, Philippe opened up the back of the cathedral radio and replaced two frayed wires. Foreign Minister von Ribbentrop's voice was the first to speak when he screwed the plate back on again, and the voice said haunting things. Philippe turned the radio off and kept it off for a week or more. He placed his faith in the Maginot Line, and went on taking his coffee in the mornings at Café du Dôme and making his photographs in the afternoons. The pictures came even easier than before. His job was to remove the mask of false guilt in order to reveal the truth and beauty that lay beneath. It was a good job; it made people happy; it involved many beautiful women; and it had begun to pay well. He bought Yvonne a warm coat to wear once the baby was born. She could hardly believe she'd ever fit into such a tiny thing again.

2. Farewell

On the day when everything would seem to be lost, the
world will see what France is capable of.

French Premier PAUL REYNAUD, speaking to
the Chamber of Deputies, 16 May 1940

The baby screamed. Yvonne got out of bed in the dark and
the second siren joined the first.

Philippe pulled on his robe and went to the salon, where
they kept the crib. 'Irene,' Philippe said to the baby, though
he couldn't hear himself speak. 'Irene, it's just the *sirènes*.
Don't worry.'

Yvonne yelled something from the kitchen. He could
smell the gas from the stove.

Philippe lifted Irene from the crib with her lamb named
Annie (once white, now gray) and he felt Irene's wet lips
against his rough face. 'Sir. Sir,' she said.

Philippe pulled back the posterboard that was taped over
the window. He couldn't see any planes or any fire. The Seine
was barely visible, winding away in a sleepy dusky moonlight,
dark except for a few ripples twinkling where it turned
beyond the Pont de la Concorde. It was what Paris must have
looked like in the last century. Then tracer fire lifted into the
sky and shadows fell into the streets like the ones made by
fireworks, falling, turning, stretching, then gone.

When the milk was warm, they went down to the cellar

together. Madame du Motier had her little cat already, so Philippe didn't need to chase it out for her with his broom. Philippe was so tired his eyes hurt. He himself had not been able to sleep at all of late. The sound of the air-raid siren was loud enough, probably, to hear across the whole of Île de France, a whine like that of a massive wind. And worse than its final amplitude was the sound's long, slow rise, which more and more demanded release as it built and built in intensity, building until one's heart was bursting, then rising still more. When it was quiet, Philippe would lie awake waiting for it.

He went to the darkroom sometimes and worked then, thinking often of the stormtroopers pushing the Jewish men into the muddy stream in the Leipzig Zoo, and the rioters sitting in the broken glass trying on one pair of shoes after another with receipts and carbons flying in the air. And the following morning, the owners of Leipzigerstrasse, the children's furniture store where Papa had once bought him a little wind-up dog, taking measurements for a new plate-glass window! Just what Papa would have done!

The newspapers were a conundrum. If he studied the blank spaces between paragraphs long enough, he felt sure he could figure out what was going to happen. Surely, the government knew what Hitler was going to do; these days they had excellent spies. They had only prevented those parts from getting into the paper, that's why there were all the blank spaces. Reports of terrorist bombing of civilians in Brussels. He tried to remember the population of Brussels and the energy in TNT.

Philippe bought Liouba's old Citroën, and from an Algerian at the Halles Centrales he bought a canister of petrol, which cost almost as much as the car. Liouba had been on the march again, writing her letters, and some deputy minister with one arm had made arrangements for Philippe's mother. There were no arrangements yet for Philippe, but all the women could go to America now. And in mid-May, when the Germans crossed the Meuse, Philippe told Liouba to go. Men with uniforms and guns now stood in the Paris streets, and though they said little and appeared to know less, it was in the newspapers: the Germans had crossed the Meuse. The one-armed man put them on a train at Gare St-Lazare. It would take them to Bordeaux, and a transatlantic freighter called *The Winnipeg*.

'Promise me you'll eat,' Mama said.

'I will eat. And I'll strap a colander to my head.'

'Come with us to Bordeaux.'

'Mama, I need a visa for that. I told you, the army has taken all the trains.'

Philippe emptied his wallet and stuffed all the bills into Yvonne's purse.

'You need money too,' Yvonne said. Irene squirmed in her arms and wouldn't even look at her father.

He counted their suitcases.

'Can you say bye-bye?' Yvonne asked. 'Mama and Irene are going on a trip. Papa is staying here.' Everywhere the refugees from the north lay on their suitcases and trunks in yesterday's clothes, smoking cigarettes. A man was rushing up and down the platform trying to sell them some useless *demi-tarif* cards.

Ita carried Hélène up the steps, Liliane limped. Liouba stood with one leg up on the train, and herded them through. Since René had been called up to fight, she didn't cry or bite her nails anymore.

'Sit by a window,' she said to Ita.

'Facing forwards, Mama,' Philippe said.

'I don't plan to be sick,' Liouba said. She had always had motion sickness on their trips across Europe in the old days, which never deterred Papa from planning yet another train trip.

'But Yvonne may get sick,' Philippe said.

'*Allons-y!*' a gendarme cried out, then turned back to the unruly line with the little old woman at the front, waving her useless train schedule. Some of the people were climbing aboard and many more waved papers or tickets or cash, and the gendarmes blew their whistles.

'The gods are coming back for you, Philippe! I've already written three letters!' Liouba said. She went in with all the girls. Not a man in the group to lift their luggage.

'Go into the basement at the first siren,' Yvonne said. 'Don't wait for the old lady and her cat.'

'I won't,' Philippe said. 'Do you have Annie?'

'Of course.'

'Can you say bye-bye, Irene?'

He took Irene from Yvonne's arms and hugged the baby firmly though she fought and kicked. The baby girl wriggled and writhed until her face was pressed against his shirt, and then he felt a sharp pinch.

'No!' he shouted. 'No, Irene! You do not bite!' The little teeth were bared, slick like newly minted sous.

'Do you have a ticket, monsieur?' the gendarme said.

'No,' Philippe said.

'Then step aside.'

'Let my mother help you if you're tired. Do you feel very sick?'

'I'll be fine,' she said, angry, as if the situation – not only the pregnancy, but the war – were his fault.

They climbed up into the train. Philippe couldn't find their faces in the windows. He wanted to leave before the train rolled away, but remained. No one came back out. He watched three teenage boys through the window, laughing and playing cards, as the train pulled away through the dusty shafts of sunlight descending between the girders.

Philippe stayed in Paris when everyone else, it seemed, had fled. Claude Delacroix, whose headshots Philippe had taken before he'd even had a studio, was already gone without a goodbye. The door to his hotel room stood open, a pair of trousers on the floor beside a broken lamp. Georges Hoyningen-Huene sent a telegram to Philippe from Tours: 'Parade naked.' Jean and Geneviève did not answer the phone. The door to the Institute, beside the dark movie theater, was padlocked. And René was gone without an address.

Philippe listened to the radio and rationed his food. On his family's behalf, he ministered to himself as he had in Meran, as if he were his own physician. Between futile phone calls and telegrams to the consulates and relief agencies in Bordeaux and Marseille, he took long walks, all the way to the Bois de Boulogne on the western edge of the city, and he carried all his food and water with him. If the Nazis came now, he thought he might hide there in the park. But others strolled under the trees of the Bois in the fine evening air as if nothing at all unusual were happening.

Out walking one night, Philippe saw candles burning under the colonnade of the Panthéon, where Painlevé and all the great men of France lay buried, and listened to the crowd hoarsely chanting prayers below its mighty pillars. In the street, one hapless fellow had belted out the *Marseillaise*, with no one to join him.

In the morning, fire and smoke arose on the horizons of Paris. The city was ghostly. The sound of German planes infested the skies like a sound of locusts, and every now and again there was the dull and distant sound of a bomb, a little distortion of the air around his ears. Taxis disappeared from the streets. Buses were parked empty on the Champs-Élysées to prevent the landing of the German airborne, some said, and the intersections were barricaded with sandbags. The weather had been flawless, without a cloud, and the evening air that week was warm and pleasant, but it also carried a faint odor of burning wood.

It was almost thrilling to the imagination: all Paris vacant, this vast warren of rooms and passages filled with belongings, abandoned to any thief or adventurer – as in the sacred ancient crypts of Egypt, but instead of jewels, the treasure was the imprint of four million lives – empty bakeries with bread still in the window, bald tablecloths and sleeping kitchens with copper pans hanging in silence, empty banks, cafés, apartments, unmade beds with the people vanished out of them, their underwear still folded in their dressers, secret notes and letters and faded flowers pressed into books on shelves, dark halls of the Sorbonne, doors locked, birds perched on the monuments wondering about the cloudless sky, no *bateaux mouches* on the Seine headed for Saint Cloud, just one or two men on bicycles riding past shuttered shop windows and quiet panes of glass, glass enclosing empty spaces like the still dioramas in a natural-history museum.

On 10 June, Philippe learned that the government had abandoned them during the night. That night, the sirens began before he'd undressed for bed, so Philippe spent the night in the cellar with another man's empty boots one inch from his nose. It was so noisy that he couldn't help but climb out every hour or so into the eerie stillness of Rue St-Honoré to listen to the booming of guns and to watch the flashing of light in the cloudless air both east and west of the city. 'It's getting closer, no?' a man asked, nervously tapping his cigarette.

'I can't really say.'

The man went on smoking and humming *Paris sera toujours Paris*, the Maurice Chevalier song.

Philippe retreated inside and lay down beside the shoes again. He slept fitfully for an hour or more. At four A.M., he hauled himself off the floor with a stiff neck. An old woman lay under a sheet and a man who lived downstairs from Philippe was pointing to the body and shouting hysterically in Portuguese. The sound of the guns was very loud now, even in the basement. People were rushing up the cellar stairs. Philippe went with them.

Once inside his apartment, he riffled through the drawers in the office. He wanted to select some of his best photographs but soon gave up. He slipped the Gide and a dozen random prints into a folder, took his twin-lens Halsman camera, scooped up his camera bag full of rations – three loaves of stale bread, some raw broccoli, a milk bottle full of tapwater, a wedge of stinky cheese, some cured ham – and ran to the bedroom. Lying folded on the bureau was the yellow silk blouse that Yvonne had been wearing the day they met. He snatched it up, stuffed it inside his shirt, slung the gray camera bag around his neck, and dragged the mattress off the bed. When he'd wrestled it down three flights of stairs, he leaned the mattress against the wall and went back for a casserole tin, which he tied to his head with shoelaces. Anything might help, you never could tell. Plus, he had promised his mother. He took one last look at home, at his father's old view camera leaning against the kitchen wall, and left. True to his word, he didn't stop for the old woman, or the cat, though he saw Noisette slinking along the wall. The cat froze on the hallway floorboards when she saw him there in his funny helmet.

By the time he was in the old Citroën, the sun had risen

and the guns had mostly stopped. Vast columns of smoke drifted up from the western suburbs, hanging in the sky in formation and slowly drifting downwind. 'Maybe the bombs will bounce off,' Philippe said to the three Spanish girls who rode with him. He pointed to the roof, where the mattress was tied. Nobody made a sound. They were dark-skinned girls with black hair and spoke no French at all. One of them was pregnant, though she couldn't have been more than fifteen. Her friends made her urinate into a bottle.

In silence, Philippe and his hitchhikers caravanned with the other cars and trucks, the donkeys and horses, everyone moving at the speed of the slowest cart. There were old ladies and cripples walking in the early morning light, people pushing their belongings in wheelbarrows. Two girls dragged a trunk on wheels. Mothers had fashioned ingenious knapsacks out of bedsheets, by which they carried their babies in the front, clothing and food in the back. Philippe felt he ought to help them somehow. An old priest walked by them leading a column of nuns, their belongings in pillowcases, black robes swirling in the wind.

3. Marseille

The trolley took us along the broad avenue du Prado to the sea, then turned left and followed the Mediterranean coast for fifteen or twenty minutes. It was a hot August afternoon. Landscape and climate reminded me of the coast near Athens – arid gray limestone hills, closely packed beach houses, umbrella pines, date palms, dry heat, dust. It was so hot that I had difficulty keeping awake.

VARIAN FRY, on Marseille in August 1940,
Surrender on Demand

The halls of the Villa Air Bel did not smell so good. There was not a cake of soap in all south France. What little *savon* they had Varian Fry had brought back from Lisbon, where the lucky ones weighed anchor for America or Africa. And at Air Bel, there was no water anyway. The well was low, and when the valves were opened the pipes only groaned and dripped.

Philippe rolled on the hot, humid sheets toward the splintery blind. He'd slept on a stack of attic linens. All of the big mahogany beds in the ruined old Marseille mansion were full, and would be for many hours more, judging from the number of empty wine bottles lying around the fountain and in the overgrown garden below. He peered out. The rising sun lit the cold bottles in the weeds and the wind drowned a few more dead leaves in the fountain pool. He prayed for one of those great men who had rescued him from jail to remember him and come back for him. He prayed to Albert Einstein and told him there was a little girl who needed him.

Philippe pulled on his pants and shirt and half walked, half fell down the steep back stairs to the kitchen, where a pot of coffee sat on the long coal stove. He rummaged in the cupboards, loud in the empty room, and poured himself a cup of the sludge that had replaced coffee in these desperate times; there was no coffee anymore, just burned malt that everyone pretended was coffee. With a dirty knife he wiped some bitter brown *confiture* on a crust of stale bread.

Cool air wafted through the open kitchen door. Outside, the Davenport girl was picking empty wine bottles from the weeds. Miriam Davenport was the only other person he knew at the villa.

'Would you like some milk to cut that poison?' she said, standing up and placing an empty wine bottle on the table beside a bottle of milk.

'Yes. Thank you.' Miriam Davenport was one of those young women from whose features an old woman already peered out. Her cheeks were already falling, or about to fall, her neck thin, and a terrible cough vibrated her ribcage at least every ten minutes. She had rejected him after looking at his photographs at the little café on the Canabière, where demobilized French soldiers jammed the streets, delivered from every corner of the French empire, soldiers with fezes, black Senegalese, Alpine *chasseurs*, all tired, all lost, all on the way to someplace else.

Varian Fry said this girl was the talent assessor for the Centre Américain de Secours, but when Philippe had called her that at the café, the young American had said, 'That's crass. We can't help everyone. And we have a charter: artists, writers, and scientists.'

Philippe had opened the folder of prints before her. 'There are more, but I had to leave them in Paris.'

'Photographs?' she had said, and shook her head.

'This one is of André Gide,' he'd said.

'Yes?'

'Well,' he'd said, 'I'm also an engineer.'

Fry had mentioned a charter too. That seemed to be their code word. What they really meant was: *we will provide you an exit visa if you are important. If we haven't heard of you, then you must be able to sing or draw.* The artists would be spirited away from the Nazis' clutches like the diamonds of Antwerp. Well, he could draw a bit. There was that self-portrait, anyway. So he had drawn a horse in Davenport's notebook. But she'd merely looked out the window at the Senegalese soldiers and said, 'Imagine coming all that way and then going back home without firing a shot.' *No American visa for you. No room on the boat. You'll have to die.* The American consulate in Marseille said their quota for Latvians was full. But they could gladly offer him a visa sometime in 1947.

The young American now plopped some milk into his cup of sludge.

'Can you wait here?' Philippe said to the girl.

He went back up the steep steps, all the way to the musty linen room in the attic, and returned with his large-format twin lens on a tripod.

'Here?' she said.

He walked out into the weeds so that she stood before the wall of dawn light rising on Villa Air Bel. 'Put the bottle on the table,' he said.

'Okay,' she said, sounding bored.

'Keep your hand on it.' Philippe remained crouched behind the camera. 'Tell me how you came to Marseille. How you met Varian Fry.'

The sun had by now filled the leaves of the plane trees with light, begun to warm the mountains, and awakened the sea far below. She told him of her childhood in Boston and her brother and dead parents. Philippe heard about the girl's wanderings in Europe, her distant fiancé and her tenuous friendships with various famous people, connections of which she was enormously proud. André, Jacqueline, and Aube Breton were her family now, she said.

Philippe didn't need Davenport, not to get to Lisbon anyway. Fry hadn't granted money, false papers, an American visa, or even an escort, but he had told Philippe how to get a Portuguese transit visa – with a stamp from the Chinese consulate that no one could read. The Chinese marking was presumed to represent still another transit visa, but according to Fry the stamp really said, 'This person may not enter China.' The Spanish consulate in Perpignan gave Philippe a transit visa on the strength of his Portuguese one. So it would be in Lisbon that he'd see once and for all the nature of things – whether reality was made solely of murdering apes and dark heartless mountains or whether there was any hospitality to it, or any goodness among people, or any power available to those who were good – whether there was any such thing as a hero.

It took him just a few hours of hiking on the windy moonlit hill to cross the border into Spain and spy the lights of Portbou. He showed his transit visa to the authorities at the train station and received the *entrada* stamp in his passport. In the morning, he took the train to Barcelona, and from Barcelona to Madrid, sitting in the choking air of a third-class car where the fleas flew into his ears. And by the time he reached Lisbon, an American visa was awaiting him. Albert Einstein had remembered him and with a goodness of immense reach and power, like a field of gravity, he had shifted time and space just a little on Philippe's behalf.

4. The Persistence of Memory

I doubt about my success in life. But I have known one
man who always believed in me and my success, and that
was my poor father.

PHILIPP HALSMANN, letter from Stein Prison, 1930

'I can't,' he said.

'You can.'

Sometimes Jane wailed because of the hole in the window
shade. The tape over the hole dangled and fell, every day,
often into the crib, often directly onto her head. Philippe
wouldn't replace the shade, since to do so was to concede
they'd be staying. He refused to look into the future at all, so
that he wouldn't see the boarding house there. And the shade
continued spilling light into baby Jane's face when she turned
around in the crib, rotating herself like the hands of a clock.
Irene too seemed to know that families were not meant to
live in such places, all together in one room. 'Too small,' she
often said. 'Too small for Jane.'

'I can't,' he said.

'You can,' Yvonne said.

'I cannot.'

To think he was working for free – when he couldn't afford
an apartment with an extra room. Living off their American
friends. Shooting another beautiful but unknown face, some
model named Connie Ford. Beauty was a tiny thing here

beside America's monolithic industries, tight-fisted, rationing, sucking all the money and labor off the New York streets, filling the nation's chest for war. All his women, Yvonne, Irene, Jane, Liouba, and Mama, had come to greet him at the terminal, where rain was soaking the gray waves of the Hudson River, and Liouba had a list of phone numbers and addresses. But still, here he was, without any work.

He almost said, What's the point? But he couldn't say such things now that there were children.

On the other hand, the words 'starting over' caused a pain on his vocal cords.

Yvonne bounced Jane against her shoulder. The little one had been up all night and so they all had.

'I want a candy,' Irene said, tireless.

He pulled his tripod from its canvas sleeve. 'Tante Liouba will have chocolate for you,' he said, and sighed. He looked at his wife. 'The model will be here soon.'

'We're going, we're going,' she said.

Yvonne set the baby down in the crib and began to hunt for the toy lamb amid the detritus of the little room. Philippe hadn't the energy to clean up for his guest. Besides, where would he put any of it? In the wet bathtub? They simply pushed their piles of junk from one side of the room to the other. Jane began to wail.

'What's the matter with *you*?' the girl said. She stood by the shelves of tacky china, a young and quite beautiful brunette in a blue hat cantilevered forward over her brow and a blue suit. She was rapidly chewing gum.

'Yes,' Philippe said. He could understand English but his vocabulary was still arrestingly small.

The girl stepped over a stack of diapers and set her handbag down on the sofa. She untied her scarf and wrinkled her nose as she looked around at the soiled walls, cheap furniture, and piles of junk. 'Was that the janitor downstairs? He sure did get an eyeful of me when I came in.'

'How old are you?' Philippe said.

'Didn't I already tell you that at the agency?' she said, as if her youth were a flaw.

'I am practicing my English.'

'I'm eighteen,' she said. 'So what's wrong? Your dog die or something?'

'So young and so . . . how do you say in English?' He picked up the little blue dictionary.

'My mother calls it "strong-willed."' The girl chewed her gum vigorously and looked at him with skepticism.

'So young and so . . . advanced of body,' he said. By the strange look on the girl's face, he could tell that his word choice was incorrect.

As if by clairvoyance, the phone rang then. It was the girl's mother. He pinned the receiver between his shoulder and chin and held up to the light the paper American flag. 'I don't like the idea of my Connie hanging around in a furnished room with a Frenchman,' the woman said. 'She's a child, now, you understand? In America, that means hands off.'

'Of course,' Philippe said. 'I am married.'

'That never stopped any Frenchman I ever heard of. I'll call back in fifteen minutes and you had better answer. Goodbye. Make it ten minutes. Goodbye.'

Philippe hung up and knelt in the center of the floor beside a basket of dirty laundry. He pinned one corner of the flag under the leg of a floodlamp.

'This is your place?' Connie said.

Philippe looked up. 'We are soon to depart.' He pushed himself up and began to circle around the girl. The face was as he remembered at the agency, with a strong chin, an almost masculine jawline, and skin and eyes like an Egyptian queen. Philippe reached up to the top of the tall girl's head and pulled out her hat pins. The hat dropped into his hands and he placed it on the imitation altar table that sat before the hideous brown sofa. 'Clothes off, please. The *chemisier*. The top.' He tugged at his own shirt.

'What?'

Again the phone rang and Philippe answered. 'Madame Ford,' he said, 'it is only two minutes till before. Seconds, perhaps.'

'She may think she's thirty-five,' the woman said. 'But she is in fact eighteen years old and her virginity is intact and shall remain so. No clothing shall be removed. Not even her shoes. Do you hear?'

'I understand, Madame.' He placed the hat pins beside the hat on the altar table.

'Now,' the mother said, 'let me speak to her.'

Philippe handed the phone to the young model and went to draw down the window shade.

'I know, Mother,' the girl said. 'I know. I'm more worried about the pictures he's going to take. This place is a real dump.'

Philippe crouched and made a few mental calculations. He tore a few pieces of dirty masking tape from a roll, turned the two-cent paper flag, and taped its corners down. He stood and pointed the floodlamp down and set a reflector on a stand on the opposite side. The reflector would soften the shadows, especially on her wonderful long neck, and would add a little bit of contour to her shoulders, making them round and touchable on film. 'Remove the shirt,' he whispered. 'I require to see the skin to here.' He placed his hand perpendicular against his own sternum.

'Yes, Mother. I have to go. He's trying to start the shoot.'

'Naked shoulders,' Philippe whispered.

'Mother – I heard you. Bye.'

The model handed him the receiver and he laid it back on the cradle. She unbuttoned her suit jacket and rested it carefully across the arm of the sofa. Then she pulled the white blouse over her head, revealing two full and jutting bosoms in a pink brassiere with a little pink bow between them.

He pointed to the bra. 'Off,' he said.

The young girl blanched. 'No.'

Philippe looked around the room, wishing Yvonne were there. He went to the closet and from the bottom shelf extracted an old sheet, which he gave to his subject.

'Are you any good or are you just hoping to trade on my looks?'

Trade on her looks? He was shooting her for free. 'Trust me, please,' he said.

'I want respectable work from this, you know.'

He pointed to the brassiere again. 'Off.'

'My mother was right about you Frenchmen, boy,' the girl said. She wrapped the sheet around her shoulders and turned away from him.

The phone rang again. Philippe picked up: the girl's mother again. 'Is she still fully clothed?' she asked.

'*Oui*,' Philippe said and hung up. The phone rang again instantly, and Philippe pulled off the receiver and held it out to the girl, a finger held upright before his lips.

'Mother, I am still a virgin. Goodbye.' Connie hung up the phone and continued wriggling out of her bra. 'I don't want to end up on a deck of dirty playing cards, okay?' He heard the bra uncupping itself from her bosoms and then saw the detached cups lying on the sofa like the shells of a hard-boiled egg.

'I would like to make a photograph *tout nu*, of course,' he said. 'But I not require *tout nu*. The shoulders naked only. Now, please. Lie on the floor.'

'Lie on the floor! Really! You don't understand America, Jack!'

'No, I understand *le monde*. Lie on the floor with the head on the colors American. The flag. Please.'

'It's dirty,' she said.

'Please. On the floor. And the shoulders – very naked.'

She knelt down and lowered herself to the floor. 'Like this?'

'More naked,' he said, pulling the sheet down a bit on her breasts. He dragged the Halsman camera over on its tripod and stood it beside the floodlamp. 'The chin down. The head right. More. Good.' The stripes of the flag slanted against her face at a near right-angle to her nose. Stars hovered about her head above the hairline. Shadow faintly veiled her eye as if to suggest the fatigue of American hard work, and her strong jawline was traced by a thick boomerang of shadow, showing America was up to any task. He had created a real American goddess if he didn't say so himself, Lady Liberty in the flesh, born there on the squalid floor of the boarding house. They ought to put this photograph on the national currency.

'I don't see what naked shoulders have to do with patriotism,' she said, 'but whatever you say, fella.'

Don't you want to beat Germany? he wished to say, but he hadn't the command of the English words. *You win a war with naked shoulders.*

1959, the Halsman Studio, 33 West Sixty-seventh Street, the Upper West Side, New York City.

'You did pretty well, after all, Halsman,' Yvonne said. There was little else left to do, so while they waited they both

265

continued looking up idly at the pictures on the wall. There was Connie Ford with the American flag behind her. The photo had been the emblem for Elizabeth Arden's Victory Red lipstick and had been printed in the *Times* again and again beside the pictures of the GIs fighting in Europe. There was the 1934 Gide with the shy old master at his piano, and the Einstein portrait, made at Princeton in 1947, the physicist's sad eyes reflecting the abysses of war. Einstein told him that day how he feared the devastating instrument he'd helped to deliver into the hands of politicians. There was 'Dalí Atomicus,' made the following year with his friend Salvador, who contrary to Einstein leaped joyously into the atomic age – with three black cats, a stream of water, an easel, and a chair, all suspended above the floor. And Churchill, who had looked on the same abysses, looked at all Europe in flames, and casually remarked, 'Whatever happens at Dunkirk, we shall fight on.' The portrait clearly depicted Churchill defying despair, though he'd in fact been defying a disgruntled photographer.

Then there were all the beautiful women, Bacall, Bardot, Bergman, and the rest. In their midst he'd placed Imogene Coca, whose expression seemed to say to the other women, 'Big deal. Your careers end at forty.' The portrait of the comedienne amused him every time he looked at it.

'Do you remember how you worried?' Yvonne said.

'You say that now, two decades later,' Philippe said. He was irritable because Marilyn Monroe was late. She was always late. But then he put his arm around Yvonne and the edge of the pad she wore on her hip, because of the old scoliosis, touched his fingers, and he leaned over and kissed her.

When the movie star finally did arrive, she was very nervous about the idea of jumping and had to be talked into it again. 'You told me last time that a picture of a jump reveals the soul,' she said, peeking out from behind the fake Byobu screen. She tossed her white socks out onto the chair.

'I know your soul already,' Philippe said. 'It is as beautiful as all your exterior assets.'

When Marilyn emerged barefoot in the black evening gown and saw Yvonne there holding a floodlamp, she froze.

'This is my wife, Yvonne,' Philippe said.

Yvonne put the lamp down and walked to her, touched her arm. Marilyn stiffened.

'We saw *Some Like It Hot*, dear,' Yvonne said. 'You were so funny!'

Marilyn looked surprised and somewhat relieved. But as Yvonne crossed the studio floor again to retrieve the lamp, Marilyn watched carefully, as though any female, even a kind one, could at any moment circle back and bite her.

Philippe examined her face. The makeup was perhaps a bit too harsh. 'I won't make you redo it this time,' he said. He checked the Weston light meter, picked up the Rolleiflex, and took a few shots. Then he told Marilyn to jump.

The shoot proceeded at its usual frenetic pace. Yvonne literally ran, jumping over the cables, when another Rolleiflex or an extra lamp was needed. Photographs actually were precious moments in time, and moments in time could never be recovered. Philippe and Yvonne ran around like people trying to catch gold falling from the sky.

'One . . . two . . . three . . . JUMP!'

Marilyn jumped like a little girl, with her legs tucked up underneath her.

'Did you really like the movie?'

'Yes, Marilyn. Everyone did.'

Philippe remembered the day in 1951 when he'd photographed her in Los Angeles. He'd asked to see what dresses Marilyn had and in her closet saw that she had only a few formal pieces, and not particularly pretty ones. He'd taken out a white evening gown with a huge bow on the left hip and tried to help the young woman acquire some taste: the bow made the dress look cheap, he'd said. She'd listened with rapt attention. Clean lines were more elegant, he'd said. She'd nodded, then found a scissors and snipped off the bow. He'd made her scrub off all her makeup, too, and apply it again with a lighter hand.

There had been a whiff of tragedy about Marilyn from the beginning, from the moment she arrived late that day in California. She'd parked her beat-up old Pontiac convertible in the street and come up the walk with hands in the pockets of her blue jeans, cuffs rolled up above her white Keds sneakers – the same ones she'd worn today. When she'd led him upstairs, he'd seen that the apartment had almost nothing in it but a fold-out bed, a bench with dumbbells on the floor beside it, a single framed picture of Eleanora Duse, and several bookshelves loaded with heavy reading – Dostoevsky, Ibsen, writers like that. She'd told him how she'd never known her father, who'd abandoned the family and died in a motorcycle accident when Marilyn was three, and how her mother was mentally ill and locked away. In one of the foster homes, she'd been raped, she said.

Marilyn jumped again, thudded back to the ground, and pushed the hair from her eyes. 'You really did like it?' she said.

'Yes, Marilyn. Now, remember, this is supposed to be fun. You're a great success now. You have nothing to prove.'

He took a few more photographs and then gave up. A shadow of some former thing had darkened Marilyn's face.

After Marilyn left, Philippe looked from the studio window out onto West Sixty-seventh Street. He looked at the silver wristwatch where it was clasped around the outside of his shirt cuff and rubbed his thumb over the initials P. H., monogrammed on his breast pocket. He took the watch off.

A memory was like a thing fallen. Or, like a view of something fallen that could not be retrieved. Ruth, for example, Ruth, as if under glass, like Ophelia under the river. Or that day when in Switzerland Papa had told the dirty joke to the man in puttees, the snow lighting their faces. *Papa*, he would like to ask, *do you think I have savoir faire?*

The Russians had taken over Latvia again. He wondered if the cottage in the Blue Lakes was still standing. He couldn't remember it much. A desk and a slanted blue wall. An arc of lamplight on robin's egg blue. The paint was cracked. People like him and Marilyn, they were great forgetters. Dark continents of lost time. Sometimes in the summer Papa took them to Jūrmala by the sea. You could wade out to a sandbar where the water was only up to your knees. He and Liouba put wooden boats in the trough and waited to see whose boat would strike the sand first. That was when his sister was always following him around. When his friend Paul was there or if he wanted to impress the girls, he used to send Liouba on errands to make her go away. Go ask Papa for the tag to the beach chairs. Could you bring us some ice water from the cabana? She liked to do it, and the warm wind and sound of the waves was gentle to him, and allowed him to believe he was indulging her, and not the other way around. Then she turned twelve and she didn't follow him anymore. Then she huddled in the cabana with the other girls, comparing bathing suits and gossiping about boys, and she told him to go away.

At one of the beaches, there were many smooth stones, and when the tide was low, the sun would heat them. One could stand on the stones and feel the warm sun on the soles of the feet. There were mussel shells, too, that were easily crushed underfoot, and cockleshells. A biologist had once come to visit them and he'd shown Philippe the barnacles on the mussel shells. Papa didn't notice details like that, only the big picture – sunsets, mountains, seas. He and Uncle Moritz had once tied a rented umbrella to a chair and carried Grandma in it over the sand like a maharani. The brothers tromped over all the stones, calling out in spirited mocking voices, and crushed the shells beneath their heels as if their skin were impervious to pain. Papa's foot had bled, and he'd insisted it was nothing. He'd walked across the stones with sand and blood on his foot and had given a wad of cash to the young biologist, who was newly married.

The boys and girls at Jūrmala made campfires in the dunes. The boys kept the liquor in a boat and returned from the waves with wet sandy feet. Philippe didn't drink. He always found a girl he liked and he talked a lot and stood near enough to breathe in her perfume, but he never touched any of them. His cousin Esya had come once, with her husband David. They were older, looking for liquor. Her slip was showing. In the morning Paul had led him back through the dunes to spy on the women; before lunch the beach was reserved for women bathing in the nude. That afternoon Philippe had a tennis lesson and afterwards ice cream. Then he had stood beside a girl with small pointed breasts, and she'd wanted to hold his hand and he'd been too ashamed.

A river, a sea, a lake. Sometimes it was easier to remember shame. In Papa's office long ago, looking up at the Chinese fan with the white dragon, above the dental drill. Philippe tried to tell a joke, and Papa had laughed a charitable laugh, not a genuine one, but then a real smile had come over his face, the gold gleaming at the corner of his mouth. It was a smile that made Philippe feel foolish.

Masks upon masks upon masks.

Finally, he remembered something more of the Blue Lakes. A ceramic ewer filled with dripping cold water. When the plumbing was being fixed, they had shut the water off at the cottage and, for a week, had to bring cold water in from the neighbors in big white ewers. Yes. And Papa let other people use the house in June, and some of the linens were invariably missing. On the first day, he and Papa would go register at the little police station by the linden tree, and then Philippe would go straight to the lake. He wished he could go back there now, to the edge of the birch forest where the gnats tumbled in the light of the sunset, back to that place where he'd gotten lost chasing a butterfly in the woods and Papa had come for him, crashing through the weeds in the red shirt with the ox-horn buttons.

He just wanted a decent book to read ...

Not too much to ask, is it? It was in 1935 when Allen Lane, Managing Director of Bodley Head Publishers, stood on a platform at Exeter railway station looking for something good to read on his journey back to London. His choice was limited to popular magazines and poor-quality paperbacks – the same choice faced every day by the vast majority of readers, few of whom could afford hardbacks. Lane's disappointment and subsequent anger at the range of books generally available led him to found a company – and change the world.

'We believed in the existence in this country of a vast reading public for intelligent books at a low price, and staked everything on it'
Sir Allen Lane, 1902–1970, founder of Penguin Books

The quality paperback had arrived – and not just in bookshops. Lane was adamant that his Penguins should appear in chain stores and tobacconists, and should cost no more than a packet of cigarettes.

Reading habits (and cigarette prices) have changed since 1935, but Penguin still believes in publishing the best books for everybody to enjoy. We still believe that good design costs no more than bad design, and we still believe that quality books published passionately and responsibly make the world a better place.

So wherever you see the little bird – whether it's on a piece of prize-winning literary fiction or a celebrity autobiography, political tour de force or historical masterpiece, a serial-killer thriller, reference book, world classic or a piece of pure escapism – you can bet that it represents the very best that the genre has to offer

Whatever you like to read – trust Penguin.